CRIMSON PEAK

THE OFFICIAL MOVIE NOVELIZATION

CRIMSON PEAK

THE OFFICIAL MOVIE NOVELIZATION

FROM DIRECTOR
GUILLERMO DEL TORO

SCREENPLAY BY
GUILLERMO DEL TORO AND MATTHEW ROBBINS

NOVELIZATION BY
NANCY HOLDER

LEGENDARY
TITAN BOOKS

Crimson Peak: The Official Movie Novelization
Print edition ISBN: 9781783296293
E-book edition ISBN: 9781783296309

Published by Titan Books
A division of Titan Publishing Group Ltd
144 Southwark St, London SE1 0UP

First edition: October 2015
10 9 8 7 6 5 4 3 2 1

LEGENDARY

LEGENDARY.COM   **TITAN**BOOKS.COM

"Love looks not with the eyes but with the mind."

—WILLIAM SHAKESPEARE,
A MIDSUMMER NIGHT'S DREAM

CRIMSON PEAK

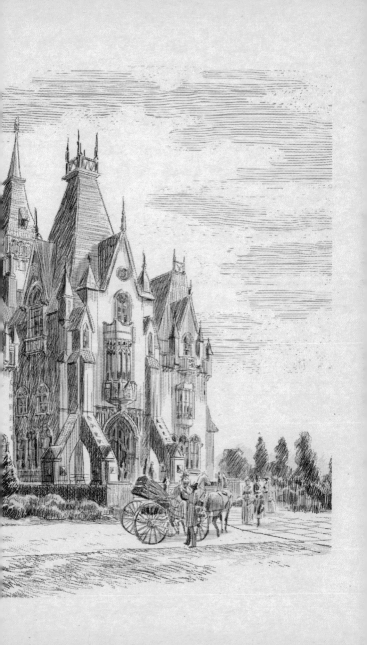

PROLOGUE

Love.

Death.

Ghosts.

The world was drenched in blood.

A scarlet fog veiled the killing ground, then dripped down through the greedy, starved mineshafts into the tortured vats of claret clay that bubbled and gasped on the filthy, bone-white tile. Crimson earth seeped back up through the walls of mud. Allerdale Hall was ringed with brilliant red—a stain that clawed toward Edith's bare feet.

But that was the least of her troubles.

Hell's own child was coming for her. Implacable, unstoppable, a creature fueled by madness and rage, that had maimed and murdered and would kill again, unless Edith struck first. But she was weak, coughing blood and stumbling, and this monster had already claimed other lives—other *souls*—stronger and heartier than hers.

Snowflakes blinded Edith's swollen cornflower-blue eyes; red droplets specked her golden hair. Her right cheek had been sliced open; the hem of her gauzy nightgown had soaked up blood, rot, and gore.

And crimson clay.

Limping on her injured leg, she moved in a slow circle, shovel raised as her chest heaved to the rhythm of the machine that had been built to plunder the earth of treasure. A clanking contraption that might still serve as the means of her destruction.

The sound pounded in her ears as she braced herself for the last battle. Nausea rolled through her as her heart skipped a beat. Sweat beaded on her forehead and her stomach clenched. Her bones ached and throbbed, and she could barely walk.

Everywhere she looked shadows loomed, red on red, on red. If she did survive, would she join them? Would she haunt this cursed place forever, enraged and afraid? This was no place to die.

Ghosts are real. That much I know.

She knew much more. If only she had pieced the whole brutal story together sooner, heeded the warnings, followed the clues. She had uncovered the truth at a terrible cost, but the ultimate penalty now awaited her and the one who had risked so much for her sake.

Behind the snow and scarlet gloaming, she caught a flash of running feet. Her grip on the shovel was slick in her clammy grasp. Her ankle throbbed and she was freezing, yet her insides burned so fiercely she expected smoke to plume from her mouth.

She backed up, whirled around, eyes searching, breath stuttering. Then time stopped, and her heart froze as she caught sight of a blur of sodden fabric, and bare feet sucking at the red muck as they came at her. The sharp blade, fingers smeared with blood, the fury that wielded it. Death was no longer coming.

Death was here.

And her mind cast back to how it was that she, Edith Cushing, had come here to fight it.

Once upon a time…

BOOK ONE

BETWEEN DESIRE AND DARKNESS

*"For now we see through a glass, darkly;
but then face to face: now I know in part;
but then shall I know even as also I am known."*

—1 CORINTHIANS 13:12

CHAPTER ONE

BUFFALO, NEW YORK, 1886

THE FIRST TIME I saw a ghost, I was ten years old.
It was my mother's.

It was snowing on the day they put Edith Cushing's mother in the ground. Large wet flakes wept in a leaden sky. The world was colorless. Dressed for deep mourning in a black coat and a hat that framed her stricken white face, little Edith leaned back against her father's legs. The other mourners wore black top hats, heavy black veils, ebony coats and gloves, and jewelry wrought from the hair of their own beloved dead. The living folk of Buffalo owned entire wardrobes of fashionable ensembles designed for weeping and tossing clods of earth and rose petals on freshly dug graves.

The coffin—locked—gleamed like obsidian as the pallbearers conveyed the corpse of Edith's mother to its final resting place beneath the monument raised in hopes of eternal repose for the members of the Cushing family. Swirls of weeping angel wings enfolded generations of the dead.

Her mother's shriveled body had been so black that it looked as if she had died in a fire—or so Edith had overheard Cook describing it to DeWitt, their butler. Edith had been struck dumb by the horrific revelation, but had no way to confirm it. In the Cushing home, no one spoke to her about her terrible loss; all the servants fell silent whenever she walked into a room. She felt as invisible as a ghost; she wanted, needed someone to see her, wrap their arms around her and rock her, and tell her a story or sing her a lullaby. But the staff kept their distance, as if the little mistress was bad luck.

Now, in the churchyard, she spotted Alan McMichael and his sister Eunice. A year older than Edith, yellow-headed Alan with his ruddy cheeks was Edith's boon companion in all things. His blue-gray eyes, the only spot of brightness in the graveyard, found her gaze and held it, almost as if he were holding her hand. Beside him, Eunice was fidgety and a trifle bored. Though Eunice was but nine, she had already been to a plentiful number of funerals. They were Victorian children and death was not uncommon.

But Edith had only one mother to lose, and that was

new and bewildering. Heart-crushing. Tears wanted to come, but they only hovered at the rims of her eyes. She was not to make a fuss; well-bred children were seen and not heard, even when their worlds were falling apart. Alan, watching her, seemed to be the only one who understood her unbearable grief. Tears sparkled in his eyes.

Eunice shifted her weight and played with one of her ginger ringlets. Alan tugged gently on his sister's wrist to make her stop and she batted at him. Their mother smiled wistfully down on them both as if she had not seen Eunice's unseemly display. Mrs. McMichael was still pretty, still alive.

Alan kept hold of Eunice's wrist. She thrust out her lower lip and their mother reached in the pocket of her sable coat, offering her daughter what appeared to be a sweet. Eunice grabbed it, jerking free of her brother's grasp. Now it was Alan who pretended not to notice what was going on—or perhaps he truly did not see it. All his attention was fixed on Edith as a huge sob threatened to burst out of her aching chest. There would be no more sweets from Mama, no smiles, no stories.

Black cholera had taken her. A horrible death, agonizing and slow. Edith's father had ordered a closed casket, and asked her not to look. So there was no parting kiss, no goodbye, no last words.

That is, until she came back. Three weeks after she died.

* * *

Time did not heal all wounds.

Her mother had been dead for almost a month, and Edith missed her more than ever. The black wreath still hung on the door and the servants wore armbands in the mistress's memory. Cook had not wanted the maids to remove the black drapes from the mirrors. DeWitt said she was too superstitious and Cook had answered that she was merely *careful*. That you couldn't be too sure when the dead were concerned. Back in Ireland, the spirit of a maiden aunt got stuck in a mirror in 1792 and had been haunting the family ever since. DeWitt had replied that as the drapes had gone up before Mrs. Cushing had expired, and she was now buried, there was no chance that the mistress was trapped.

Yet the drapes stayed up.

Edith was lying in her little daybed, weeping quietly in the dark with her stuffed rabbit for company. The hurt in her heart seemed deeper and more painful with each passing night. Shadows of snowdrifts mottled the dusty covers of the books her mother and she had read together, a few pages every night. She could not bear to open them.

The grandfather clock at the end of the hall ticked between her sobs like an axe striking wood. Outside her bedroom window, the ever-present snow fell silently over the eastern shore of Lake Erie and the headwaters of the Niagara River. The Erie Canal had fostered the fortunes of Edith's family. Wind and frozen water. The beautifully appointed Cushing home was cold that night, as it had been every night since Mama's death. Edith felt as if it were she who had turned to ice, and could never hope to be warm again.

I wonder if she is cold, down in the ground. Edith couldn't banish the thought, even though she had been told a dozen times—a hundred—that her mother was in a better place.

She remembered when her room was the best place: the soft, gentle voice of her mother reading as she snuggled beneath the coverlet with a cup of hot chocolate and a hot water bottle.

Once upon a time.

Playing lullabies on the piano when Edith couldn't sleep.

There was no music tonight.

Edith cried.

The clock ticked, counting off the seconds, hours, nights of life without Mama. Endless. Relentless. Heartless.

Then Edith heard a strangled sound that was halfway between a sigh and a moan. She jerked and clapped a hand over her mouth in surprise. Had she done that?

Her heartbeat stuttered as she cocked her head, listening hard.

Tick, tick, tick. Only the clock.

There it was again. A sad, low keening. A whisper of grief. Even… agony.

She bolted upright and slipped out of bed. As she crept across the chilly floor, the floorboards creaked and the rustle of silk caressed her ears. She was not wearing silk.

Cook had told DeWitt that Mama had been laid out in her finest black silk gown, and that her skin had turned just as black in the hours before she died. Cook had used words like "revolting, ghastly. A horror." She had been speaking of her mistress like a monster.

Of *Mama*, who had been so beautiful, and smelled always of lilacs, and loved to play the piano. Who told her the most wonderful stories about plucky princesses who thwarted evil sorcerers and the princes who adored them. Who promised Edith that her own life would hold a "happily ever after" with a man who would build her a castle—"with his own two hands," she would say, smiling very dreamily, then add, "like your father."

But now, as Edith stared into the gloom, she couldn't keep that Mama in her mind's eye. Her thoughts kept returning to the monster, the horror, and she wondered if the shadows kept shifting of their own accord, or if that was the play of snowflake silhouettes on the wallpaper. She looked from the wall to the end of the hallway. It was not quiet there. The air seemed to flutter, and then to thicken.

Her blood chilled as a shape began to emerge from the gloom—a figure cloaked in shadow, floating at the end of the hall. A woman, swathed in once-fine black silk now tattered like the aging wings of a moth.

Was it just her imagination? A trick of the light?

Edith broke out in a cold sweat. *It's not there. It's not.* She's *not.*

Her pulse raced.

It was not gliding toward her.

She was *not.*

With a gasp, she turned away and darted back toward

her bedroom. Her skin prickled and her cheeks felt hot. She tried to listen but could only hear a roaring in her ears and the thud of her bare feet on the carpet runner.

Edith did not see the thing that was trailing after her as she ran, or feel the skeletal fingers of a shimmering hand as they caressed her hair. Moonlight shone on finger bones, revealed a quicksilver glimpse of a tormented face, flesh eaten away.

No, Edith did not see. But perhaps she *sensed*.

A shade. A spirit compelled by inextinguishable love to return, by desperation to speak. Gliding, with the rustle of silk, and the clack of bone and withered flesh.

Edith saw none of that as she scrambled under the covers and clung to her bunny, quivering in terror.

But seconds later, as she turned on her side, she went absolutely rigid with shock. She felt the decaying hand wrap around her shoulder, smelled the damp earth of the grave, and heard the desiccated lips, a hoarse distortion of the voice she had known better than her own as it whispered into her ear:

"My child, when the time comes, beware of Crimson Peak."

Edith screamed. She shot up and grabbed her eyeglasses. As she looped them over her ears, the gas lamps came back on. She hadn't even realized they'd gone out.

There was nothing—no *one*—in the room.

Until, alerted by her shrieks, her father rushed in and gathered her up in his arms.

* * *

It would be years before I heard a voice like that again—a warning from out of time, and one I came to understand only when it was too late...

CHAPTER TWO

BUFFALO, NEW YORK, 1901

IT WAS MARKET day, and puffy white clouds tatted the sky like fine lace as Edith sailed over the muddy yard in her high-buttoned shoes. She had selected her burnished gold skirt, a white blouse, and a black tie to wear on this auspicious occasion. The skirt most closely matched her blond hair, which she had wound into a smooth chignon and topped with a smart new hat adorned with a modesty veil that identified her—to her way of thinking—as something more than a fashion plate and something less than a Bohemian. A bright young woman with ambition, then. And *talent*.

For the first time in her life, she had something she had created, a product to sell—and a potential buyer. She hefted the heavy parcel and smiled secretly to herself.

Livestock, street vendors, carriages and the occasional motorcar threatened to splash mud on her clothes. Unblemished, she crossed into the busy commercial building where she, Miss Edith Cushing, had business to conduct, and started up the stairs.

She took it for a good omen when Alan McMichael, now Dr. Alan McMichael, hailed her as he came down the stairs, stopping to meet her as she ascended. They hadn't seen each other in ages; he'd been in England studying to become an eye doctor. She was rather startled to realize that he truly was all grown up, his face angular in that way adult men's faces were—baby fat gone—and his shoulders quite broad beneath his coat. He was not wearing a hat, and his hair was nearly the same color blond as hers.

"Edith," he said delightedly, "you know I'm setting up my practice?" He seemed to assume that she knew he'd returned.

Eunice never said a word to me, she thought, a bit put out. But on the other hand, Edith hadn't been calling on the McMichaels. She hadn't been calling on anyone, and in polite society, that was rather rude. One asked after one's friends. Except that Eunice was not friendly, not in the least. One called on one's acquaintances, then. One inquired after their health and kept up with the important events in their lives—which in Eunice's case would include the minute details of parties, balls, and galas.

How extraordinarily dull, Edith thought. *Oh, dear, I'm only twenty-four, and it appears that I'm already a crotchety misanthrope.*

"At ten I'm going to see Ogilvie," she informed him, regaining her sense of excitement. "He's going to look at my manuscript and see if he wants to publish it."

She had begun the book before Alan had left for medical school, reading sections to him when they chanced to meet—rather more often than one would have anticipated, given that they were only friends. He had been the one to whom she had confided her mother's ghostly visitation, although of course Eunice had eavesdropped and told the whole world. And the whole world had mocked and ridiculed Edith. From that day to this, Edith had decided to exploit the wild imaginings of her grief-stricken ten-year-old self—for such they must have been— as the metaphor for loss in her novel. Though the memory of that nightmare still haunted her, she was grateful for the terrifying experience, as it had provided riveting grist for the mill.

His smile grew at the mention of the completion of her book. "You do know that it's only nine o'clock," he ventured.

"I have a few corrections I wish to make first." She began to go through a mental checklist of her revisions, then became aware that Alan had just asked her to stop by his new office soon, and was saying something about some uncanny pictures he wished to show her.

She gave him her full attention. She truly was glad to see him. So perhaps she wasn't precisely a crotchety misanthrope. Perhaps she was simply selective about whose details to keep track of. New business ventures were far more exciting than the latest fashions—although she did not consider herself a frump.

"I'm to help Mother," he was saying. "She's throwing a party tomorrow for Eunice's suitor. Why don't you come?"

As if on cue Eunice, some of her social-climbing hangers-on, and her mother, Mrs. McMichael, appeared on the stairs. They were dressed to the nines, and Eunice was glowing.

"We met him at the British Museum," Mrs. McMichael announced. "Last fall, when we were visiting Alan."

"You wouldn't believe it. He's so handsome," Eunice gushed, all rosy blushes.

Edith was able to feel happy for Eunice. The other girl's dream was to be well married. She would lead a husband a merry dance, that was for certain.

"And he has now crossed the ocean with his sister only to see Eunice again," Mrs. McMichael continued, preening.

"Mother, he's here on business," Eunice protested mildly, but her words were only for show.

"Or so he *says*," one of Eunice's sycophants trilled, and Eunice blushed. If she'd been carrying a fan, she would have fluttered it like a butterfly to cool herself.

Mrs. McMichael pressed on. "It seems he's a baronet."

"What's a baronet?" another of Eunice's companions asked, and Mrs. McMichael shrugged with studied nonchalance.

"Oh, well, an aristocrat of some sort—"

"A man who lives off land that others work for him. A parasite with a title." The sharp words tumbled out before Edith had a chance to hear herself. Alan grinned behind his hand. But Mrs. McMichael arched her brows.

"I'm sorry," Edith began.

But Mrs. McMichael could clearly hold her own when any sort of challenge was raised regarding a matter close to her heart. Or more accurately, her pride.

"Well, this *parasite* is perfectly charming and a magnificent dancer. But that wouldn't concern you now, would it, Edith?" she added with asperity. "Our very own Jane Austen."

"Mother," Alan remonstrated her gently.

"Though I believe *she* died a spinster." Mrs. McMichael's gaze was flinty, her mouth set in a tight, insincere smile.

"Mother *please*," Alan said.

"It's quite all right, Alan," Edith assured him. She met the older woman's gaze full on. "I would prefer to be Mary Shelley," she said sweetly. "She died a widow." Savoring her sally, she took her leave.

She found a space in the public library's reading room and set down her manuscript, pushed her glasses onto the bridge of her nose, took out her pen and ink, and set to making her changes. Her pen leaked and smudged her fingers, so that when she smoothed back tendrils of her hair, she unknowingly left her own fingerprints on her forehead.

She had no idea of her somewhat disheveled state when at last she made her way to Mr. Ogilvie's office.

Early. Which the great and powerful publisher pointedly mentioned as she took a seat before his desk. She churned with well-concealed anxiety as page by page he read her cherished magnum opus.

She could have sworn she heard a clock ticking. Or maybe that was her knees knocking.

He sighed. Not a good sign.

"A ghost story. Your father didn't tell me it was a ghost story." Each syllable was laden with disappointment.

She was determined not to give up hope. "It's not, sir. It's more like a story… with a ghost in it."

She pointed at the manuscript with her ink-stained fingers. He pulled away. Undaunted, she said, "The ghost is just a metaphor, you see? For the past."

"A metaphor." He could not have sounded less enthusiastic. He read on a bit. "Nice handwriting. Firm loops."

Oh, no. He hates it.

He put the manuscript down and rearranged it slowly, rather like a child's nurse folding up a soiled nappy.

"So, Miss Cushing, how is your father?" he asked. "In good health, I hope?"

"He said it needed a love story. Can you believe that?"

Edith was incensed all over again. She leaned forward in her chair, which sat catty-corner to her father's in the golden dining room of their home, where they were taking their evening meal together. It was sunset, and light spilled over the damask wallpaper and alabaster sconces. The silver serving dishes glittered.

"Everyone falls in love, dear," he ventured. "Even women." He was dressed for dinner, every hair on his head carefully combed, his beard immaculately trimmed. Though her father was nearly sixty, the pains he took bore fruit: he looked considerably younger.

"He said that just because I'm a woman," she grumbled as the maids carried in elegant platters. "Why? Why must a woman always write about love? Stories of girls in search of the ideal husband—being saved by a dashing young prince? Fairy tales and lies."

An expression she couldn't read flittered across his face. Then he said, "Well, I'll have a word with Ogilvie on Monday morning at the club."

Edith huffed. "You most certainly will not. I will do this. Alone."

The look he gave her was gentle, and she braced herself for his objections—which she had no doubt he would intend as fatherly concern and nothing more, but which could certainly not sway her from her decided course. Then he frowned slightly and leaned toward her, as if examining her under a microscope.

"When you met Ogilvie, were your fingers ink-stained like that?"

She grimaced, recalling the smudge on her forehead as well. She had only discovered it after her appointment. "I'm afraid so. It won't come off."

He brightened. "Aha." Then he set a small package

before her with a flourish. "I was hoping this would be a celebratory gift but…"

She opened it and lifted out a beautiful gold fountain pen. It was the most magnificent writing instrument she had ever seen, and evidence of his faith in—and support of—her ambition to become a writer. Deeply touched, she kissed his cheek. Though he was flustered, the color in his face assured her that he was equally pleased.

"I'm a builder, dear. If I know one thing, it's the importance of the right tool for the job."

"Actually, Father, I would like to type it in your office," she informed him sweetly.

She almost missed his flash of disappointment as he regarded the gleaming pen, which was suddenly obsolete. "Type it?"

"I'm submitting it to *The Atlantic Monthly*," she said. "I realize now that my handwriting is too feminine."

"Too feminine?"

"It gives me away. I'll sign it E.M. Cushing. That'll keep them guessing."

He looked pensive. "Without a doubt."

CHAPTER THREE

THIS DAY IS mine.

Despite yesterday's rejection, Edith was light on her feet. Her hopes buoyed her on confident wings. Once she had a fair hearing—her work read by someone who was not prejudiced against her gender—she was confident that publication would be hers.

She almost—but not quite—imagined how proud her mother would be if presented with a book her own daughter had written. But she held that thought at bay, refusing it a place to land. The image of that blackened hand on her arm, that stench, that horrible voice—

It was only a nightmare. I was mad with grief.

No, you weren't. You know exactly—

She had arrived at last at her father's busy engineering offices. Dominated by huge models of buildings and bridges encased in glass, the airy rooms with their high ceilings proved a beehive of activity as engineers, clerks, and assistants examined miniature models, executed blueprints and measured drawings, and conducted the vast business of Mr. Carter Cushing. Her father had built some of the finest buildings in Buffalo, and in many other cities as well. Buildings of stone, brick, and iron that would carry his name and his vision down through the centuries. He was as much an artist in his world as she hoped to become in her own—in her case, the world of books and stories.

To that end, she sat ensconced in the chair of her father's secretary, her manuscript at her elbow, as she peered through her small round glasses at the alphabet keys, which were arranged in no discernable pattern. Hunting for each letter, it took a span of time to peck the title and opening line of the story. Several spans more to fill a page. Then, with a bit of coaching from the secretary, she touched the return lever and the carriage zipped across the top of the contraption with thrilling speed. Edith was delighted.

"It'll take me all day, but it does make it look rather handsome, don't you think?" she said.

The secretary busied herself with hefting a box file onto a shelf. Edith settled back to staring at the odd arrangement of letters on the keys when she became aware that there was some sort of shadow being thrown on the typewriter. She squinted, the merest bit vexed.

"Good morning, miss," said a voice. Male, English.

She looked up.

The bluest eyes she had ever seen were focused on her. She blinked, riveted. The visitor's face was chiseled, his dark hair neatly arranged, yet some curls had refused to be tamed. Her writer's brain conjured words to describe him: *astonishing, elegant, winning.* He was dressed in a blue velvet suit that had at one time been resplendent—yes, another good word—perfectly cut to mold his slim build, but was now nearly threadbare at the cuffs. His ensemble did not speak of poverty, precisely, but he was certainly not well off. Yet he acknowledged her look with a sort of courtly grace that did speak of good manners and a cultivated upbringing.

Other words sprang to mind: *uncommonly handsome.*

She revealed none of this as she waited to see what he would say next. For her part, the secretary was quite breathless. The man also carried a box, wooden and polished, under his arm. It looked heavy; he would have made short work of the task.

"Forgive the interruption," he said, his upper-class British accent falling tantalizingly on her American ears, "but I have an appointment with Mr. Carter Everett Cushing, Esquire."

Her father, in other words.

"Goodness. With the great man himself?" Edith asked, assuming a bland tone. She was rather taken with him, but it was not considered proper for a lady to behave too warmly to a man she did not know. And on occasion, Edith had been known to behave properly.

"I'm afraid so." His smile was a bit tentative and she realized that he was nervous. That only added to his attractiveness, as far as she was concerned. Dashing as he was, he was still human. She kept her eyes fastened on him as he produced a business card and presented it to her.

"Sir Thomas Sharpe, baronet," she read aloud. Then it dawned on her that this was Eunice's aristocrat. Her *parasite*. Good Lord, she *was* a crotchety misanthrope. She was the Elizabeth Bennett of her day. In *Pride and Prejudice*, Jane Austen's heroine had come to the exact same foregone conclusion about Mr. Darcy, who had been rakishly handsome and debonair—yet upper-class, and therefore worthy of Elizabeth's middle-class contempt for a do-nothing snob.

"I will call him." The secretary moved swiftly to do just that.

Sir Thomas Sharpe crooked his neck as he looked down at her desk.

"You're not late, are you?" Edith asked. "He hates that."

"Not at all. In fact, I'm a bit early."

A man after my own heart. So to speak.

"Oh. I'm afraid he hates that, too." She wasn't certain why she was teasing him so. It didn't matter; she was failing to get a rise out of him. His nervousness had dissipated. In fact, he seemed rather distracted. She was a bit crushed.

"I'm sorry, I don't mean to pry. But—" he gestured at her manuscript, and she realized then that he'd craned his neck in order to read it "—this is a piece of fiction, is it not?"

She nodded, concealing her consternation. She wanted to explain that the ghost was a metaphor, and to assure him that she had already decided that it was just too silly for the heroine to fall in love with Cavendish on page one and she was going to change it back to the way it had been before Ogilvie had turned it down. She shouldn't have listened to him, even if he was a famous publisher. Love stories *were* fairy tales and lies as far as she was concerned and… good Lord, he was reading more of it.

"Who are you transcribing this for?" he asked, genuinely interested. But she couldn't tell if he was intrigued or horrified by the text on the page.

She decided to dodge his question. If he hated it, that would be altogether mortifying. "It's to be sent to New York tomorrow. *The Atlantic Monthly.*"

He took that in. Read another page. "Well, whoever wrote this is quite good, don't you think?"

Delighted, she tipped back her head, the better to read his reaction. "Is it?" she tested.

He shrugged as if to say, *Isn't it obvious to you that it's good?* "It's captured my attention."

He was being sincere. He truly liked it. He liked her book. Not since Alan had anyone read any of it… until Ogilvie. And Alan had listened carefully, but hadn't provided commentary except to say things such as, "That's a nice description of the countryside," or, "I'm sorry, I'm confused. Is the ghost real or not?"

But Sir Thomas Sharpe, baronet, had pronounced it *quite good.* No doubt he'd attended superior boarding schools and studied at a great university such as Oxford. He probably had a vast library in his castle and had read Virgil in the original Latin. How could her little book compare?

Favorably, that was how. He had said so himself. She was galvanized. Here was a kindred spirit.

Should she confess? Why not?

"I wrote it. It's mine." She heard the pride in her voice.

He brightened measurably. His lips parted and he was about to say something more when her father's deep voice boomed out.

"Sir Thomas Sharpe. Welcome to our fair city."

Carter Cushing approached. As he regarded the Englishman, a cloud crossed his face, then vanished when he turned his attention to her.

"I see you've met my daughter, Edith."

Edith enjoyed Sir Thomas's flicker of surprise and smiled at the speechless man as her father escorted him toward the meeting room. The younger man carried his wooden box as if it were a precious object, and Edith determined to find out why he was there. Everything about him was immensely interesting. She rose from the desk, leaving her manuscript where it lay.

By then the two men had entered the meeting room. She peered through the open door and saw that some of the most prominent businessmen in Buffalo had taken places at the polished desks positioned in a circular arrangement. It was a high-profile gathering; she spotted Mr. William Ferguson, her father's lawyer. All eyes were on young Sir Thomas Sharpe, who stood in the center. No wonder he'd been nervous. It was like facing a dozen Ogilvies.

"The Sharpe clay mines have been Royal Purveyors of the purest scarlet clay since 1796." His voice was firm and authoritative, all traces of the jitters utterly vanished. He held up another wooden container, this one much smaller than the box. Inside lay a deep scarlet brick with some sort of seal on it. He passed it around to the august bewhiskered men, and each examined the intensely hued clay.

Intrigued, Edith walked into the room and shut the door after herself. Her father's colleagues were used to her observing from the perimeter and paid her no mind. But Sir Thomas's gaze flickered, and she was both abashed and pleased that she had proved a distraction.

"Excessive mining in the last twenty years caused most of our old deposits to collapse, which crippled our operations and endangered our ancestral home," Sir Thomas continued.

He has an ancestral home. Just like Cavendish in my novel, Edith thought.

"You leeched the life out of the land, is that what you're saying?" her father asked sharply. "Bled it dry—"

"No," Sir Thomas protested, still quite calm. "New clay shales exist but have proved elusive to reach."

Well said, Edith thought approvingly. Her father was even more intimidating than Ogilvie. She decided to observe Sir Thomas in action and learn what she could of the fine art of salesmanship. Authors often watched the world so that they could properly render it on the page.

However, during her musings on the subject of being

more observant, she had missed a portion of Sir Thomas's demonstration. He had opened the larger wooden box and pulled out a scale model of what Edith recognized from her many days in her father's office as a mining drill. He had connected the drill to a little brass boiler and with a theatrical hiss of steam, the burnished brass levels and gears started moving. The drill spun. The miniature was charming, and clearly also quite impressive, for the men leaned forward as they studied it. Little buckets crept upward and she could just picture them scooping out ruby-red clay and depositing it on a wagon.

"This is a clay harvester of my own design," Sir Thomas said. "It matches the output of a ten-man crew. Transports the clay upwards as it digs deep. This machine can revolutionize mining as we know it."

The men began to applaud, and Edith was pleased for the earnest young aristocrat. What a clever inventor he was. Clever and handsome, then. Eunice was a lucky girl… though Edith doubted her impeding engagement to this man had anything to do with luck and everything to do with her mother's ambitions. If she knew Mrs. McMichael, the lady had lain in wait for Sir Thomas at the British Museum and "happened" to engage him in some way that, while perhaps somewhat forward, would not have been considered indiscreet or ill-mannered. And the hours Eunice had likely spent primping just in case the meeting was successful would have been time well spent. She *was* a very beautiful young woman.

Then Edith noted that among all those present, her

father was the only one *not* applauding. In fact, he was scowling.

"Turn it off," he barked, then softened his command, "please. Who built that?"

Sir Thomas inclined his head. "I built and designed the model myself."

I'll bet he could build a more sensible typewriter, Edith thought. *Honestly, the arrangement of the letters makes no sense at all.*

In the ensuing silence, the other businessmen regarded her father, whose cold smile bespoke his skepticism.

"Have you tested it? Full scale?"

"I'm very close, sir, but with the funding—"

"So all you have is a toy and some fancy words," her father interrupted.

Sir Thomas's face fell, and Edith felt a rush of protective indignation on his behalf. Carter Cushing had every right to question him, of course, but his tone was quite biting. Dismissive. *Just* like Ogilvie.

Her father picked up a document that had been lying at his elbow and scrutinized it before he spoke again. "You have already tried—and failed—to raise capital in London, Edinburgh, Milan."

The Englishman raised his brows just a bit, obviously surprised. "Yes, sir. That's correct."

Her father stood. "And now you're here." His voice held a sharper edge, and Edith unconsciously pushed away from the wall. However, she was in no position to argue whatever point her father was about to make. This was Sir Thomas's battle, and if she spoke up, it would only embarrass him.

"Correct again," Sir Thomas replied.

"The men at this table, all of us, came up through honest, hard work. *Almost* all of us. Mr. Ferguson is a lawyer, but even he can't help that."

It was a tired joke, but the titans of Buffalo industry laughed anyway. They gave each other looks that indicated that Cushing had a point. They *had* "come up" through honest, hard work. By implication, Sir Thomas had not. The men in this room held the same inverted snobbery Edith had held herself until very recently—perhaps an hour ago at most.

The titled, very English Sir Thomas stood alone in a room filled with hardscrabble Americans who put stock in results and not in charming presentations. Edith sensed that the tide was turning in favor of her father and his disdain, though of what—Sir Thomas's invention or the man himself—she wasn't certain.

"I started out a steel worker, raising buildings so that I could own them," her father went on. He approached Sir Thomas with raised hands. "Rough. They reflect who I am. Now, you, *sir*…"

He gripped Sir Thomas's hands; the younger man's back stiffened slightly, and Edith recalled reading that English people were more standoffish than their American counterparts. Perhaps he didn't like to be touched. She wondered what it would be like, however, to touch his fingertips. Perhaps even his unsmiling lips.

And *she* should not be thinking of such things.

"You have the softest hands I've ever felt," her father announced. "In America, we bank on effort, not privilege. That is how we built this country."

But he is being unfair, Edith thought. *Sir Thomas told him that he designed and built the model himself. It must have taken some doing to visualize and construct such a revolutionary device.* It occurred to her that he was a creative person like herself— and he too was about to be rejected.

Her father moved away from Sir Thomas. The baronet's deep blue eyes flared with passion, and he raised his chin.

"I am here with all that I possess, sir." He spoke most respectfully and with humility, a counterpoint to her father's patronizing, judgmental tone. "A name, a patch of land, and the will to make it yield. The least you can grant me is the courtesy of your time and the chance to prove to you, and these fine gentleman, that my will, dear sir, is, at the very least, as strong as yours."

Well done, so very well said, Edith thought, and as Sir Thomas glanced toward her, she sensed that it was time for her to withdraw. Sir Thomas was intent on standing his ground, and perhaps he might feel his speech constrained by a lady's presence. He was in total command of himself and fully prepared to stand up to her father. Many other men had withered in the attempt.

He is not going to wither. I can feel it. A shock jittered up her spine. *I have strength of will, too. I am like him.*

What she felt was more than that. It was something

she had only read about, and before now, never believed in. She blushed and turned away. As she left the room, she began to tremble, and it took all her own strength not to turn back for one last gaze at Eunice McMichael's suitor.

CHAPTER FOUR

EDITH LOOKED OUT on a great and dirty city. Dickens would have termed it thus, a city saturated with gloom and soot. Slanting torrents of rain turned the streets of Buffalo into fields of mud as thick as clay.

Huddled in their greatcoats, under umbrellas, pedestrians hurried past Cushing Manor, anxious to avoid the deluge, while inside the Cushings' servants turned on the gas lamps. A warm glow emanated from the prosperous redbrick building, dissolving into the gloaming.

Edith wore a mustard-yellow dressing gown as she fondly regarded her father, while he scrutinized his reflection in the mirror. He looked dapper in his tails, and his waistcoat was her favorite gold one. His birthday was in a couple of weeks, and she had a wonderful surprise planned for him—a bound presentation book of watercolor sketches of his most important building projects. It was being completed now.

"I need a corset," he said with a sigh as he appraised the slight girth of his middle.

His vanity touched her because of the vulnerability it revealed. She went to him and tied his bow tie.

"No, you don't."

"I wish you'd change your mind and come along tonight. Mrs. McMichael's gone to a lot of trouble." He grunted. "Little Lord Fauntleroy will be there."

She almost chuckled at his choice of names, but didn't. He had been too stern with Sir Thomas, and she didn't want him to think she shared his contempt. Far from it.

"You mean Thomas Sharpe?" she said pointedly.

"*Sir Thomas Sharpe, baronet.* Apparently he has taken an interest in young Eunice."

And she wondered if Eunice appreciated him beyond the allure of his title and charm. He was an intelligent, innovative man who would thrive when matched with a partner who enjoyed the life of the mind. Eunice preferred shopping and dances. But perhaps that was all *he* expected from a wife. Her father had raised her differently. As an heiress, she could afford to be quite particular about what she wanted in a husband. In all honesty, she had very seriously entertained the notion that she might never marry. Were Sir Thomas free, she might consider it. But he was not.

Even so, she couldn't stop herself from rising to his

defense. "Was his proposal so outrageous as to merit such a harsh answer from you?"

"It wasn't his proposal, my love, it was *him*. There's something about him that I don't like. What, I don't know." He shrugged. "And I don't like not knowing."

"You were cruel," Edith insisted.

"Really? Maybe that's how I conduct business, child."

"What I saw was a dreamer facing defeat. Did you not notice his suit? Beautifully tailored—but at least a decade old. And his shoes were handmade but worn." *And I'm not sure I'm helping his case. My father is a successful businessman who deals with other successful people.*

"I can see you observed far more than I did." He quirked an eyebrow and she fought down her flush. "At any rate, he'll have his chance. The boardroom wants to hear more about it. In spite of my reservations."

That pleased her. She was about to say so as she helped him on with his jacket when the doorbell rang.

"That'll be young Dr. McMichael," her father declared with real warmth. "He's brought his new motorcar to collect me. Come and see it. Say hello to him. He's just opened his new practice." He headed toward the hallway. "He's always been awfully fond of you."

They descended the staircase together. "I know that, Father." Alan had been her childhood playmate and had grown up to be her friend. She knew that there was no romantic spark between them. After all, she was about to welcome a visitor wearing nothing but her dressing gown. If he were a serious suitor, her father would not have permitted such a breach of etiquette.

Nonsense. He never even notices such things.

The door opened to pouring rain and Alan, who cut quite a figure in his formal wear. His blond hair was swept back and neater than usual, and his eyes shone when he caught sight of her. She grinned back at him, not at all embarrassed to be seen looking less than her best.

"Good evening, Mr. Cushing. Edith."

"My, don't we look smart, Alan," she said easily.

"Oh, you like it? It's just something I threw together," he bantered.

"It's Edith who should be the belle of the ball, don't you agree, Alan?" said her father. A servant brought his hat and coat and Edith hoped his good mood lasted long enough for him to be a bit kinder to Sir Thomas.

"I was rather hoping it would be so." Alan cocked his head. "But Edith takes a dim view of social frivolity."

"As I recall, you're not so keen on it yourself," she shot back.

He made a face. "Tonight, I have no choice. Eunice would never forgive me."

That's true, Edith thought. *If anyone can hold a grudge, it's Eunice McMichael.* She had watched Eunice shun former best friends for the flimsiest of imagined slights.

Edith regarded the two men fondly. "You lads enjoy yourselves." Then she whispered sotto voce to Alan, "Please don't let him drink too much."

* * *

The door to Cushing Manor closed as firmly as Edith's refusal to attend the soirée. As Alan held out an umbrella for Mr. Cushing and they walked toward his motorcar, he was disappointed but not surprised that she was staying home. He would have skipped the party, too, if it weren't being held in his home, by his family. Still, if Eunice married the young aristocrat, she would leave home and perhaps then Edith would call on the McMichaels more frequently. He certainly understood why she kept her distance. He loved his sister, but she could be quite mean.

"So she's not coming." It wasn't a question. It was an opening gambit to find out precisely why. He had his opinions, but it stung him a bit that though he was but newly returned, she had not found that sufficient reason to put on a pretty dress and take a turn on the dance floor with him.

"I tried," Mr. Cushing said. "Stubborn to the bone."

"And where does she get that from?" Alan jabbed playfully. "I like it."

Her willfulness indicated that Edith had a mind of her own, and he did like her mind. She was a prodigious wit and very creative, too. He was a man of science, not given to flights of fancy such as hers. He'd loved hearing her read passages from her book so long ago, but had never known exactly what to say in response. "I like it" had always sounded so weak.

"So do I," her doting father admitted.

They climbed in and Alan guided the car into the

rainy street. Next stop: social frivolity. If only Edith had consented to attend. She would have brought a ray of sunshine into a tedious, rainy night.

I couldn't go, of course. I had so much to do: I was busy reading about clay mining in the north of England. And about the Sharpes' home, Allerdale Hall. One of the most elegant homes in Northern England.

Edith knew that she would never see Sir Thomas's ancestral home, but she was curious about it. And about him. She had already decided to rewrite Cavendish so that he more resembled the inscrutable young man—a common practice of authors she had learned from her research about the literary life. After her father and Alan's departure, Edith lay sprawled on her large bed and studied a thick book replete with maps of England and intricate engravings of daily life. Cumberland, England, was the location of the Sharpe clay mines and their "family seat": an enormous, castle-like building. Carriages entered and exited via a porte cochère; ladies with parasols strolled alongside gentlemen in top hats carrying walking canes.

It was enchanting. She imagined Sir Thomas drinking tea and discussing his invention with beautifully dressed visitors in a room decorated with oil paintings of his noble ancestors and a coat of arms over the mantel. She had never been to England, although she had read all the important British authors and some of the popular ones as well. She liked Charles Dickens very much, and her secret guilty pleasures were the ghost stories of Sheridan Le Fanu and Arthur Machen. She and her mother had read the Shakespeare plays, of course. Her mother's favorite had been *A Midsummer Night's Dream*. But for her money, she would take *Hamlet* or *Macbeth*. Stories with ghosts in them. She could imagine Thomas taking her to see a Shakespeare play in London.

Sir Thomas, you twit, she remonstrated herself. *And he's practically engaged to Eunice. They'll probably make the announcement tonight.*

Which was the real reason, of course, that she was not attending the ball. One must be philosophical about these things. And while she had no hopes of being with him, she fully intended on escaping into the charming, mysterious man's world, even if just for a few hours, by burying her nose in these books. The old world. Titles and privilege. So much depended on the accident of one's birth. If you were the oldest son, you got everything. But if you were a younger brother, or a sister…

She wondered if Sir Thomas had siblings. She imagined him with doting parents. And a dog. Several. Hunting dogs, perhaps, though the notion of actual hunts repulsed her. What were they called? Blood sports.

Outside, raindrops spattered the windows. Thunder rumbled. The sky was unnaturally dark, and a sharp wind whistled down the lane. Father and Alan would be at the party soon, where there would be crackling fires and hot rum punch, and candles everywhere. She could just see Sir Thomas in his white tie and tails.

She smiled wistfully as she memorized the lines and angles of his grand family estate. Her father had visited many of the opulent homes of American tycoons, some even designed to look like English castles.

The handle to her door turned slowly.

Edith raised up on her elbow and watched it. It kept turning, as if by someone whose hands were too full to push open the door.

She rose from the bed, more curious than afraid.

"Father?" she called. "Did you forget something?"

She heard no reply. The handle kept moving, jittering wildly. Then suddenly the door swung open.

She jumped. No one was there. Wary and confused as long-buried memories bubbled toward the surface, she moved into the hall toward the upper-floor parlor, telling herself that she wasn't afraid, that every chill down her spine was not an echo of something that had happened to her fourteen years ago.

When her mother—

She balled her fists and kept walking along the hallway.

Halfway down, she froze. She saw a shadow; she could *see* a woman in black, a dead woman, a *thing* of bones and decay and grave dirt—

No. I do not see her. I am not seeing this. I am asleep on my bed thinking of Macbeth.

But she was awake, and though the shadows were very deep, she *was* seeing something…

Gasping, Edith turned on her heel and raced back to

her room, shut the door and held firm to the handle. She trembled, teeth chattering, trying to make sense of what she thought she saw, trying not to panic. Denial was her instinctive response.

I did not see that. It was my imagination, like that first time. It was—

Her heart pounded. There was no pressure on the handle. No sound on the other side of the door. She listened harder, ear pressed close to the wood.

Then came the rustle of silk…

And then… the turn of the handle once more, this time moving against her fingers.

Chills raced down her back as she held the handle with both hands, fighting to keep the door shut. If the door opened—

If she saw—

"What is it?" she cried. "What do you want?"

Two withered hands burst straight through the door and grabbed her by the shoulders. They were burning cold blocks, sticks of ice, painfully strong. Then a horrible, blackened head that stank of the grave crashed through the wood, the figure's features crushed, the face a ruin.

No, not crushed; the face was *rippling*, like water.

And the voice that had read her to sleep so many childhood nights, the voice that now rushed forth from long-dead lungs was likewise quavering, distorted almost beyond recognition.

"Beware of Crimson Peak!"

Edith fell backwards and scrambled away. The room

tilted, then whirled. She couldn't breathe, could only gape. There could be no doubt this time it was her mother, her long-dead and buried mother.

Then her face, her hands vanished. The door was unmarred. Edith heard herself gasping.

The door handle turned again, and Edith choked back a scream as Annie, one of the maids, cracked it open and leaned in.

Mute with horror, Edith could only stare at the girl.

"Are you all right, miss? Whatever is it?" the maid asked anxiously.

"Nothing. You—you startled me, that's all."

Oh, my God, I saw a ghost. Or else I am mad.

Annie did not press her mistress for further explanation.

"There's a Sir Thomas Sharpe at the door," Annie said. "He's dripping wet and most insistent on coming in."

"Thomas Sharpe?" Edith fought for composure. "At this hour? Did you tell him Father was out?"

Annie bobbed her head. "I told him that, miss. He won't go away. He wants to talk to *you*."

Edith was stunned. "It's out of the question, Annie," she said, forcing the quaver out of her voice. Beyond the impropriety of receiving a gentleman in her dressing gown and without her father in the house, Edith felt barely coherent. She had just seen a ghost.

Had she not?

"Send him away."

The maid shrugged helplessly. "I tried."

"And?"

"He won't go away."

Nonplussed, Edith found herself in a kind of fog descending the stairs. The situation was untenable.

I saw a ghost. She was here.

But she had no proof of that. Her door was unblemished. She had been working very hard on her novel—revising with a sharper, tougher eye since Sir Thomas had commented on it, she had to confess. A dream would have churned up horrific images, memories. She had read of the lengths to which her fellow author, Edgar Allan Poe, had gone to wrest the grotesque and phantasmagorical from the humdrum, mundane outer life he had endured as a magazine editor. And Samuel Taylor Coleridge had smoked opium to bring such deeply buried visions as the Ancient Mariner to life.

So perhaps this simply means that I am digging into my own mine—into a rich vein of metaphors for my own loss, as I told Mr. Ogilvie. Perhaps this happened because I am changing. I thought never to leave Father's side, as he would then be alone. I believed I had no interest in a husband of my own. I had assumed I would be content to serve as Father's hostess for as long as he lived.

Perhaps this is my fear that my father will not always be here. His birthday is coming, and he is growing old, no matter how he may try to disguise it. And I have a true calling to write. I cannot deny it. I should embrace these specters that I see. They are a gift.

Still, she was quite shaken. But good breeding and manners took over as she saw Sir Thomas in the foyer, his long, wavy hair damp with rainwater. He was wearing a black coat, perfectly cut, a white vest and tie, trousers revealing the polished tips of a pair of leather dancing boots. No more elegant man had ever crossed the threshold of Cushing Manor in her lifetime, not even her father. She was confounded.

He is spoken for, she reminded herself. *Well, almost.*

"Miss Cushing, are you all right? You seem quite pale." His deep-set eyes narrowed with genuine concern.

If I summoned the courage to tell him what just happened upstairs, he would no doubt think me hysterical, or mad.

"I am not all too well, Sir Thomas, I'm sorry to say. And Father's not home." She spoke in a clipped fashion in an attempt to maintain her control.

"I know that. I saw him leave." He paused and then added, "I waited in the rain for him to leave."

Despite her distress, she understood, with a shock, that he was calling on her.

"Oh?" Edith managed.

"I know he is going to the reception at the McMichael house," he continued. "Which is my destination, too."

Now she wasn't quite following again. Concentrating took a supreme effort. Too much had happened. Was happening.

"But that's Bidwell Parkway, sir. This is Masten Park. You are very, very lost."

"That I am," he concurred. "And I desperately need your help."

"Help with what?" she asked cautiously.

"Well, Miss Cushing, the language, for one." His

smile was rueful. "As you can plainly see, I do not speak a word of American."

At that, she mustered a small smile. He had a wit. The master of Allerdale Hall had come calling. He cut a breath-catching figure in his evening clothes. And yet…

"Sir Thomas, I simply can't."

"Please, am I to make even more of a wretch of myself?" he beseeched her. "Why would you want to stay here, all alone?"

Why indeed? She gazed back up the stairs toward her room. Had that happened? Had it really happened? Perhaps she had dreamed it.

I know that I didn't. I know what I saw.

Fear bubbled up.

She swallowed it down.

They are gifts, she reminded herself.

CHAPTER FIVE

This party can't get any worse, Alan McMichael thought as he gazed around at the glittering assembly of Buffalo high society. The ladies were dressed in the finest fashions from Paris, bare-shouldered, draped with pearls and glowing, the gentlemen in their tailcoats and gloves. Candles gleamed and a profusion of artfully arranged flowers lent an air of magic to the McMichael home. *Poor Eunice.*

For his sister, the night could not get any less magical. Though she was holding her own, chin high, it was becoming quite apparent that the guest of honor, her suitor, Sir Thomas Sharpe, baronet, had stood her up.

She and Mother had presided over a frenzy of home preparation—the floor polished, the piano tuned, and the lavish midnight supper arrayed in all its splendor: caviar, truffles, snipe, partridge, oysters, quail, grouse, pressed beef, ham, tongue, chicken, galantines, lobster, melons, peaches, nectarines, and specially imported jams and biscuits. Champagne, of course, flips, toddies, and the punch Alan had learned to make in London while in medical school. Eunice had insisted that he recreate it in their sterling silver punchbowl, and the few sips he had taken to test it had set him back on his heels. Tea, coffee, lemonade, white wine, claret, and sweet Madeira were also going to be served, along with negus, orgeat, and ratafia, accompanying the proper courses. There were towers of fruit, sugared almonds, and marzipan, custards, and cakes.

They had gone to all this effort and this expense, publicly declaring the regard in which the McMichael family held Sir Thomas and his sister, and the blackguard was not here. After having accepted the invitation Sir Thomas was duty-bound to appear. He had not sent his regrets—though nothing short of a death in the family would have excused him—and Buffalo society was left bearing witness that he was snubbing Eunice on the most special of evenings. It was the height of rudeness, and sufficiently hurtful to break even the flintiest of hearts. And Eunice was not precisely flinty. She was spoiled, yes, and jealous when it came to focusing attention on herself. And on occasion, less than sweet to Edith.

But she did not deserve this humiliation.

Alan had inquired of Lady Lucille Sharpe, Sir Thomas's lovely dark-haired sister, where she thought her brother might be. Discreetly, of course, and phrased in such a way as to not embarrass her. Lady Sharpe had been unconcerned, nonchalantly assuring him that Sir Thomas would arrive soon. He knew he should not press, but he was angry. Then Alan's mother had announced that Lady Sharpe had graciously consented to play some pieces on their piano, and any further conversation on the subject was terminated. Mercifully so, for it really was bad manners of him to put her on the spot.

Lady Sharpe's upswept hair was a rich chestnut; it was dotted with scarlet stones too impossibly large to be actual rubies. A similar gem graced her finger, a garnet, deeply red and rich. Perhaps it was real. Her green eyes were enormous, set in a porcelain face of striking features. As she seated herself on the piano bench, the rich folds of her antique gown seemed to shimmer, drenching the fabric in deeper shades of jewel-like crimson. She looked almost Elizabethan, the back of the dress elaborately laced, with a high-necked ruff the color of fresh blood.

The lush, romantic strains of Chopin drifted from the keys beneath her fingers and the partygoers, most of whom were standing, drew a collective breath. The English beauty sat very straight, bending slightly toward the keyboard. Her musicianship was flawless and she played with depth between the swelling crescendos. Yet, surrounding the lady herself was an air of unapproachability, almost coldness. Alan knew from having lived in London that the upper classes of English society were raised to betray very little emotion in public, and perhaps that was what he was observing. It could be that she, too, furtively glanced at the gilt clock above the mantel and silently cursed her brother's name.

Lady Sharpe concluded the piece with a flourish. Alan realized then that there was real passion in the soul of Lucille Sharpe, expressed through music. She was more than the decorous traveling companion of her brother. He wondered what she dreamed of, what she wished for. She was two years older than Sir Thomas and, apparently, unmarried; certainly she must have had chances. Perhaps she had been widowed? Would she welcome an American girl into the family, step aside as Sir Thomas's hostess and allow his new wife to shine?

As the assembly broke into applause, Lady Sharpe rose and dipped in modest acknowledgement. Then attention turned from her and murmurs rippled through the room. Like the others, Alan turned from the lady to see what the cause was, and his lips parted in surprise.

Sir Thomas Sharpe, the hallowed guest, had arrived at last.

And Edith, stunningly dressed in a gown of champagne satin that Alan had never seen before, was on his arm. Their appearance bespoke a couple, and Alan was bewildered. She had said she was not coming, yet here she was. He looked to Carter Cushing and found he too appeared astonished at his daughter's arrival. What was Sir Thomas's part in all this? Did they not see that this dramatic entrance was rather scandalous?

I should see to Eunice, he thought. *This will upset her, and she has every right.* But he couldn't stop staring at Edith. She was a vision, cheeks rosy, hair tenderly gathered up to reveal the slender column of her neck, the smoothness of her shoulders. The little girl who had wept at her mother's grave had grown into a beautiful woman, and he could not help the way his heart played its own melody of yearning. He doubted, however, that her heartstrings were strumming a tune for him. He was still her childhood playmate, not a man who might win her affections. Certainly no match for the dark-haired aristocrat before whom the crowd parted like the Red Sea before Moses.

Someone who, he feared, may have already won her affections. As they joined the party, Edith's smile was mysterious, like the Mona Lisa's. As if they had shared a confidence before crossing the threshold of Alan's home and had sworn to keep it always to themselves.

He swallowed his consternation as the pair approached. Edith regarded Alan gently as she and Sharpe faced him together. She said, "Alan, may I introduce Sir Thomas Sharpe?" Then she turned to Sharpe and said, "Sir Thomas, this is Dr. McMichael. The best man in town if you're feeling poorly."

Perhaps she meant it as a compliment, but Alan felt damned by faint praise. Was that all he was to her? However, he said politely, "That's quite a glowing presentation. I'm Eunice's brother, sir. I've heard so much about you." There. He had reminded Sharpe that the baronet had offered Eunice hope back in London, and politeness required that a gentleman treat her with decorum now.

"A pleasure." Sharpe bowed slightly.

Sharpe gestured to his own sister, who joined them. Eunice and their mother approached on Sharpe's other side, their faces carefully composed. "And, Edith, this is Lady Lucille Sharpe—my sister."

"Charmed, Miss Cushing," Lady Sharpe said. "You've managed to delay my brother quite a bit." She waited for that to sink in, and then she continued. "Eunice was growing awfully desperate. You see? She claims that no gentleman in America knows how to dance a proper waltz."

She kissed Sharpe's cheek. "I trust you will oblige."

Out of the corner of his eye Alan saw his sister smile. So all was mended then. Good. He felt so relieved. And now Edith would be released to consent to a dance with him; he savored the prospect. The bright side was that she was here now, and that was delightful.

"I will if you play it for me, dear sister," Sharpe said.

Lady Sharpe regally inclined her head. "With pleasure."

When Edith moved to stand beside Eunice, Alan noticed the distance she had put between them. Then Mr. Cushing stepped close.

"Interesting development, don't you think?" he said in a low voice.

Alan heard the disapproval in his voice and wondered if he had missed something. He nodded. And then he tensed as his mother approached Edith. Her smile was forced, and her eyes were hard as diamonds.

Mother, please don't stir up a hornet's nest.

"Edith, what a surprise this is," Mrs. McMichael bit off.

Edith flushed, indicating that she knew that she was rather in the wrong. She had already sent her regrets, and to show up on the arm of Eunice's suitor was an affront.

"We were not expecting you for dinner," his mother added, in case Edith did not fully understand the gravity of her social faux pas.

"I know," Edith said contritely, "and I am terribly sorry for this imposition. I am sure there is no place for me and—"

"Oh, don't worry, my child," she interrupted her. "Everyone has a place. I will make sure you find yours."

Alan inwardly winced at the barb.

Over at the piano, Lady Sharpe arranged herself and flashed a tiny, complicit smile at Eunice. With a theatrical sweep of his hand, like a magician, Sir Thomas took a candle from a nearby candelabrum.

"The waltz," he began, playing to the gallery. "Not a complicated dance, really. The lady takes her place slightly to the left of the leading gentleman. Six basic steps. That is all."

Alan's sister and their mother were attentive, eager. What woman wouldn't be, about to be swept into the arms of a true-life Prince Charming?

"However, it is said that the true test of a perfect waltz is for it to be so sweet, delicate, and so smooth, that a candle flame will not be extinguished in the hand of the lead dancer. Now *that* requires the perfect partner."

Eunice, of course, Alan filled in. His sister would be so

enthralled that he doubted her dancing shoes would touch the ground.

Sir Thomas turned… and held out his hand to *Edith*. "Would you be mine?"

Everyone in the room gasped. Edith's eyes widened, and then she looked demurely down. Alan saw her lips move, but he could not hear her reply.

Edith looked at Sir Thomas's outstretched hand and wondered if he had any idea of the scene he was causing. A brewing scandal, and the shame it would bring on her. There were murmurs among the guests, and she couldn't make herself look in Eunice's direction. In the heat of Sir Thomas's gaze as he had challenged her to come with him to the party, Edith had thought of herself as a New Woman, freed from the strictures of the old century. But now that she stood before him with eyes downcast, wordlessly begging him to observe propriety, she realized she wasn't quite as modern as she had supposed herself to be. These were her friends, and she wanted their good opinion… no matter how desperately she would love to dance with him.

"I don't think so, thank you," she said in a voice meant only for him to hear. Ladies *never* refused a gentleman's invitation to dance. However, this was beyond the pale. Yes, she had arrived on his arm, but she was not here *with* him. She had felt almost Bohemian, an artistic nonconformist making an entrance… but having anticipated that Sir Thomas would propose to Eunice tonight, she had fully expected to bid him adieu soon after. "But I'm sure Eunice would be delighted," she added bluntly, further bolstering her awkward but nonetheless sincere desire to put right her foolish indiscretion.

His smile did not waiver. "I daresay, but I asked you." To the onlookers, he said, "Please make some space."

Somehow she found herself moving to the center of the ballroom. Which was worse? To stand there while he stretched out his hand for an eternity while everyone awaited the apparently inevitable outcome? Or to get it over with? Eunice and her mother were stricken, and Edith didn't blame them.

"Eunice is a very sweet girl, you know," she murmured. "Kind and loyal. I am flattered, but—"

"Is it so hard to accept that you're beautiful?" he said softly. "As well as delightful and intelligent?"

"I can't do this, I can't. Please," she protested.

Lady Sharpe put her hands to the keyboard. And Sir Thomas's gaze was unwavering. Insistent.

"I've always just closed my eyes to things that made me uncomfortable. It works wonderfully. Won't you try it?" he urged.

And she knew that she was going to waltz with Sir Thomas Sharpe.

"I don't want to close my eyes," she replied. "I want to keep them open."

A sweeping melody rose from the piano as Edith's fingers descended lightly into Sir Thomas's outstretched palm. His touch electrified her, and the dance—their dance—began. Gliding, his hand firm on her back, he led her in the simple but majestic steps. Gazes locked, his face swimming before her, his expression confident and… joyous? He was finding real pleasure in waltzing around the ballroom with her. And she with him.

The flame on the long white taper in his grasp fluttered but remained lit, attesting to his mastery as he traveled the floor with her. Her hand in his, his smile, the grace with which he moved and caused her to move. She felt so different. The connection she had felt in the meeting room held, grew, binding them as they glided together, perfectly matched. Faces blurred and the requirements of civility no longer took precedent; they had entered a private world where no one else existed. At least, not until the last notes of the dance drifted away and then, of course, it was over.

The candle Sir Thomas held still glowed, and Edith, utterly transformed, made a wish deep inside her heart and blew it out.

What that wish was, she would never say out loud, but Sir Thomas's satisfied smile and courtly bow seemed to answer it with an unspoken *yes*.

Then Sir Thomas's sister rose from the piano and left the room. With one more gentle look at Edith, he took his leave and followed her out. He took Edith's heart with him. Surely he knew that.

CHAPTER SIX

CARTER CUSHING STOOD before the mirror in the shower room of his club. His shaving things and a fine breakfast of ham and eggs, coffee and a small glass of port were spread before him. The attendant, one Benton, had just hand-cranked the phonograph and it played an old sentimental tune that his dear, departed wife used to hum. Her voice had been so sweet; he had loved to close his eyes and listen to her singing lullabies to Edith. And reading to her. The nursery had been a refuge from the hard dealings of the male world—a world he had tried very hard not to deny his headstrong daughter, since she was determined to make her way in it. But in this instance, he must protect her if there was anything to protect her from.

And after Sir Thomas's display at the McMichaels' ball, he was even more sure that there was.

Unwelcome business, this, Carter Cushing thought as he detected the familiar footsteps of the odious man about to enter his employ once more. *I wish I felt no reason to proceed.*

As if on cue, the gaunt, young figure of Hezekiah Holly approached, gingerly making his way across the tiled floor in hopes of keeping his nice leather boots dry. He wore spats and imagined himself quite the dandy. He was not.

"Mr. Holly," Cushing said. "I like the club first thing in the morning. I have it all to myself."

"A great way to start the day, sir," Holly replied officiously.

"Isn't it? And perhaps a good time to end certain things, too." He paused, but he had come to a decision, even if it might lead to crushing disappointment for his beloved daughter. "There is a young gentleman and his sister. Something's not quite right about them."

He handed Holly a slip of paper with *Sir Thomas Sharpe, baronet* and *Lady Lucille Sharpe* written on it. "These are their names. I need you to investigate for me. Spare no expense. I want results." He handed Holly a check. "As soon as possible."

No sense prolonging her agony, if that is what it comes to.

It was a brilliant day in Delaware Park, the most recent in a number of brilliant days Edith had spent in the company of the Sharpes. A band played; families picnicked. The weather was absolutely glorious. Edith strolled with Lady Lucille Sharpe, a parasol protecting their complexions from the bright sunlight. She wore her burnished gold skirt accessorized with the belt of two ivory hands clasped one over the other, a personal favorite because it reminded her of the illustrations in her cherished childhood copy of *Beauty and the Beast*. The Beast's enchanted castle was populated by magical servants who did his bidding, and although they were supposed to be invisible, in the pictures, they were shown as spectral white hands outlined in black. When first they had read the story together, Edith had asked her mother if they were ghosts. Mama had replied that there were no such things, and if anyone—perhaps Cook, who was Irish and therefore superstitious—told her otherwise, she was not to listen.

The Sharpes were both dressed in deepest coal black, which reminded Edith of Dickens' many descriptions of the impenetrable soot that hung over London. Lady Sharpe's costume was punctuated with a large red flower at her breast and a lace collar and cuffs. Sir Thomas was a tall black shadow with a slice of white collar and a dangling silver watch chain. They both wore round black spectacles to shield their eyes from the sun.

Thomas sat a ways apart with Alan, Eunice, and a few of Eunice's friends. Heads turned as Edith and Lady Sharpe promenaded; Edith's head was buzzing with excitement, though she maintained a pleasant yet placid exterior. Lady Sharpe had come with tweezers and a specimen jar, and was busily collecting butterflies.

"*Papilio androgeus epidaurus*," she announced, as she placed a pretty, fluttering insect into a jar.

"They're dying," Edith murmured, somewhat stricken.

"They are," Lady Sharpe concurred. "They take their heat from the sun, and when it deserts them, they die."

"That's so sad."

"Not sad, Edith," Lady Sharpe riposted. "It's nature. A savage world of things dying or eating each other right beneath our feet."

Edith grimaced. "That is absolutely horrid."

"Not all of it." Sir Thomas's sister plucked up a cocoon attached to a tree limb, and examined it.

"Look at this. Everything it needs is in there. A perfect world. If I keep it warm and dry, a pretty little thing will hatch. A dollop of sunshine with wings." She smiled at Edith as she held it up. "Back home we have only black moths. Formidable creatures, to be sure, but without beauty. They thrive on the dark and the cold."

She wrapped the cocoon in a handkerchief and folded it carefully.

"What do they feed on?" Edith queried.

"Butterflies, I'm afraid." She sounded almost bored.

She was gazing down at something on the ground, and Edith followed her line of sight. An army of ants had pinned down a lovely butterfly; they were devouring it as it quivered. Edith was repulsed.

But Lady Sharpe watched avidly.

* * *

"The specter started to move in a hunched posture, as if in pain… and it was then that she realized, both with horror and relief, that the specter was that of her mother."

Sir Thomas read aloud from Edith's manuscript as she, Lucille, and Alan picnicked on the grass.

Lady Sharpe arched a perfectly shaped brow. "Ghosts? Really? I never imagined that's what you wrote about."

"Edith saw a ghost when she was a child," Alan said, and the long-suppressed heat of embarrassment rushed up Edith's neck and spread across her cheeks.

Lucille blinked. "Really?"

"But now she's more interested in a love story," Alan said, and Edith's flush deepened. Was he teasing her?

"The ghosts are a metaphor," she replied.

"They've always fascinated me," Sir Thomas said, catching Edith's eye.

"It seems to me the only people who witness such apparitions are those who feel themselves in need of consolation or reproach," Lady Sharpe declared.

"I assume you're beyond both," Alan said, and she raised her chin as if looking at something in the distance. Soon the Sharpes moved away and were deep in conversation.

"Visit me, Edith. Come to my office," Alan said. "I'm still setting up but I think you would find some of my theories quite interesting."

Theories? Edith wondered if she had missed something. About what? She replayed the conversation. Was he speaking of ghosts?

* * *

Shaded from the blazing American sunshine, Lucille said quietly to Thomas, "I don't think she's the right choice."

He leaned closely toward her, murmuring, "You have to trust me."

He was different; this was different; this was not what they had agreed on. It was too bright out; she could not think. Trust was so hard to come by in this world. But of course she trusted Thomas.

Who else was there?

Carter Cushing was an observant man; details were important in his line of work. And so, a few days later, as Mr. Holly approached him, he knew that the man had information for him, and that it boded ill.

Ah, child, I am sorry, he thought.

"It's not often I am the bearer of bad news," Mr. Holly said by way of greeting. "But when I am, I insist on bearing it myself."

He was holding an envelope, which he extended to Cushing.

"Open it alone," he advised.

More money changed hands, and Mr. Holly left.

Edith was so proud of Alan. Though his office was still half in boxes, he was consulting with an actual patient, and he moved with the authority of a trained scientist. In dimmed light, he was using a device to examine the eyes of an elderly gentleman, and Edith politely stayed on the sidelines. She recalled observing Sir Thomas showing off his mining machine to her father and her cheeks warmed. Occupying herself, she began to scan his bookcases and other belongings.

"You have not been using the drops regularly," Alan said gently. "I must insist you do so." He turned and saw Edith, and she smiled at him. He began to write on a pad of paper. "Take this to the druggist and ask him to prepare it exactly, then resume the dose."

The man departed, and Alan turned his full attention to her. She beamed at him.

"What are you reading?" she asked him. "*Morphology of the Optic Nerve. Principles of Optical Refraction.* And…" She touched the spine of another book. "Arthur Conan Doyle? Alan? You fancy yourself a detective?"

He shook his head. "No, not really. But he is a doctor. An ophthalmologist, just like me."

She smiled. "Just like you."

"I met him, in England. I attended one of his lectures."

"You did? How was he?"

"Fascinating. The lecture was not on fiction, but on spiritualism. Let me show you something that might interest you."

Sitting, she watched as he arranged a wood-and-brass projecting device. The color of her dress with its mutton-chop sleeves matched the brass hue of the device's fittings. Alan busied himself arranging a tray of photographic plates.

"Photographic work is simple," he began. "The

image is captured using a coating of silver salts and it stays there, waiting, invisible to the naked eye. It's called a latent image. Then we use a developing agent: mercury vapors, say, to reveal it."

He gestured to the glass plate before them. The primary image, darker, was of a little baby in a crib. Then Edith's blood turned to ice as she spotted a blurry shape hovering above the baby: a stretched, eerie face with black holes for eyes and a mouth caught in a scream, whether in fury or agony or both, she did not know. She looked back down at the baby, and suppressed every impulse in her to snatch the child out of the crib, unreasonable as that was.

"It is my belief that houses—places—be it by the chemical compound in the earth or the minerals in the stone, can retain impressions, just like this plate. They can record an emotion or a person that is no longer alive. It's called an 'impregnation.'"

Can that be what has happened in our house? Edith thought anxiously. And what she had seen… *twice*… within its walls? They were not products of her imagination, but things that were actually present?

"But not everyone can see them," she said quietly.

I did see them.

I saw her.

Her stomach clenched.

"Right." Alan went on, unaware of her discomfiture. "That man that just left, amongst other ailments, is color blind."

More of his collection of phantom images paraded

before her—cloudy and half-formed, increasingly disturbing, elongated and unreal... Were they aware, these *things*? Were they memories, recordings? Did they have a reason to come back?

"He will *never* perceive the colors red or green," Alan went on blithely. "He only accepts their existence because the majority around him does."

Ghosts, did they exist? Were these images of real ghosts? *And in that picture, that one... did one just move?*

"These... *specters*—" he used her word deliberately, favoring her with a quick nod "—may be all around us and only the 'developing agent'—those with the specific aberration—can see them."

"Or perhaps we only notice things when the time comes for us to pay attention to them. When they need us to see them," she said. Then she realized how intently he was staring at her, and she colored and looked away. He had been her confidant, the one she had entrusted with her whispered secret that Mama's ghost had appeared to her. He had been the witness to her humiliation at his sister's hands when she had learned of it. And he had seen Sir Thomas relish every spine-tingling word of her manuscript, and beg for more.

"Conan Doyle spoke of an 'offering,'" Alan continued. "A gesture—an invitation to communicate. 'Knock once if you mean "yes,"' or, 'Touch my hand if you are here.'"

She was perplexed as to why he was bringing this up. She had not spoken a word of the most recent... appearance to anyone, so it seemed strange that he would revisit a past event that had proved so painful. But he had seen how interested Sir Thomas was in her ghost story. Could this be an attempt to draw her attention away from the Englishman in order to compete for her affections? Or had he realized that in the past, as her friend, he had not been particularly supportive of her work?

"You've never spoken to me about these interests of yours, Alan," she said, and waited for his reply.

His face softened. "I feel sometimes, Edith, as if you can only think of me as that childhood friend that climbed the orchard trees with you."

She took that in. Was this something more than an invitation to see his new practice?

"Edith, I understand your fascination with the Sharpes, but…" He hesitated a moment and seemed to come to some kind of resolution. "In your own best interest, proceed with caution is all I ask."

I am right, she thought, a little dazed. *Alan has feelings for me.*

"I can take care of myself, Alan. Don't presume too much." Did she sound defensive? "You've been gone a long time and now…" She tried to couch her words more gently. "I've managed somewhat."

His face was unreadable. "You're right, Edith. I am sorry. My deepest concern has always been for you. If you are happy, then I am happy."

And you are a true friend, she thought, grateful that he cared enough to be concerned for her. He had certainly given her something to think about. She had assumed these… what could she call them—visitations? nightmares?—were the product of a creative imagination. But what if Mama really had been there?

Her blood ran cold.

Those pictures aren't proof, she thought, perhaps a little desperately. *The process of making the images could have been manipulated. And I don't really know where Alan stands on the subject. He is a scientist of the eye, of vision, and the repair of distortion. He said that Conan Doyle believed, but he did not say that he did. For him, this may not be more than an interesting puzzle.*

She thought to pursue the topic, but another patient was announced. And it was with some frustration, but more relief, that she took her leave.

In his grand boardroom, Carter Cushing had convened a group of geologists to observe Sir Thomas's machine. The Englishman's miniature was rattling away, and he had brought a topographical model of Allerdale Hall complete with hills and valleys, and crowned with a model of his house. The geologists were agog.

"The new deposits lie right beneath and around the house," Sir Thomas elaborated, "in this stratum here—the reddest clay. The purest. And with enough ore in it to make it steel-hard after baking."

Cushing watched as Sir Thomas managed the questions and took every opportunity to put forward his plans.

William Ferguson came up beside him and murmured,

"I don't know about you, but I am impressed."

"I must say that so am I," Cushing replied. *But not in the same way. Most definitely not.*

Sir Thomas smiled at him, having overheard the exchange. Cushing decided to make the next move.

"Gentlemen, we should continue our discussions tonight at dinner. At my house," he said warmly, returning Sharpe's smile. But his mood was anything but warm; he felt positively glacial. "Who knows? We may have a toast to make."

The group broke up and walked in twos and threes out of the room. His secretary drew him aside, and there he found Mr. Holly with the additional document he had asked him to acquire. He perused it. So. It was true.

"Well done, Sir Thomas," Ferguson said to Sharpe as he passed by him on his way out. "Well done."

Not so fast, Cushing thought grimly.

CHAPTER SEVEN

GUESTS MILLED; SERVANTS bustled. Dinner at Cushing
Manor was to be a grand affair. The fragrant scents of
meat and wine tantalized Thomas's senses as he and Lucille
prepared to enter the dining room. The atmosphere was
charged with the same excitement that had accompanied
his demonstration this afternoon, and he knew that, at last,
success was to be his.

Edith's home was lovely, so different from their own.
Yellow light gleamed from the candles; gas lamps shone
through panels of stained glass. It was the palace of a
fairy princess, and Thomas could well envision a younger
Edith and her mother reading stories, blond heads
knocked together as they pored over pictures embellished

with all the colors of a butterfly's wings.

We are going to get the funding from these good men of Buffalo, Thomas thought. *There is no need to go elsewhere.*

And then there she was, Edith, golden and glowing like the sun. Romeo had said the same of Juliet; that love had been doomed, but for them—

Beside him, Lucille murmured in his ear, "Give her the ring."

The Sharpe garnet no longer graced his sister's hand. He remembered how it had gleamed on her long slender finger when she had played the piano at the McMichaels' ball. It had been meant for Eunice, but once he had met Edith, he had known in his soul that Eunice had not been the proper choice. He knew Lucille was not entirely convinced that Edith was better, and that she had only acquiesced because she loved him so much.

Now as his sister moved apart from him, he felt a twinge of guilt, for he had not been entirely honest with her. He would give the ring to Edith, oh, he would, but not in the manner they had imagined. Not for that reason. Life was new for him. The sun had come out at last, and all those years in darkness—

—those secrets—

were over.

Such a weight rose from his shoulders, it was almost as if he himself had wings.

Before he grew too nervous, he approached Edith.

"May I have a word?"

She looked from him to the throng of guests and back

again. "Right now, Thomas?"

She has stopped using my title, he thought, very pleased. He had asked her to do so, and at first she had demurred. To hear his name on her lips…

"Yes, now. I am afraid I can't wait," he replied. He sighed, genuinely twitchy, and fumbled in his pocket for the ring. She was waiting, attentive. He had to do this well.

"Miss Cushing… Edith," he amended, "I really have no right to ask this, but…"

Then, of all times, Edith's father suddenly appeared. Thomas put the ring back in his pocket.

"Sir Thomas, may I see you in my study? You and your sister? If you would be so kind as to fetch her?" Cushing asked. He turned to his daughter. "Child, please see that the guests are seated. We will join you shortly."

The skin of Thomas's face prickled. He watched Edith recede into the distance like the sun sinking beneath the horizon. And then he went to find Lucille, as Mr. Cushing had asked—no, more correctly, *ordered*—him to do.

I take no satisfaction in this, Carter Cushing thought, as Sir Thomas and Lady Sharpe joined him in his study. But truth was, he did. He had pulled himself up by his bootstraps, and each time he won out over any challenge, he felt a thrill of victory. Perhaps it was petty of him, but it was the truth.

"Now, Lady Sharpe, Sir Thomas." He regarded them both. So pale and dark, the two of them, practically twins. "The first time we met, at my office—"

"I recall it, sir. Perfectly," Sir Thomas assured him.

Cushing raised a brow. "I imagine it wasn't hard for you to realize I didn't like you."

Sir Thomas took his frank statement manfully. "You made that plain enough, sir. But I had hoped that now, with time…"

"Your time, Sir Thomas, is up." *And thank God for that.*

"Could you speak plainly, Mr. Cushing?" Lady Sharpe cut in. "I'm afraid I don't follow you."

He was astonished at her brass.

"Plain I will be, missy. Plainer than you might like to hear. I have no idea what your implication is in the matters at hand, but in the past few days, your brother has deemed it fine enough to mix business with pleasure by repeatedly engaging socially with my daughter. My *only* daughter," he added for emphasis.

"Sir, I am aware that I have no position to offer," the young man said. "But the fact is…"

He fumbled, and Cushing regained the upper hand.

"You love my daughter, is that it?" He restrained his anger. There was no point to it. He had an end game in mind, and the sooner there, the better.

Sir Thomas matched his gaze. "Yes, sir, it is."

"You play the part well." An honest statement. "A few days ago, my daughter asked me why I didn't like you. Honestly, at the time, I had no good answer. But now I do. I obtained some interesting records on you. English peerage, property records…"

He pulled out the envelope from Mr. Holly containing

the documents he had paid an extra sum to acquire, and slid the contents across the table, toward the Sharpes. As he had anticipated, the corner of one piece in particular attracted Sir Thomas's attention.

"But that document there, the Civil Registry, that's the real find," Cushing declared, nailing the coffin lid shut. A single glimpse of the seal was sufficient; the young man turned stark white.

"I believe that's the first honest reaction I've seen from you."

There was silence. Lady Sharpe was impossible to read, but Sir Thomas was a study in misery as he ground out, "Does she know?"

"No," Cushing answered. "But I will tell her if that's what it takes to send you on your way."

Sharpe's expression broke as he leaned forward, perhaps unconsciously. He said, "I am sure you won't believe me, but—"

"You love her. You're repeating yourself." He opened his book of checks and wrote out the one on top. "Now you…" He held it out to Lady Sharpe. "You seem to be the more collected one, dear."

Her eyes widened as she saw the amount. He took grim satisfaction in her avarice as it reinforced his very dim view of this nefarious pair.

"It's more than generous, I know. But if you want that check to clear, there are two conditions." He handed them two train tickets. "A train for New York City leaves first thing tomorrow morning. You and your brother better be on it. Do we understand each other?"

"We do."

She was angry, and that made him angrier. She had no right to any emotion except shame. She took the check and the civil certificate. That damned, damning certificate. He was astonished at their arrogance, assuming that a foolish American from a backwater town wouldn't think to check their credentials. Their days were not only numbered, they were over.

"What is the second condition?" she asked.

"That concerns my daughter." He looked hard at the lecherous parasite that was her brother. "Tonight, you must thoroughly break her heart."

The banquet was served, and Edith was busy ensuring the comfort of all her father's guests. She had been the manor's hostess ever since her mother's death, and she was quite skilled at it. But tonight she was preoccupied, aware that Sir Thomas had begun to ask her a very important question—perhaps the most important question a woman was asked during the course of her entire lifetime—only to disappear with her father for a private discussion.

Which signified to her that she was correct about the nature of that question.

Her heart was fluttering in her chest; there were legions of butterflies in her stomach. She was unable to read Thomas's expression as he and Lucille, seated as the two guests of honor, ate but little. If she *was* right, then Thomas had every prerogative to lack an appetite. According to her reading on the matter, men about to propose marriage tended to be very jittery. Could it be that his sister shared his anxiety because she wanted him to be happy? Edith had never had siblings, but had often wanted them. Lady Sharpe could be her sister, then. She was overjoyed at the prospect.

Stay calm, Edith, she told herself, but the very air crackled around her.

Her father raised his glass.

"Ladies and gentlemen, we have an unexpected announcement to make. Sir Thomas?"

Oh, God. Here it is. But he would speak to me first, yes? So am I wrong? Perhaps it's not that at all. Perhaps the announcement is about their business partnership. I shouldn't get my hopes up. It is too soon, and I am swooning like a foolish heroine in an Ann Radcliffe novel.

But no, he was looking straight at her and he raised his glass. Lingering on her face with those soulful blue eyes. He looked like a man about to announce a partnership of a far different kind.

"Thank you, Mr. Cushing," he said. "When I came to America, my heart was brimming with a sense of adventure. Here the future actually seemed to mean something."

She met his gaze. He was speaking of the future… their future?

"I have found warmth and friendship among you all. And for that, I am ceaselessly grateful." He fell silent for a moment. Edith lived a lifetime in that pause.

His expression shifted, his gaze steady as before, but now it was sad. A tiny flash of alarm darted through her. Something was amiss.

"But for now, farewell. May we meet again. Perhaps on a different shore. My sister and I depart for England just in time for the winter."

His little joke brought laughter and cheers around the table. But not from Edith. He was not proposing. He was *leaving*. Passing her by exactly as he had passed by poor Eunice.

But I thought… I thought he… loved…

Devastated, she murmured her excuses and escaped.

She did not know he had followed her until he spoke her name.

"Edith."

She swallowed down her pain as she had on another snowy day, as true a death as this one visiting upon her breaking heart. She had thought… she had hoped…

"You are leaving us." Each syllable was a struggle, but she betrayed nothing. Her voice was as steady as his gaze had been seconds before he delivered the killing blow.

"We must go back immediately, tend to our interests," Thomas said. "The pit digging must commence before the depth of the winter." There was another beat. "And with nothing to hold us in America…"

Could he be any crueler? Did he know that he was?

"I see."

She had reached the stairs; she caught sight of her father hovering in the background. Her dear father, perhaps aware that this decision would cause her pain, was standing sentry in case he was needed. She was not unloved.

"Your novel," Thomas said. "I read the new chapters. I will have them delivered in the morning."

"That's good of you." Her mind spun back in time to their first encounter, his admiration of the as-yet-unknown author of her novel. There had been a connection between them, there *had*. The pain in her heart ratcheted up to agony.

"Would you still like to know what my thoughts are?" he asked.

She nodded, and he reacted with a bit of a start, and then took a breath, as if the entire conversation had become nothing more than an odious and perfunctory task.

"Very well. It is absurdly sentimental. The aches that you describe with such earnestness… the pain, the loss. But you have not lived at all. In fact, you seem to know only what other writers tell you."

She could not have been more mortified than if he had spat in her face. What was he saying? How *could* he say such things in public? Humiliate her in her own house?

"I thank you for your frankness, sir," she said tightly.

He took a step toward her, an act of aggression. "I am not done, child. You insist on describing the torments of love when you clearly know *nothing* about them."

Why must he be so awful to her? Had her gestures of familiarity… of hope… embarrassed him? Was she… did he see her like Eunice, all misplaced presumption, beneath serious consideration for his affection?

"You've made yourself more than plain." Was that her voice? Were those her words? She sounded like an ice princess, cold and hard and angry.

The guests were wandering in, attracted by the quarrel and now witnesses to her humiliation. He was relentless, approaching her, mocking her:

"…I advise you to return to your ghosts and fancies. The sooner the better, Edith. You know precious little of the human heart or the pains that come with it. You are nothing but a spoiled child playing with—"

That was as much as she could take. *She* knew nothing? At least she had a heart.

She slapped him hard; he flinched but took it.

She turned and fled.

Darkness. Her room. Tears.

The door handle moved, and Edith, lying in her bed, tensed.

Then it opened, and there stood her father. She longed to be comforted, but her feminine pride lay in tatters already. He had called her a child, and so had Thomas. But she was a grown woman who had endured an excruciating rejection, and her father was not the person to offer proper comfort at such a time. If there was anyone who could, which she doubted.

"I am not blind, Edith," he said delicately. "I know you had feelings for him. But give it time. Perhaps you and I… we could go to the West Coast. You could write and

I..." He trailed off, and she saw a future in which he was a widower and she was a spinster, and they kept each other company, and she could not bear it.

"I love you, Father. But can't you see? The more you hold me, the more I am afraid." She didn't want to speak the words she was thinking. "I just don't want to talk any further tonight. I just can't." Weariness overcame her. "Good night."

He was sorrowful as she closed her door, shutting him out.

For now, anyway.

"My love is like a red, red rose…"

The next morning, the sweet old tune that had been his love song to his wife played on the phonograph. Cushing stood in the locker room of the gentlemen's club in his robe, pensive and triumphant. Edith had been prevented from making the mistake of a lifetime. If Sir Thomas Sharpe had managed to pull off his loathsome scheme, Edith would not have *had* a life. The scandal would have ruined her.

That morning, Cushing felt especially close to his dear departed wife. When he gazed into the mirror at his gentlemen's club, he could almost see her beautiful face. Not the horror that they had buried, but the sweet girl she had been when they'd wed.

I've kept our daughter safe all these years, he silently told her. *She is still safe.*

Edith was an heiress, and he supposed there would be other Sir Thomas Sharpes who would come sniffing after her money. He would do whatever it took to protect her. But he hoped he would never again plunge her into such pain and suffering.

Morosely, he prepared to shave. The attendant arrived with clean towels, making all ready for Cushing with a twist of the washroom basin's hot water faucet.

"How's the water today, Benton?" he asked with forced cheerfulness.

"Piping hot. Just the way you like it, sir," Benton replied as he turned on one of the showers as well. The room began to steam up.

"Very well, then," Cushing said. "Be kind enough to order me some ham and eggs. I'll start with coffee, if it's hot. And a sip of port."

"Right away, sir. And the *Times*?"

"If you'd be so kind." Perhaps there would be a short squib about the departure of Sir Thomas Sharpe, baronet, from the fair shores of America. And good riddance.

Mist clouded his vision as he prepared to disrobe. Then a shadow flitted behind him, startling him, and he turned to see if Benton had returned.

There was no one there.

But there had been someone. And he had the distinct feeling that he wasn't alone. Any member would announce himself. It was curious and rather off-putting that they had not.

Perhaps it was his imagination.

And still…

Feeling rather silly, he checked the lockers. Of course they were empty.

Hot water was spilling over the basin; in his distraction he had let it run too long. His flat razor fell, the soap brick too. With a grunt, he bent to pick them up, nicking his finger. Clay-red blood swirled down the drain.

There it was, the shadow again. Then someone grabbed him by the cuff of his robe and the back of his head. Before he could react, his head was slammed down against the basin's corner. There was no pain, only shock. He staggered, went down. The figure loomed over him, grabbed his head, and smashed it again and again against the porcelain. He heard his bones crush as his nose shattered.

Edith.

As his forehead fractured.

Again.

Edi—

As gouts of scarlet blood gushed out of the ruin of his skull.

Again.

E—

As he did not move, and the blood plumed into the clear, boiling water.

CHAPTER EIGHT

How she had managed to doze off, Edith had no idea. But she woke slowly to awareness sprawled on top of her sheets in her bedroom, still fully dressed. What a trite cliché; she had cried herself to sleep.

Annie was in her room, and she was holding a sheaf of papers that Edith recognized at once: the most recent chapter of her now-hated manuscript. Thomas had made good on his promise to return it, and the sight rekindled every bad feeling that had haunted her that night.

"What is it, Annie?" Edith murmured.

"This was delivered this morning, miss. But I didn't want to wake you up any earlier."

"It's all the same, Annie, thank you." She indicated

the wastebasket, but the maid hesitated.

"The letter, too?" Annie asked.

"The letter…?" Edith fished for her eyeglasses and looped the ends over her ears. Red wax in a coat of arms with a skull design sealed the flap of an envelope of thick parchment paper. Her name was written across the front in a bold but elegant hand. Edith didn't know if she dared read it, but she ripped it open anyway. The room seemed to dim as she devoured the lines:

Dear Edith,

By the time you read this, I will be gone. Your father made evident to me that, in my present economic condition, I was not in a position to provide for you. And to this I agreed. He also asked me to break your heart—to take the blame. And to this I agreed too. By this time, surely I have accomplished both tasks.

But know this: When I can prove to your father that all I ask of him is his consent—and nothing more—then, and then only, will I come back for you.

Yours,
Thomas

Elation surged through her; euphoria. He had not abandoned her, had not proven a heartless cad. But when had this been delivered? What time was his train?

Am I too late?

Frantically, she rushed for the stairs, shouting for Annie.

She dashed out into the hall, crying, "Annie, my coat!"

Then through the streets, past so many monuments to her father's pride, through traffic and crowds, fighting to get to the hotel where the Sharpes had been staying; dodging, weaving, then into the lobby and at last to the front desk.

"Thomas and Lucille Sharpe?" she asked breathlessly.

The manager studied the guest registry. "One-oh-seven and one-oh-eight," he said, "but—"

Edith bolted, rushing past some guests and a porter; at last she reached the door to one hundred and seven, to find it ajar—

—and two young, dark-skinned maids inside a room devoid of luggage or personal belongings, making up the bed.

One of them said, "They checked out this morning, miss. In time for the early train."

Edith stood stock-still, panting, defeated. No, it couldn't be. To have found out, to *know*, and to have missed him… it was too cruel.

"Are you all right, miss? Miss?" the other maid asked.

Would she ever be all right again? Would she—

She became aware of another presence; someone standing close by. She turned her head.

It was Thomas.

Unimaginable joy blazed inside her. She managed to rein in her instinct to throw herself into his arms as his dear face sought understanding in hers. Forgiveness. Hope. Her heart thundered in the silence. Surely he could hear it.

"Lucille has gone," he began, "but I could not. Your

father bribed me. To leave."

He reached into his pocket and produced what she recognized as a bank check. Then he tore it in half.

"But I cannot leave you, Edith. In fact, I find myself thinking of you at the most inopportune moments of the day. I feel as if a link, a thread, exists between your heart and mine. And that, should that link be broken by distance or time… well, I fear my heart would cease to beat and die. And you'd soon forget about me."

Edith found breath to speak. "Never. I would never forget you."

She looked in his eyes and melted. This was happening. This was real, a dream after the nightmare.

He pulled her close, and kissed her. Her world became Sir Thomas Sharpe. His arms, his wild heartbeat. The softness of his lips as they brushed her mouth, then pressed harder. Edith closed her eyes, waltzing again, her wish come true.

She felt his restraint, as if holding back; she was about to open her eyes to assure him that there were liberties that he could take now. He had broken her heart, and only he could mend it. Then he relaxed against her and gathered her up, and all was right, so very right, with this beautiful new world, this shining, golden day. Perhaps Ogilvie had been right to insist upon a love story. The endings were so wonderful.

But this is not the end of our story, she thought. *It is only the beginning. He declared himself in his letter. He has asked me to marry him.*

Arm in arm they took their leave of the room, and Edith couldn't even care where they went, or what they did next. She supposed he would present himself to her father and they could begin again, on better terms. Surely Papa's consent would be given once he saw that an honorable man stood before him. A man who could not be bought, and who prized her, Edith Cushing, above the wealth he required to fulfill his mining plans. He could have kept the check and made his way back to England where any number of young ladies were no doubt waiting in line to become Lady Sharpe. But he loved his American commoner with his whole heart. What father would not wish such a man on his only daughter?

I am so incredibly happy.

But as they crossed the lobby, she saw her father's lawyer, Mr. Ferguson. And her maid, Annie, stood with him, pointing at her. She and Thomas slowed and her heart thudded so hard she felt her pulse in the soles of her feet. The agonized looks on their faces, wrenched, horror-stricken... hollow eyes, speaking of tragedy. She had seen that same expression on her father's face when he had come to tell her that her mother's suffering had ended.

Of her *death*...

Of death.

Here was proof that a terrible mistake had been made: Her father, who so loved grandeur and elegance, could not possibly have been taken to such a filthy, disgusting place.

The Buffalo City Morgue was more vile than a stable, anyone could see that. No one who knew him would have brought him here. And so… there had been an error and someone else's poor father lay dead inside.

And though it would be a simple thing to enter and point out the blunder, she found she could not do it. Fear was drowning her denial: Mr. Ferguson would not make such an error; and in the lobby, Annie, who had been with them for three years, had burst into tears and embraced Edith as soon as she had come within arm's length.

But this is my day of greatest happiness. It cannot be. It cannot.

Thomas and Mr. Ferguson stood with her, and she felt the warmth of Thomas's body through the frozen block of terror encasing her.

There was a clatter of footsteps, someone catching up to the trio. It was Alan, quite out of breath, and his appearance gave weight to the reality she was fighting so hard against. She stared at him as if through a snowstorm, barely able to see. She couldn't sense her feet on the ground. She began to feel as if she were dissolving, as insubstantial as one of the specters in Alan's spirit photographs.

"I'm so sorry," Alan said. "I came as soon as I heard."

No, don't say that, she silently begged him. And then Thomas's hand gave her substance again, and some modicum of courage. She must be here for her father. If a mistake had been made—

—Please, please, please let it be a mistake. Oh, please.

She started holding her breath.

Alan faltered as the coroner opened the door to the

morgue. Edith turned to follow the man.

"Wait," Alan ordered. "Don't look."

Edith's throat was so tight that it took a great effort to speak. "I am told that I have to."

Alan appealed to the coroner. "No. Please. I'll give you a positive identification. Don't make her look. I was his physician." He turned to the family lawyer for support. "Ferguson, you know that."

That wasn't the truth; perhaps Alan had fitted him for eyeglasses. He was trying to spare her.

Unless Father was ill and didn't want anyone to know… and that is what has happened… some kind of seizure…

The renewed possibility that they were all supposed to be here squeezed her chest even tighter. She was afraid she was going to faint.

No. It is not he. Please, if it is not he, then I will do anything. I will give everything I have or want. I will not marry Thomas…

But her heart wailed in anguish at the thought of losing the man who was holding her up even then. Whose arm encircled her and protected her as she swayed forward.

Mr. Ferguson set his jaw and gave his head a little shake. "And I'm his lawyer, Dr. McMichael. I am sorry. It's not just a legal formality. It's obligatory, I'm afraid."

I'm afraid. The words echoed in her mind. She was so very, very afraid.

Thomas was there, and he loved her.

Alan was there, and he was her dearest and oldest friend.

But in her fear, she was all alone.

Her knees wobbled. She couldn't breathe enough to remain conscious. She could not draw sufficient air to hold body and soul together.

I am afraid.

She and the men walked across a tile floor that was slippery, pitted, and dirty. The room stank of blood. There were flies. An abattoir. Carter Cushing could not possibly lie beneath that stained winding sheet, on that steel table.

And yet, the profile was his.

Time stopped utterly. This moment must last forever. This must be where she existed for the rest of eternity, because right here, her father could still be alive. Right here, they were together, and Thomas too. In this ticking heartbeat, this strangled breath, this sunlight in amber. Her world hanging in the balance, teetering until the pendulum swung back the other way. Balanced on the head of a pin. This was where she must always *be*.

Then the coroner took hold of the sheet, pausing a moment as if he, too, wished that the earth would stop spinning. That he could spare her. Then he lifted the drape.

And everything stayed frozen, everything: heart, thought, breath. Edith only stared as Thomas's hand tightened, tightened…

He did not look like her father.

He did not look human.

His face, destroyed. The bones crushed. Blood pooled and coagulated. The damage to the features beyond her ability to comprehend. A mistake, a mistake. This was not her father.

It is.

Oh, dear God, it is.

If she gave a sign that it was her father, she was unaware. But the tension in the room thickened; she felt a heavy weight pulling her downward as if she would sink through the floor, and the men grew even more somber as they shifted and someone cleared his throat, as if signaling that it was time to move to the next step in a hellish ritual. Was Thomas keeping her on her feet? She could not tell. The candle that they had held on the night they had waltzed… *Night's candles are burned out. Thomas… oh, Thomas, this cannot be happening.*

What had she wished for when she had blown that candle out on the dance floor? Could she have not wished for long life for her father?

"How did it happen?" Alan asked hoarsely.

"An accident," Mr. Ferguson said. "The floor was wet."

Alan's brow furrowed as he scrutinized the body… her father… *Papa.*

"May I, sir?" Alan said to the coroner. "Help me turn him."

Edith watched numbly as Alan inspected the poor, ruined head. The head that could not be her father's. Then, with the aid of the other man, he began to turn the deceased on his side and she saw shaving cream on his cheek. *Shaving cream. An accident. A wet floor, like this one. Slipping. The porcelain sink.*

The sheet began to fall away, revealing—

This is my father. It is, it is!

"Stop it, stop!" she cried, rushing forward. "Don't handle him like that, please don't."

Alan drew back. "Forgive me, I was trying to—"

She strangled on her tears as Thomas drew alongside, steadying her, though hardly steady himself. His face was stark white; he was as horrified as she was. But now she must act; she must shield her beloved father from their eyes and their poking and prodding. Cook and DeWitt had gossiped about her mother—

—*Black as a charred lamb shank, she was. Sight of her is going to give me nightmares for years, I can tell you that. And the stink! They don't pay me enough to lay her out; I told her lady's maid to do it, and she up and quit and so I got the belowstairs to take it on. Master says the young lady is not to see and I'm all for that. One look and she'll grow up in an asylum, sure as my family's in Dublin. Are all the mirrors covered, DeWitt? Because you cannot be too sure. You certainly cannot. They hate the grave, the dead. And when you leave behind a sweet little girl like our Edith… well, you just don't go.*

"This is my father," she said staunchly. She took possession of him. He was hers. She moved through the haze and took her stand as his daughter. "He—he is turning sixty next week, and he is afraid of looking his age, you see? That's why he… dresses so well, why he loves taking long walks with me." She cradled and kissed his hand. "It feels cold. Why is it so cold?"

They looked at her with such pity. And then as the horrible reality finally sank in—that he was truly dead—she crumbled.

CHAPTER NINE

THE CEMETERY, AGAIN. Fourteen years vanished like phantoms as Alan once again regarded his dearest friend lost in grief. It seemed only yesterday they had gathered to bury Edith's mother, who had died horribly. And now her father, too. Alan could not support the coroner's cause of death: There had been far too much damage, and at the wrong angle, for a fall.

But that was a matter for another day. Now he must be there for Edith. She should have never been forced to see that. Ferguson and his obligations be damned. There were things that once you saw them, you could not unsee. Such had it been when he had witnessed his first surgery upon a human eye, popped from the cadaver of a beggar woman in the operating theater in London. Only the certainty that by observation he might save the sight in others gave him the fortitude to remain at his place, although the fellow beside him had covered his mouth and excused himself, running for the door.

He remembered the way Edith had looked to him for comfort when she was but ten and he eleven. Even as a callow lad, he had known how her heart was aching, seen the tears that would not fall.

What had Conan Doyle said during his spiritualism lecture? "Of all ghosts the ghosts of our old loves are the worst." Alan had loved Edith Cushing all his life.

But today she wasn't even looking at him. Too much a boy back then to think of marrying her, he was also here today to bury his hopes as a man. Upon her finger glittered the large red ring that had graced Lady Sharpe's hand the night Edith had waltzed with Sir Thomas. A family heirloom, clearly; for Edith, a new acquisition, and it sucked in the watery light of the gloomy day, casting no reflection. Alan knew what it signified: She was engaged to be married to Sir Thomas Sharpe.

Sharpe, whose pale English face seemed to vanish into the sleeting rain as he sheltered her beneath an umbrella. In tribute to the man who would have become his father-in-law, the Englishman wore deep mourning, and Edith was likewise swathed in black from head to toe. Alan remembered her childhood story of seeing a woman in black in her nursery, likely her mother, and how Eunice had laughed at her and called her mad. Now Edith was a woman in black, and as she leaned against Sir Thomas's chest, dazed and unfocused, Alan knew that she would haunt him for the rest of his life.

Sir Thomas's arm was around her, which would have been a breach of propriety had they not been affianced. It was all too soon, under circumstances too horrible to comprehend, and perhaps he was looking through the prism of his jealousy, but when he regarded the way Sir Thomas held Edith, it seemed that the man was determined to keep her in his grasp rather than to ease her suffering. She looked trapped, not protected.

Then Sir Thomas noticed his gaze and held it, steadily. It was an unspoken duel. Edith saw none of it. Alan knew that he had already lost, and so he tipped his hat, as one would do under such a circumstance to salute a grieving relative of the deceased. Encumbered by umbrella and fiancée, Sir Thomas was unable to return the gesture, and so, inclined his head. Sharpe was the model of gravity and sorrow, and Alan wondered if he himself was being unfair because of his jealousy. Sir Thomas's feelings for Edith could be pure. It *was* possible to fall in love deeply and quickly.

Just ask Eunice.

Three short weeks later, a few of the same guests who mourned my father's passing would attend my wedding at Asbury-Delaware Church. It was a small affair, the details of which I now struggle to recall.

* * *

Edith the bride was dressed and veiled in white, like a phantom. The bouquet of red roses that she held as Ferguson walked her down the aisle reminded Alan of a beating heart, and of her father's favorite song, "A Red, Red Rose," which Cushing had listened to nearly every morning as he showered and shaved at his club. She looked dazed. Like every man present, Alan included, the groom wore a mourning band. It was macabre that they should marry now, and when the minister asked if there were any present who knew of any impediments to their union, Alan wanted to speak up. He wanted to say that it felt wrong, her father had not approved and Edith was making a terrible mistake, but he held his peace. He wished her well, he truly did.

But as Sir Thomas kissed his bride, her garnet ring cast a slash of red light against her pale, wan cheek, and it looked so much like a wound that Alan gasped. Heads turned his way, including Eunice's, and she favored him with a sad, tight smile. She was sending him a signal: He must accept that the kiss sealed the two as husband and wife and the hopes of the McMichaels were dashed. Eunice would love again, of that he was sure, and he tried to convey confidence in her future happiness by taking her hand and giving it a squeeze.

And he was equally sure that he would never stop loving. He would go to his grave married in his heart to Edith Cushing, and perhaps, if there were such things as ghosts and the fates were kind, he would be able to watch over her, and her children, and her grandchildren and keep her free from danger.

Let her be happy, and I will be happy, he thought. *It is all that I want out of this life.*

BOOK TWO

BETWEEN MYSTERY
AND MADNESS

"No ghost was ever seen by two pair of eyes."

—THOMAS CARLYLE

CHAPTER TEN

CUMBERLAND, ENGLAND

THE HILLS WERE barren and the sky was clotted with fog. Warmed by blankets and her traveling coat with the magenta bow, Edith, who was dozing in the open carriage, got lost in a hazy dream that she was riding in a hearse toward a cemetery. Not so much riding as being conveyed to the graveyard, which signified that she was the one who had died. The last of the Cushings. But she was a Cushing no longer. She was Lady Sharpe.

Through the chill, she felt the warmth of her husband and knew that she was dreaming, and roused herself. Then Thomas said, "Edith, Edith, wake up. We are here."

When her eyes opened, she saw Thomas. His dear face, the angles as keen-edged as the facets of her garnet ring, his eyes bluer than the exquisite cameo Wedgwood belt clasp she had eyed, then rejected, while shopping in London. Thomas had encouraged her to allow the purchase but she wanted all possible funds to be spent on developing his clay-harvesting machine. She had a wonderful trousseau that would stand her until his own fortune was restored.

If only her father could be there to see that.

The horse brought the carriage closer to the gates of the Sharpe family seat, and in some ways, the place matched the engravings she had studied in her book. The bones of the grounds and the house were still there. Short columns supported an iron arch dominated by the family crest, which was often wrought in pictures in brilliant red as a nod to the crimson clay from the Sharpe mines, and included the image of a chained skull, very dark and Gothic, in her view. The crest had been impressed in the red wax seal on the back of Thomas's desperate love letter. Below the crest wrought in iron were the words ALLERDALE HALL.

The bleak house stood at the end of a red clay path, surrounded by dead brown grass and skeletal trees and backed by a dark gray sky. Gone were the boulevards lined with trees and topiaries. No porte cochère to shelter aristocrats' coaches as they disgorged visitors; indeed, no visitors. No servants, either, just one man, she had been told. Thomas and Lucille could no longer afford staff, and so had given up entertaining.

I will change all that. Upon the death of her father, control of the family fortune had passed to her. She would restore Allerdale Hall and its master to their former glory. The worry lines on her beloved's dear face would disappear. They would waltz in their own home surrounded by friends and family. And children.

She blushed.

As to the hall itself, two Gothic spires of unequal height dominated the asymmetrical silhouette as it sat wedged between life-size versions of Thomas's mining equipment. It had been built on over the centuries, in many styles of brick and stone; there were walkways, turrets and towers, numbers of which had deteriorated so badly as to fall. Glazed glass panes stared at her beneath eyebrows of arched brick. Allerdale Hall looked at once to be simultaneously unfinished and too tired to go on, as if it were alive and slowing dying. What was the saying? Giving up the ghost.

Thomas had prepared her, but the sight of the once-magnificent estate now fallen into such terrible ruin stunned and saddened her. There was a desperate dignity about her new husband as he gazed at her taking it in. Like his beautiful but dated clothing, his home spoke of a life begun in refinement and elegance, but without the means to maintain it. It spoke of loss. She remembered what he had told the captains of Buffalo industry: that he was possessed of an indomitable will. It seemed to her now that Allerdale Hall stood aboveground only through the sheer force of that will; that if owned by a lesser man, it would have disappeared into the fog like a mirage.

The carriage rolled to a stop and a manservant approached and greeted Thomas deferentially, bobbing his head to Edith. He was arthritic and quite old, his eyes milky, and his homespun clothes were even more threadbare than Thomas's dark blue suit.

"Hello, Finlay. How have you been keeping?" Thomas asked him warmly.

"Never better, Sir Thomas. I knew it was you a mile off."

"Finlay, this is my wife."

"I know, I know, milord. You've been married a while," the man—Finlay—replied. Then he went round the carriage to fetch the luggage.

Poor thing, Edith thought. *His mind is giving out.*

Thomas handed her out of the carriage. Together they walked toward the front steps of the house she was now mistress of. Thomas opened his mouth to say something, but at the same moment, a cute little dog scurried around the carriage and yipped in ecstasy at the sight of them.

Edith cried, "And who is this? You never told me about him! Or is it a she?"

"I had no idea," Thomas murmured.

Edith bent to examine the bouncy creature. She could feel its delicate bones beneath its icy, matted coat. "It has a collar. Is it a stray, do you think?"

"Impossible," he said, wrinkling his forehead. "There's no other house for miles and the town is half a day's walk away."

"Well, the poor thing is in a terrible state. Can I keep it? It looks famished."

"As you wish," he said indulgently. "Now, Your Ladyship, may I have the honor?"

With a flourish, he picked her up and carried her over the threshold of their home. They both burst into happy giggles. *Married.* And home at last from their honeymoon— if one could properly call it a honeymoon. They had not shared the marriage bed as yet. She was so grateful that Thomas had respected her mourning—and yet, she was ready to be a proper wife to him.

In all respects.

He set her down just inside the foyer, and as he slowly took off his top hat she was reminded of a magician drawing back the curtain of a magic trick. She had her first glimpse of the interior of the great house. There was a huge foyer, paneled in dark wood, and above it three stories of lacy balconies and Italianate galleries, profusions of finials, and Gothic arches decorated with quatrefoils. Portraits of centuries of Sharpe ancestors in gilded frames compounded Edith's impression that she was standing in the ghost of Allerdale Hall, a memory of lost vibrancy, that the actual house was gone. Yet there seemed to be a birdcage elevator of moderate size, able to hold perhaps three people—a single note of modernity—and it reminded her of Thomas's ingenious mining machine. This place *would* live again, and it *would* come into the present. She would see to that.

"Lucille!" Thomas called, his voice practically echoing. "Lucille! Lucille!"

The little dog barked a delighted chorus. Snowflakes drifted from the holes in the ceiling, soundless and melancholy. Edith found herself thinking of the rose petals she had scattered over her father's casket—their skin-like texture and dying scent—and shivered.

She said over her shoulder, "I think it's colder inside than outside."

"It is an utter disgrace," Thomas responded. "We try to maintain the house as best we can, but with the cold and the rain and the mines right below… it's almost impossible to stop the damp and erosion."

Indeed, there was evidence of damage everywhere, rust and mold and streaks and pools of red clay. Her father could have set all to rights with his engineering expertise, of that she was certain; she spared a moment for another, deeper pang of grief, felt it as palpably as if it were creeping up her body, then set it aside for her dear new husband's sake.

"How many rooms are there?" she asked him.

He blinked, surprised. "Why? I don't really know." Then he grinned at her, and there was the charm that had won her over so quickly. "Would you like to count them?"

She laughed. "Oh, I will. But how can you sustain this house, just you and Lucille?"

Mr. Finlay entered with some of her trunks. "Take it upstairs, young master?" he asked. She smiled at the old man's slip in speaking to Thomas as if he were still a child, his affection for Thomas evident. Edith's father had always told her that if you wanted to measure the character of a man, then watch how he dealt with his servants. Thomas treated Finlay quite civilly, and there was a real bond between them. That pleased her deeply.

"Yes, Finlay, please." Thomas brushed Edith's lips with a kiss and returned his full attention to her. "It is a privilege we were born into and one we can never relinquish. But we manage, darling, somehow. My workshop's in the attic. I can't wait to show you."

He turned with a "wait-for-me" air and disappeared into the gloom. To locate his sister, she supposed. It was uncanny how, with a few quick steps, he seemed to vanish. How the house appeared to swallow him up. Despite her book of engravings, she hadn't realized just how enormous it was. It could contain several Cushing Manors and a few copies of the McMichael home as well. She didn't understand Thomas's slavish devotion to it, but he came from an old family in a country steeped in tradition, custom, and duty. She couldn't imagine enduring a life in this house for any other reason than love. And love would keep her here.

With Finlay upstairs and Thomas off to find his sister, she was ostensibly alone in the large, cold room. Except for the cute little dog, of course. The pup had grown so quiet that she had almost forgotten it was there. Now, as she looked at it, she realized that its tail was curled fearfully between its legs. Slightly uneasy, Edith drew her coat more closely around herself. The dog continued to cower, and she looked around, trying to see what it saw. But there was nothing. What was it frightened of?

As if in answer, the wind slammed the front door shut with a boom. She jumped. The dog hunched lower.

With the door closed, the great hall descended deeper into darkness, and she lost sight of many of the architectural details. It was enormous, and it dawned on her that one could look down from above without being seen. What that signified, she had no idea, and she tried to shake off her presentiment of doom. She was very tired, and this was the final destination of the day's long, cold trip. This was her home now.

So she took off her hat and gloves, settling in, then spotted a large mirror, where she checked her hair. She wanted to look presentable for Lucille, whom she barely knew. Because Lucille had already left for England on that terrible day when Edith's father had died, she had missed the wedding.

Her hair looked fine; Edith recalled the day she had gone to see Mr. Ogilvie with ink smudges on her fingertips and forehead. So much had happened since then, but the one constant was that she was still working on her novel. She had packed plenty of paper and the exquisite gold pen her father had given her; aside from the garnet ring Thomas had placed on her finger when he had proposed, the pen was her most cherished possession.

The dog was still cowering and as she looked down at the poor mite, she heard a strange, soft buzzing. She glanced down at a tray by the mirror to find, to her astonishment, a handful of dying flies. She frowned; it was so odd and unexpected. She couldn't imagine how they had ended up inside the frigid house, nor why they were dying at this precise moment. She studied them and scanned the shadows for evidence of food or perhaps a dead animal.

Then the little dog trotted back into the room, startling Edith, who hadn't even noticed that it had left. The house was freakish in the way it absorbed sound.

The pup was carrying a bright red rubber ball in its mouth and trotted up, wagging its tail as an invitation to its new friend to play fetch.

"You? Where on earth did you find that?" she asked it. She could not imagine any reason for there to be such a dog-sized ball in the fabulous ruin.

The dog persisted. She was about to stretch out her hand when in the mirror, she spotted the dark shape of a woman on the far side of the room. At last Thomas's sister had emerged. Edith felt a little flutter of nerves. They were strangers who now were family.

She raised a hand, but the figure stayed well away from her, so cloaked in the shadows that Edith couldn't really make out her appearance. She seemed to be moving strangely… or perhaps that was due to one of Lucille's tightly corseted Victorian gowns, which constricted movement. Edith far preferred the more modern full skirts and mutton-sleeved blouses of the New Woman, which coincided with her image of herself as a lady novelist.

"Lucille?" she said by way of greeting.

The lady moved away, and Edith was perplexed. Should she follow after her? Was there some reason

Lucille was not speaking to her? And—dear Lord, was she *smoking*? The light caught some sort of trail wafting behind the woman in a strange way, faint strands that appeared to be glowing as they floated upward. She simply could not imagine such a refined lady as Lucille Sharpe puffing away on a cigarette.

"Excuse me," Edith called, walking toward her. It was not Lucille; she could tell that much. For one thing, her height was wrong.

Ignoring Edith, the stranger entered the elevator cage. The mechanism hummed to life and the elevator ascended as Edith hurried over to it and peered upward. Too late; all she saw was the bottom of the cab.

Then Thomas walked back in, and Edith waved her hand at the lift just as it stopped at the top of the house. Or at least so she assumed. The machinery had stopped humming, but she wasn't certain that the elevator door had opened yet.

"A woman, Thomas, in the elevator," she told him.

He raised a brow. "You mean Lucille?"

"No, no, Thomas, it wasn't Lucille," she insisted.

"That contraption seems to have a mind of its own," Thomas said, almost fondly. "The wiring gets affected by the dampness in the house. It connects to the clay pits, you see. Promise me you'll be very careful when using it, and never, ever go below this level. The mines are very unstable."

She wanted to make it clear that there *had* been a woman in the elevator. It hadn't just "decided" to go up.

As she opened her mouth, the little dog started barking

and bounded toward the foyer. The door opened and Lucille walked in, wrapped in gloves and heavy woolens, and her eyes widened when she saw the dog.

"What is this thing doing here?" she asked curtly. "I thought that you—"

"Dear Lucille," Thomas broke in happily. "It's so good to see you!"

As he went to embrace her, she threw off her cape, preventing him. Then she regarded Edith with a cool eye.

"I see you made it, Edith," she said, which was a rather strange thing to say. "How was London?"

"A blur. A dream," Edith said, putting aside her concerns about the woman. Perhaps Lucille had engaged someone from the village to prepare the house for their homecoming. And truly, London *had* been a dream. Despite her father's wealth and position, she had not traveled much. She and Thomas had seen many of the sights that had been in her book about England, just as depicted, and Thomas had seemed so happy revealing his country to her.

Thomas said happily, "We went to the Albert Hall, Lucille. A concert. So grand. So wonderful."

Indeed, they had listened to a Chopin program, and Thomas had remarked that Lucille would have loved it. He had spoken often of his sister during their excursions, and Edith had been touched by his devotion to her. It had reminded her of Alan and Eunice, and she had felt a pang of homesickness. She occasionally caught herself talking about her father, and would cut herself short because she did not want Thomas to think she wasn't happy. But

Thomas had encouraged her to talk about him, reminding her that she was still grieving.

Lucille bristled a little. "I see. Well *I* went to the post office. Your machine parts are here from Birmingham. Two heavy crates. You'll need Finlay to fetch them." She spoke stiffly, clearly a bit jealous of their fine time. But one went on a honeymoon with one's bride, not one's sister. Surely Lucille understood that. Perhaps they could take a trip together, the two Sharpe sisters-in-law, while Thomas worked on his machine. It would be difficult to be parted from Thomas for even a few days, however.

Lucille cocked her head. "Edith? Is there something the matter with you?"

Thomas looked at Edith too. His warm glow dimmed a bit. "Give us a moment," he told Lucille. "She's a little shaken."

Lucille hung up her winter things. "Goodness. Why is that?"

He shrugged. "She saw something. A shadow, a reflection. It frightened her."

Lucille favored her with a condescending smile. "A shadow? Oh, darling, all that lives in this house are shadows and reflections and creaks and groans. So you'd better soothe that boundless imagination of yours from now on."

Edith considered. She was tired and Allerdale Hall *was* filled with "shadows and reflections and creaks and groans." After all, she had imagined that the woman had been having a cigarette, yet she smelled no smoke.

And as she turned her head, she caught her own reflection in another mirror, and she had to admit that despite presentable hair, she looked a sight: pallid complexion, dark circles beneath her eyes. She barely recognized herself.

She determined not to pursue it, at least not when they had just arrived home and she needed to create a bond with her new sister-in-law. However, the house was much more unsettling than she had expected, and she *would* have to rein in her imagination.

"I need a proper welcome, that is all," she declared, embracing Lucille. "From this day forward, the house will contain nothing but friendship and love and warmth."

From Lucille's posture, Edith could tell that her new sister-in-law was looking over Edith's shoulder at Thomas. Smiling at him, she hoped. Letting him know that she was pleased by Edith's overture.

"Warmth would be an excellent start," Lucille said. "Thomas, your bride is frozen."

Lucille unhooked the key ring from her waist and turned to go. She seemed harried and a bit tired.

Thomas smiled at Edith. "I'll take you upstairs, my darling. Start a fire at once. You can run a hot bath. You'll need to let the water run. The pipes will carry some red clay at first but then the water will clear."

Abashed that Lucille should perform housekeeping tasks while she bathed, Edith thought to reject the bath in favor of assisting her. But truthfully she *was* frozen, and so exhausted that she would be of no use to anyone.

She vowed that she would lift the weight from Lucille's shoulders, or, at the least, take on her fair share. She herself was not used to performing work customarily given to servants, but she was game to learn, and did know how to run a house.

"Lucille, whenever it's convenient, may I have a copy of the house keys, please?"

"You don't need one," Lucille said quickly. Then, in a more measured tone, she added, "For now. There are parts of the house that are unsafe. It will take a few days for you to familiarize yourself. Then, should you still feel that you need them, I'll have copies made."

Edith let herself be satisfied with that answer, but she made a pledge to herself to be useful to Lucille. The other woman had carried the burden of maintaining this enormous house for too long, and it was clear to Edith that the house was winning.

We shall turn that tide together, she vowed.

Then she followed her bridegroom toward the lift, anticipating a nice hot bath and then, perhaps then… the bridal chamber.

CHAPTER ELEVEN

IT WATCHED.

The bride was in the bathroom, standing in her chemise and corset as she turned on the taps. Steam spilled from the faucet and the first few sputters were red as blood.

"Oh, God," she cried.

There is no God here, it thought. *Abandon hope, all ye who enter here.*

The recalcitrant heaters on both sides of the tub began to knock, the pipes vibrating like a death rattle, then growing louder, a horrible sound. Rude and demanding. Then the water ran clear and hot. Not everything was ruined and decaying. Not yet, anyway.

She removed her eyeglasses and placed them in the basin. She climbed into the tub. Quite a dainty thing. Blond hair, a distinction. American. A novelty.

Above her glasses, in the mirror, a handprint bloomed.

Busy tonight, then, inspecting the bride. What was she like?

Belowstairs, in the scullery, it made another observation:

"What is this?" the sister asked. Her voice was clenched with worry, a tinge of panic. "What is she playing at?"

"I have no idea," the brother replied, graduating the flame in the copper heater. Ah ha: caring for the comfort of the innocent in the tub. Making sure her bath was hot, and the water for her tea as well. Laying the traps. These two, these dark two. How it loved them. Wind them up—

"The dog." The sister was agitated. There were beads of perspiration on her forehead. "You said you'd killed the dog."

His face tensed. Was it with apology, or excuse? "I left it on its own," he confessed. "I thought…"

"How has that thing survived? All this time?" she wondered aloud. "On scraps, I suppose. As we all do."

Then his face softened, and the love he bore his sister came through. "We won't have to do that anymore." His voice held promise, certainty.

"Won't we?" She scowled. "The money is not here, is it?"

"Not yet, but soon."

She stomped to the stove and readied a kettle of boiling water. Then she selected a red tin of tea and poured the water through the leaves into the pot. Next she inspected the cups and rejected the one with a chip in it, placing perfect cup and saucer together. The tea service was *cloisonné*, a family heirloom. Beautiful. There were so few treasures left.

Lucille moved close to her brother, perhaps as close as his bride would stand, and he did not move aside. Distracted, perhaps, as she prepared a tea tray for him to take upstairs to Edith. Perhaps... guilty.

Haunted.

"Once she signs the final papers, she will be gone," Lucille said. "In the meantime, don't make another mistake."

Looking troubled, yet saying nothing, he put away the red tea tin and picked up the tray.

Edith would never have thought it possible, but she was beginning to warm up as she soaked in the claw-foot tub. It had been lovingly cleaned and she had added a few handfuls of the fine bath salts she had packed in her trousseau. The scent of roses brought vague memories of their wedding. She had moved through the ceremony like a sleepwalker, and she wished she remembered more of it. She had still been in shock.

The wind blew past the windows, howling; the panes rattled in the round leaded window above her. Edith sank a little deeper into her bath.

Then she thought she heard a noise: a whisper, perhaps, or someone… crying? She tried to hear over the sudden triphammer of her heart. Lucille had been right about the need to rein in her active imagination. She leaned back and allowed the steam to relax her. Yet she found herself replaying the episode with the elevator. It *was* an enormous house, and Lucille had not been there when they'd arrived. Someone could have slipped into the house while Finlay was unloading Edith's trunks from the carriage. True, there were no other homes for miles around, and the village was far away, but a disgruntled servant, perhaps, or some other person… Thomas and Lucille hadn't shown the slightest bit of curiosity about the possibility of an intruder.

They've lived here all their lives, she reminded herself.

There was a rustling in the bedroom. She jerked, listening.

"Thomas?" she called. He had promised to bring her some tea.

Then the little dog trotted up to the edge of the tub with the red rubber ball in its mouth.

"No, not now," Edith murmured.

But the winsome pup whined and wagged its tail, insistent. She smiled; she could see how the plucky little thing had survived out on the heath.

"Oh, all right." She reached out—the air was bracing—and took up the ball. "Fetch!" She threw it and the dog took off like a shot, flying out of the bathroom into the gloom.

Edith thought she heard the rustling again. But still no Thomas. Perhaps he hadn't heard her call. They had yet to be… *familiar* with one another. He had never even seen her in her nightdress. The mysteries of the marriage bed remained such. But now, in their home… perhaps he was laying a hot water bottle between the sheets and stoking the fire. It moved her that a baronet should perform such menial duties. This would not stand. As soon as she could transfer her funds, the Sharpes would live as they once had.

The dog returned victorious, miniature jaw champed down on the ball, and it dropped the prize at the base of the tub once more.

"Shh, quiet now," she told it, still listening for Thomas. She wondered what she should do; she had not brought all her nightwear in the bathroom, assuming she could slip into the bedroom to make herself more presentable. Or not, if Thomas was of a mind…

The dog yipped and tapped its nails on the tile, impatient.

"Oh, all right, fetch," she said again. And she threw the ball once more. It ran off; in a flash, the furry creature reappeared, ball in mouth, barking, even more excited.

She threw the ball yet again and the pup ran after it *again*. She waited, one ear pricked for the sounds in the bedroom. She could still hear someone in there. Dear Lord, could it be Finlay? If he was the only servant, he might even be unpacking her clothing. The thought embarrassed her. She would have to do something. But first, she'd gather up the dog and keep it with her. There was no telling which parts of the house were unsafe, as Lucille put it, and she wouldn't want the pup to crash through a weak section of the floor or lose itself in a warren of cluttered rooms.

Seconds ticked by, and the dog did not return. Perhaps a full minute. Her anxiety began to rise. She half-rose from the water, absolutely certain that someone was in the bedroom. Someone who by now should have made their presence known.

This is off, she thought. *This is strange.*

She thought again of the woman in the elevator, and gooseflesh broke out all over her body, even the parts submerged in the steaming water. Then the dog trotted back into the bathroom. But this time it did not have its toy. It sat proudly, awaiting praise.

"Doggie? Come on, silly. Where is the ball?" she prompted it. It just stared at her in its merry way.

She heard a *thump*.

And the ball came bouncing back.

By itself.

It watched.

Blurred by shadow, a slender figure moved in the bedroom. Dark, ghostly, lurching awkwardly, long scrawny arms groping the air like a blind beggar, movements spectral and disjointed. Staggering, unnaturally stooped, as if this time and place were not its time and place.

The bride, so innocent, rose like Venus from the tub

and reached for her spectacles. Her trembling made her clumsy and she only succeeded in dropping them. They clattered on the hard tile but did not break.

In the bedroom, the figure jerked. Then, drawn by the sound, it peeked around the corner, almost timidly, and pulled the sliding door open.

Would they see one another?

The bride finally succeeded in retrieving her foggy, wet glasses and she looped them around her ears. As the condensation cleared, she stepped from the tub and wrapped herself in a robe.

Half-hiding, the figure watched her draw near and crouched.

Still, surely she would see it.

But why? Others had not seen it.

Did not see it.

It glided away.

And as the bride entered the room, she saw no one there, until her husband entered with a tray.

"Lucille made you tea," he told her with a smile. Then he stared hard at her. "Are you all right? You look rather pale."

She did not tell him. She did not confide. After all, while she loved him, she didn't know him all that well. She still had a lot to prove.

A lot to discover.

* * *

Creeping along, creeping along, creeping along.

Bathed in blue midnight, leaves scattered along the floors of the galleries; curtains shifted. Creaks and groans, reflections, shadows.

In the snow, on the heath, Allerdale Hall stood by itself against the hills, holding darkness within.

Edith was relieved and happy to be nestled in bed with Thomas, who was fussing over her—raking the fire, pouring and bringing her tea in a lovely cup that spoke of fine things and better times for the Sharpes. Then she took a sip and found it quite bitter. He raised a brow at her grimace, and she was abashed to disappoint him.

"You don't like it?" he asked.

"What is it?" They had never had anything like it in London.

"Firethorn berries. Very good for you," he said.

"It's a little bitter," she confessed, and his face took on the haunted, sad expression that seemed to appear at the strangest times—often, when he should be happiest. She did not know what caused his melancholy, but she had promised herself she would wipe it from his face once and forever. She would make him so blissfully happy that he would forget whatever it was that threw a shadow over his spirit.

"I'm afraid nothing gentle ever grows in this land, Edith," he said. "You need a measure of bitterness not to be eaten. To survive."

It was so queer, the words he spoke, contrasted with

the way he spoke them. But it frightened her a bit, and reminded her of what Lucille had said back in Delaware Park when she had collected butterflies to feed her cocoon. That all they had here were insects that thrived on cold and darkness. Black moths. And wintertime flies as well? So Cumberland produced moths, maggots, bitter berries, and blood-red clay?

What was this place she had come to?

Like a reply, a low, agonized moan filled the room. It raged from one end to the other, lifting up the hair on the back of her neck. Edith was so startled that she nearly dropped her cup as she clung to her husband.

"What is that?" she cried.

"When the east wind picks up, the chimneys form a vacuum and, with the windows all shuttered, the house…" his features became pinched, as if he were embarrassed to go on "…well, the house *breathes*. Ghastly, I know."

She shuddered. It *was* ghastly. It was almost too much for her to take in. The sound was horrible enough, but what it implied was too strange. A breathing house—how terrifying, for children especially. How had Thomas endured it as a little boy?

"Can something be done about that?" she asked hopefully. She was certain that if he knew it bothered her so badly, and he could repair it, he would. And what of their own children, should they be so blessed, once the two of them consummated their marriage?

"Nothing," he replied. "I cried every time I heard it as a child. You'll learn to turn a deaf ear."

So it *had* frightened him as a boy. She concluded that he wasn't happy to be home, and that made her sad, too. As his wife, her life's work would be to bring him gladness. He had lifted her from the abyss when her father had died. She would do all she could to keep him from that dark, lonely place where she had been.

The infernal racket ceased and they settled in together again. As she sipped the very bitter tea, he placed a large wooden box in front of her with an unexpected flourish. She looked from it to him, pleased to see that his smile had returned. It was like the sun breaking through clouds, and it warmed her.

"What, pray tell, is that?" she asked.

He had dimples when he grinned. "Ah! This is a surprise. I wracked my brains for a suitable wedding present."

She was touched by his thoughtfulness. They had married quickly, and he had been stretched for funds. He had purchased beautiful mourning attire for her father's funeral, insisting that he could not embarrass himself by accepting her charity in purchasing it for him. Yet he had somehow also managed to procure her a wedding gift.

On the box was a plaque engraved with the initials E.S. How had he pulled that off so expeditiously as well?

"Edith Sharpe," he said unnecessarily. For of course she had practiced writing her new initials, as any young schoolgirl would have done upon accepting a suitor. This, too, pleased her, and she sat for a moment, savoring the sound of her name on his lips.

Then she opened the box and caught her breath at

what she saw: Inside sat a stalwart typewriter. The memory of their first meeting came rushing back and emotion rolled over her in waves. She embraced him; he held her back to look at her, really look, and there was true joy on his face, mixed with… regret? Ah, yes; he was remembering that first encounter, too. It had been at her father's offices, she typing her manuscript, which he had declared quite good. Then how he and her father had sparred. Her poor father, in the ground now, with her mother.

My mother, who walked our halls after she was dead. Who warned me to beware of Crimson Peak. Or was that she? What did I really see?

She held back a sob, then wept gently in his arms over his goodness. She was safe, protected. He closed his eyes and she fell on the bed with him. Now, now it would happen. She was a little afraid, but passion began to overtake her. And the tenderest love for this man.

His kiss was tentative. He was still reticent. She wanted to tell him that she desired him, but perhaps this was not the time. Their moment had not yet arrived.

"It's been an exhausting journey," he murmured. "You better get some rest."

He rose, easing her firmly away. Perhaps he believed that this was best for her, and she was too shy to say otherwise. She really didn't know too much about such concerns; she hadn't had a mother with whom to discuss marital matters, and the things the other girls said didn't seem to make much sense. Eunice had stolen a copy of a book from a stack she'd found in a locked trunk in the

McMichael attic and read bits aloud to a giggling assembly that had included Edith. It was mostly about whippings and canings and Edith had declared with certainty that these were not the normal acts that occurred between married people. Edith had been so vehement about it that Eunice had tossed the book at her and said, "Then tell us all about it, Edith, since you know so much. Tell us a story that begins 'Once upon a time, a trembling virgin married the ghostly lord of a haunted castle…'"

Here she was, married over a month, and all she knew was that when Thomas drew near, when he touched her, she grew warm and eager, and wanted to find out *everything*.

"I'll have a bath now," he told her. "Finish your tea, and, if you fall asleep, darling, I won't wake you up."

But I want you to wake me up, she almost said. *I want… you.*

Yet as he took one more look at her, her eyelids had already begun to droop.

CHAPTER TWELVE

IT WATCHED.

The sister spied through the keyhole in the door to their bedroom. She watched her brother refuse to perform his husbandly duties. She smiled and moved away.

It watched the house's breath scatter the dried leaves that drifted in, drifted by. The walls were bleeding from fissures in the wallpaper. Stab wounds, or a razor blade slowly drawn across a vein? Moths flew out; maggots fed.

The mad head of the house was rotting, and night was dragging her wings across the moon, tracing filigree on the floors. In the attic, more black moths were dancing because it was cold, because it was dark. Because they were hungry.

For the butterfly.

* * *

The clock struck midnight, and Edith half-stirred among the shabby elegance of the blue bedclothes.

Another noise, and she opened one eye. Someone was softly crying again. This time she was certain. She turned her head toward Thomas's side of the bed, but he was not there.

There was more sobbing, papery, whispering. She looked slowly around. The room felt busy; she saw shapes and tried to make out what they were, seeing faces and hands everywhere and telling herself that they were only chairs and her new typewriter and the fireplace tongs and her tea things. But ice water filled her veins as the memory of the black-faced phantom in Cushing Manor batted at her awareness, demanding entry. She denied it, would not think of it, but her subconscious mined the deep, consuming dread that had never left her since that night in the nursery. It had only lain dormant, waiting to emerge.

"Thomas?" she called. For perhaps it was he who was crying. She heard it distinctly now, yes, weeping, and she called to mind that he had seemed sad at intervals since they had first laid eyes on Allerdale Hall. An Englishman—a blueblood baronet—surely could not show such weakness in front of his new bride, and so of course he would conceal himself.

Then she heard footsteps, and the door to the room opened gently.

She got up. There was no one there—the loose door was simply more evidence of the house's decay, she reasoned—and she closed it.

It opened again with a slow, long *creeeeak*. A sharp chill rippled up her spine as she took a step back. Then, gathering her wits, she stepped out into the hall. Her little dog, which had been sleeping by the fire, followed her out. And she thought of the pup's little red ball, and the sounds emanating from the bedroom while she had been in the bath. Of the woman in the elevator.

In a house that breathed.

It watched.

Holding a candelabra, the bride stepped into the hall with the dog that should be dead jaunting along beside her. When did curiosity flow into dread? It was a question that waited to be answered, though it had been asked a hundred times within the walls of Allerdale Hall.

The floor was cold as a crypt, the boards and tiles frigid as stone coffin lids. Portraits stared down. Statues did not move until one looked away. And then… was it just the light?

Moths fluttered, fluttered, dipped and dove. So hungry.

Just ahead of the bride, a shadow turned the corner. Creeping, shambling. It knew its way around. It hadn't always. But there was a reason it moved in such a bizarre manner. Perhaps the bride would find out why tonight.

But no, she missed it. Didn't see it.

Or *couldn't*?

She glided on, and with her long, plaited hair and white gown, she looked like a ghost herself. Like she belonged at Allerdale Hall. Or would, soon.

Bam! A door slammed shut.

The bride jumped, a cry dying in her throat. Then she stood stock-still, attempting to locate the source, to make it make sense. She was probably thinking that her husband must have shut a door. But she didn't call out his name. Fear kept her silent. She didn't want to call attention to herself.

Curiosity met dread.

Or perhaps she still insisted that her door had opened because the wood was rotting and the hinges were rusty; that, like the elevator, dampness and age threw everything off-kilter. Creaks and groans, curtains, snowfall, a house that breathed. There were rats.

Moonlight spilled; she opened one door in the hallway. Her candlelight flickered over the threshold. Furniture was covered with sheets; dusty ashes were heaped in a fireplace. On the mantel, a candleholder was thickly wrapped in cobwebs, and two crystal goblets stood before a vase of dried roses.

She shut the door and tried the next. A white marble statue missing a face was holding a human skull, perhaps pondering the mysteries of eternal rest. At the base of the statue carved letters stood out in relief, some of them obscured by clumpy red stains: B LOVE W FE. *Beloved wife.* Clearly a funerary monument. Perhaps she wondered if some of the bodies were moved from the family plot because of the mining operations. It was clear that the statue upset her, for she shut that door a bit more firmly.

She opened the next door. That room was completely bare, although the floor was littered with leaves and rat droppings. The fourth room as well.

It watched as she opened every door in the corridor. The bride was made of stern stuff. The dog withdrew, perhaps bored, but the bride moved on, her gown and hair billowing in the breathy sighs of Allerdale Hall. Her feet must be burning with cold. It could almost see her breath in the stygian frostiness.

Then she reached the last door. As she stood before it, she reacted to the scratching and whimpering. So desperate.

Coming from the other side of the door.

"You silly dog," she chided, but there was a quaver in her voice. She was fighting to stay brave. "How did you get locked out?"

She reached her hand around the knob and pulled—

—as, behind her, the little dog barked. She startled, then turned to see it—

—and behind the door, a linen closet, not a room; and crowded in, something, something, *something crimson*—

—whimpered; it whimpered and scratched incessantly.

Of course it saw; of course it knew what it was:

Rolling eyes, a clacking jaw, scarlet fear, a ruby-red woman shape, scratching with fingers of bone. A trail of brilliant, fresh blood floated up toward the top of the closet, defying space just as the monstrous apparition defied time.

But it wanted, needed to be seen; it was wild for her to turn her head back from the dog. However, she did not turn. She did not see.

But the door slammed shut!

That got the bride's attention. She stared at the door and for a moment, it seemed certain that she would run back into her room and dive beneath the covers. Others would.

Others *had*.

But she took a deep breath, building up her courage. Excellent adversary!

Then she finally yanked it open.

The linen closet was bare of bed sheets and pillowcases—for how many did two people need when linens from Allerdale Hall could be sold for enough pence for a few buckets of coal—but it did contain a box. How it had wound up there was quite a story in itself—one best told on another night.

The bride examined the objects in the box and murmured, "Wax cylinders." She was a child of the new world; no doubt she knew that they contained recordings. Perhaps of music.

Perhaps of something else.

Her back straightened as she heard the sobbing again. Leaving the cylinders in the closet, she turned back into the hall, facing the way she had come.

It watched as she watched.

From the floor, pulling itself out, a specter of purest scarlet, a grotesque revenant, emerged painfully, struggling, sucking its essence through the floor: the spine first, like taffy, then the back of the head while an arm withdrew as from a viscous, sticky sludge. Bright red bones stretched in unnatural shapes, weirdly, wrongly jointed; the hand slapped down as if for leverage, purchase. Every part of it red; the second arm raising upward, digging itself out. And as the bride stared, paralyzed in horror, it began to crawl toward her. Faceless, scuttling. Implacable, coming to her, at her, for her.

Closer.

She bolted. The little dog that should be dead darted into the elevator and she flew in after it. With shaking hands she twisted the key and pushed the lever.

The thing was coming.

It watched.

The elevator did not move.

"Down, damn it, down!" the bride ordered the lift. Did not plead: it took note.

The elevator remained where it was as if complicit in her destruction. She was trapped now.

The crimson horror dragged itself toward her, hand over hand over hand. It was nearly there.

And then the cage jerked, swayed, and started a slow descent.

She gathered the dog in her arms; it thrashed, practically strangling in her grip. Down past the second story, then the first; down into darkness past the basement and then the cavernous walls. There was a gentle bump as the elevator stopped about two feet off the ground.

The bride set down the frantic dog and tried the lever with shaking hands, but the elevator would not budge another inch.

The things in this house had minds of their own.

At least, in some cases.

As the bride fought for breath, and sanity, it could easily read her face: Would that *thing* come down here? What had it been? What had she seen?

Blood trickling upward, like the materialization in the linen closet. Because the phantom existed in time out of mind. It was a haunter of the dark, from a place where angles did not meet and natural laws did not work.

As Edith forced herself to continue to act, the sound of dripping water echoed in the blackness. She groped through the bars and found a switch. A twist of the knob, and a clutch of sepia-colored bulbs threw off dim light. Gazing fearfully up, she climbed down from the lift onto the earthen floor.

Did I see that? Did I?

Mine car rail tracks climbed upward into a tunnel. She felt a draft. Blood-red clay had seeped in through the walls, coating large portions of the cavernous space. Six enormous vats sat on the tile floor, three on each side of a trough puddled with scarlet clay. Beyond it lay a jumble of luggage and a mountain of women's shoes and clothes, boxes of papers, and a sturdy steamer trunk.

She gave the profusion of clothing a cursory inspection, then went over to the trunk. The brass plate on the lock said ENOLA. The initials on the trunk read E.S.

Her initials.

She tried the lock. It required a key, which of course she did not have. Beneath her feet, several stones moved loose;

she lifted one up and found gold trinkets such as a lady would possess—chains, a brooch, a lady's watch—and another stone revealed bones of small animals—rabbits? dogs?

What did it mean? She had almost reached her capacity to take in information. She kept looking up at the ceiling, and then the elevator. Trembling from head to toe, she—

Tap, tap, tap.

Edith jerked at the sound. It had followed her down! It was here!

Tap, tap, tap.

It was in the cavern. Shaking, she scanned, listening, the little dog skittering around on its toenails, snuffling. Edith's racing mind was split down the middle, one half obsessively replaying what had happened upstairs, the other focused on the noise. Trying to make sense of it, fighting to *understand.* She was a dervish of confusion and fear.

Who was here? What was happening? Why had that horror—

And then she froze. She had pinpointed where the tapping was coming from.

Inside one of the vats.

A sealed vat.

Something was in there, trying to get out.

Terrorized, Edith fled.

As it watched.

CHAPTER THIRTEEN

Why did I agree to do this?

The knot in Alan's chest tightened into a fist as stalwart workers loaded another crate onto the dray cart outside Cushing Manor. Books, engineering instruments, even Edith's beloved childhood library were being put up for auction. It was as if she had wished to blot out her entire existence here in Buffalo. To be sure, much of it was tragic—the terrible deaths of both her parents—but while his hopes that they would one day marry had dissipated, surely she had *some* fond memories of their years as confidants and playmates. Was it so easy to put him from her mind as well? He would never forget her, ever.

He walked over to the cartons of her books and shook

his head. He picked up a piece of stationery, wrote out an IOU for a considerable amount, and on a second piece of paper wrote SOLD TO DR. ALAN MCMICHAEL. DO NOT LOAD. In time, Edith would be sorry that she had let these books go. God willing, she would have children of her own. He could imagine her seated in a nursery—the one at Allerdale Hall must be charming—reading her fairy-tale books to a rapt little girl, a daydreaming boy.

He wished with all his heart that those children could be his, but as his own mother might say, *If wishes were horses, beggars would ride.*

Mr. Ferguson, the Cushing family lawyer, regarded him with somber interest. He spotted the sold sign and gave Alan an approving nod. It was natural that the man had been put in charge of shutting down the house. He had been the executor of Carter Cushing's will as well. Edith was his sole heir, now quite wealthy. Alan had offered to help him go through all the Cushings' possessions; thanks to his long, intimate history with the family, he could assist with the cataloging and pricing.

"I spent a good part of my childhood in this house," Alan said, turning to him. "Our families were so close back then."

Ferguson sighed, just as heavy-hearted. "It's a pity. To liquidate all this. So quickly. So soon."

Alan cocked his head. "Too soon, don't you think?"

But Ferguson was ever the discreet retainer. He said neutrally, "It's all a matter of opinion, really."

Alan wandered over to Cushing's desk and began

transferring the contents of the drawers into a carton. There he discovered Cushing's book of checks.

And saw in the register that the very last check Cushing had written before his death had been made out to Sir Thomas Sharpe for a very substantial sum. With a chill, he verified the date on which the check had been written: October 11th.

The day before Cushing had died.

Or been killed, he thought, a terrible suspicion blooming in his mind.

Making his apologies to Ferguson, he left Cushing Manor and drove his motorcar to Cushing's club. It was a simple matter to gain entry to the locker room—he was known to the club secretary. He examined the scene of Cushing's death. A new basin had been installed. He studied it, and then the floor, trying to reconstruct exactly how such grievous injuries could have been caused by a mere fall. And even if Edith's father had hit the porcelain full on, the angle was all wrong. Alan had tried to explain that to the coroner, but the man had been affronted… and defensive. And it is very difficult to get a man to listen to reason if he is defensive.

I should have tried harder to get Edith to listen to me, he chided himself. *I did not want to pressure her.* Sharpe had turned her head… and captured her heart. In grief, she'd been so vulnerable. At the cemetery, she had trembled beneath Sharpe's arm—more like a dying butterfly pinned to a board than a bereaved woman shielded by her beloved.

This is all wrong, he thought. *All of it.*

Dismayed, he left the club.

A piano.

A lullaby.

And for those drifting moments between sleeping and waking, Edith imagined herself back in her nursery, her beautiful mother playing to soothe her busy-brained child to sleep. *Sleep, my child, and peace attend thee, all through the night.*

Then she opened her eyes to find Thomas's head on the pillow beside her. Her first impulse was to wake him up and tell him about what had happened... but what *had* happened? He had brushed off her insistence that she had seen a woman in the elevator. What would he say if she told him that a deformed, blood-coated skeleton had emerged from the floor of the second story of his house? She had no proof... but she could show him the trunk in the clay pit.

Except that he probably already knew it was there. But what of the tapping in the vat?

Again... she had no proof.

Maybe I was dreaming. Maybe I am going mad. Perhaps she had a fever; she felt her forehead. Her skin was clammy. And she didn't feel very well. Perhaps dinner had not agreed with her. She knew that Lucille had not been raised to cook her own meals, and they were stretching every penny when it came to food expenditures. Perhaps the meat had gone bad. Yet the Sharpes seemed well.

I am a Sharpe. I am Lady Sharpe.

Perhaps too much wine, then; they had opened two bottles to celebrate their marriage followed by some brandy. Edith was not used to spirits; her father had been conservative in that regard and as his hostess, she had followed his lead.

Thomas lay so peacefully; she didn't want to disturb him with her strangeness. He had been reading her novel and professed that it had given him the shivers; it would follow, then, that the authoress of the piece would be equally affected. By the light of the early morning, she began to doubt herself. In all the wild rush of events, she never had sent her manuscript to *The Atlantic Monthly*, and now she was glad. There was more to the story.

More than I imagined, she told herself firmly. Lack of sleep, nerves, the shifting shadows of the house—she could not have seen what she thought she'd seen. A horror... that tapping.

The piano played on. Bright light filtered through the windows, casting sunbeams, speaking of a morning spent in slumber. Surely it was afternoon. Her stomach growled; she felt a cramp and decided she should get up. She put on her dressing gown and left the room. The little dog stayed behind with Thomas.

She followed the notes, going downstairs, until she wandered into an enormous room lined with books and glass curio cases. In the center, Lucille sat playing an antique grand piano. Oil portraits stared down from the walls. Beneath the Sharpe coat of arms over a fireplace, a

Latin inscription spelled out *Ad montes oculos levavi.*

"To the hills we raise our eyes," Lucille said, still playing.

Edith made a moue of apology. "Oh, I am so sorry. I interrupted you. I—"

"Quite the opposite," Lucille replied. "Did I wake you?"

Rubbing her temples, Edith confessed, "I slept very little. I…"

"You did?" Lucille asked. "Why?"

She made the same decision to keep last night's visions from Lucille—if visions she had truly had.

Maybe my mother tapped inside her coffin. Perhaps the mirrors in this house were not hung with black crepe when the dead expired.

The thoughts came unbidden, and they threw her. They were evidence of a fevered imagination. Perspiration beaded on her forehead and upper lip.

Lucille was still waiting for an answer.

"I'm still exhausted." Which made little sense, really. Someone who was exhausted would fall asleep easily, would they not? She determined to change the subject. "That piece of music. What is it?"

"An old lullaby," Edith replied. "I used to sing it to Thomas when we were little."

A much more welcome topic of discussion.

"I can imagine the two of you in here as children. You playing, Thomas coming up with his inventions."

Lucille's eyelids became hooded as she raised her chin. Her expression grew faraway. "We were not allowed in here as children. We were confined to the nursery. In the attic." She spent a moment in that other place, seeing things that Edith could not, and Edith had the sense that Lucille was holding tightly to precious memories that she did not wish to share. Edith had imagined that the two of them would giggle together over stories of Thomas as a young mischievous boy, forging bonds of family and history. But so far, Lucille had maintained firm possession of all her reminiscences as tightly as the household keys, and Edith felt rather locked out.

Lucille went on. "Mother had this piano brought from Leipzig. She played it sometimes. We'd hear her through the floor." She swallowed down another emotion. "That was how we knew she was back in the country."

That seemed so sad. Wouldn't a mother rush to their children, throw open her arms, and gather them in? Perhaps playing was her special way of announcing her return, like a secret code between the three of them. Her own mother's playing had been a sort of code: *Do not fear. I am near.*

Edith had compassion for Lucille then. Of course she would be possessive of Thomas. They had only had each other to turn to. It must be difficult for Lucille to stand aside. Edith was expecting too much too soon.

Lucille motioned toward a large painting of an unsmiling, elderly woman with leathery skin stretched over a narrow, skull-like face. She had the coldest eyes Edith had ever seen, and her mouth was set in an angry, stern line. Lucille seemed to falter as the two gazed at it, and then she collected herself.

"Mother," she said.

Edith was shocked. The woman seemed more like a grandmother or a maiden aunt. Thomas had told her that their mother had passed when he was but twelve, nearly the same age she had been when her own mother had died. And her mother had been young and beautiful.

Until the black cholera. I know what she looked like now. I saw her.

And I saw something last night, as well.

There. She had said it. Admitted it. A pall fell over her.

"She looks…" Edith ventured, and had no idea how to courteously proceed.

"Horrible?" Lucille asked bitterly. "Yes. It's an excellent likeness."

Edith approached the painting and read a small brass label set into the frame: LADY BEATRICE SHARPE. Then she noticed the huge garnet ring on the ring finger of the withered left hand. It was the engagement ring Thomas had given her. It was on her hand now. She glanced down at it. Yes. The identical ring. It unsettled her.

"Thomas wanted us to take it down. But I didn't want to," Lucille said. "I like to think she can see us from up there. I don't want her to miss anything we do."

Was that a smirk? Lucille smiled at the painting as if she and that evil-looking woman were sharing a private joke.

"This is, I think, my favorite room in the house," Edith said, both to change the subject and because it happened to be true.

"Mine, too." Lucille smiled briefly, but it was a warmer smile than she had favored her mother's portrait with. "I read every book I could find. Specifically entomology."

"Insects," Edith filled in.

"Insects, yes. Jean-Henri Fabre. There's nothing random about insects. And I admire that. They do what needs to be done to assure their survival. Even their beauty and grace are only means to ensure their species—"

"Are these all your books?" Edith asked quickly. *Anything to stop her talking about how moths eat butterflies*, she thought.

"Mother selected most of these. Had them brought from afar. She was not very mobile, you see. So the world needed to come to her."

Thomas hadn't mentioned anything like that, but then, he had been quite circumspect when discussing their parents. She had assumed at the time that he didn't wish to bring up an indelicate subject so soon after her father's death. The English were far more indirect than Americans. One had to listen for subtleties. Edith didn't mind. She could listen to Thomas talk all day. Perhaps she could find a more discreet way to bring up her experiences in the house. If she could get him to talk about the house's legends and ghost stories, perhaps, or its past. Who had died here, and how… and why.

As she considered that, she skimmed a few of the titles of the dozens if not hundreds of books, recalling how she had done the same thing in Alan's ophthalmology practice. It had crossed her mind a number of times to write her old friend, but it didn't seem proper. She was certain now that he had entertained hopes, and as such, he was—had been—her husband's rival for her affections. It would not do to correspond with such a person, no matter what place he had held in her earlier life. It would be disloyal.

And yet, she wished that etiquette decreed otherwise…

"*Oratory of a Pilgrim*," she read off the spine of one of the volumes.

Lucille almost grinned. "Sounds quite virtuous, doesn't it?" She paused as if for dramatic effect. "Have you heard of a fore-edge illustration?"

Edith shook her head, and Lucille took the book. "They are images hidden in the book's fore-edge, carefully dissimulated as a pattern until you bend the pages so…"

She bent the side of the book so that it curved, revealing a colorful painting of a Japanese couple in flagrante delicto—performing sexual acts upon each other. Edith was nonplussed.

"Oh, my. Are all the books…?" The books that Thomas's *mother* had ordered?

"Surely that can't shock you now?" Lucille said. "Now that Thomas and you…"

Edith shook her head. She was actually beginning to feel close to Lucille. It was good to have another woman to talk to.

"No, no. He was so respectful of my mourning. We even traveled in separate cabins."

Lucille seemed to brighten at that. Or perhaps she was amused.

"How considerate," she drawled. "Well, my darling. In time, everything will be right."

Those were comforting words if they were true.

They will be my lullaby, Edith thought, and smiled at Lucille. But the other woman had returned to her playing, and so did not see the smile. Edith glanced back up at the portrait of Lady Beatrice Sharpe, and was very grateful that so dour-looking a woman had not survived to become her mother-in-law, no matter how uncharitable that was.

CHAPTER FOURTEEN

LUCILLE CONTINUED HER playing, and Edith went back to the bedroom, to discover that Thomas had dressed and gone out. She put on one of her favorite gowns, a dark green velvet with pumpkin appliques, and put up her hair. It was inconvenient, to say the least, to do without a lady's maid. She thought of home. Annie already had a new position; all the Cushing servants did. Her family's residence would soon be sold, and everything in it.

I wish that I had saved my picture books, she thought. Perhaps she could write Mr. Ferguson in time to stop their sale.

Edith settled in front of her typewriter to work on her novel, but the day passed drearily without Thomas and she found herself easily distracted.

As the day wore into dusk, Edith gazed through the window and saw her husband with Finlay and a couple of men from the village at the base of his harvester. She knew what she was looking at. She had grown up around similar apparatus. There were actually several machines on the grounds, quite enormous, the derrick-like poppet head towering over all of them. She made out the drill and the harvester, the several conveyer belts, one placed beside an oven intended to bake the clay into brilliant bricks such as the one Thomas had shown off in her father's meeting room. The lumpy, industrial chaos was out of place in the yard of the great old house. A hodge-podge. But looks could be deceiving. The chaos reigned in the house. The arrangement of the equipment was actually quite efficient and logical, and would yield the best results once the new clay shales could be extracted.

Thomas was a visionary, a man who could see things that others did not. She reminded herself that he loved her, and that he was her husband, and his duty was to protect her. She would go to him. Perhaps she could make sense of her own visions by asking him about the history of the house.

Alerted by her rumbling stomach, Edith went down to the kitchen and nibbled a piece of bread and jam as she made some sandwiches, helping herself to rye bread that had gone a bit stale, cold ham, and cheese. Her stomach was not much better, and she was beginning to get a headache so she brewed some of the terribly bitter firethorn tea. Steadfastly, she packed a hamper and went outside.

Snowflakes fell gently from the steel-gray sky. The air was briskly chill, and she knew that the hot tea would be most welcome. The dog trotted briskly, bounding into and out of the snowdrifts, and Edith watched Thomas hard at work on the full-scale model of the machine he had demonstrated in Buffalo. Had Father not been so overly protective of her, he would certainly have funded the invention.

"Edith, my sweet," Thomas greeted her. He was attempting to connect a part of the machine with the rest of it. By the look of frustration on his face, it wasn't going well. "What are you doing here?"

"I want to see you," she answered. "I need to talk to you."

He looked from the machine to her. Finlay appeared to be stoking the engine. They were both very busy.

"Of course, of course," Thomas said.

"I don't know where to begin." She took a breath. "Thomas, has anyone died in this house?"

His answer was a quizzical smile. "Of course, darling," he said. "What manner of question is that? The house is hundreds of years old. I would venture that many souls have come and gone."

"I understand," she said patiently. "But I'm talking about specific deaths. Violent deaths."

He blinked. "This is not a good moment, Edith. This infernal contraption won't start. It's a complete fiasco. We've been at it all afternoon."

He returned to his task. But she would not be deterred.

"Can we take a moment, Thomas?" she said more urgently. "I brought you some sandwiches and a bit of tea."

"Tea? You made tea?" He made a little face and returned to his work. She recalled a comment he had made while in Buffalo—that Americans had no idea how to make a proper cup of tea. It had something to do with boiling the water or steeping the leaves just so. "What tin did you use?"

"I'm sorry?"

"What tin did you use?" he repeated. "The red or the blue one?"

"Oh, I don't know. It's all the same, isn't it? Tea is tea." Well, except for if one was English, she supposed.

"Try it again, Finlay," Thomas told his man.

Finlay stoked the fire on the steam engine and turned a valve. The machine rattled. Some gears gyrated a little bit but then spasmed violently. Edith was reminded of the bathtub taps and, despite being thwarted in her desire to speak with him, she crossed her fingers that this tremendous racket would resolve. Thomas grabbed onto a valve and held tight.

Work, work, she told the machine.

The rattling increased tenfold, and still her husband did not let go. Then sprays of hot water and steam began to jet from seams between the pipes, then from the valve itself. Thomas held on tightly, trying manfully to hold the machinery together with his bare hands. She could see that it was hurting him. Yet he held it fast. His face was growing red from the exertion. Then a geyser of steam hissed violently, spraying Thomas's hand; he jerked back, pale face twisted in anguish as he screamed.

With Finlay's help, Edith conveyed Thomas to the kitchen. He was covered in red clay that looked like blood and she fought to remain calm as images of her dead father swirled through her mind. Even with the clay cleaned off his right hand, his skin blazed scarlet from his burns.

As was the case in many English country homes, the Sharpes kept a larder of salves and remedies, and Edith dutifully applied what was brought to her to tend her husband. She was reminded of Cook once mentioning to her that back in Ireland, they used honey for burns. In her mind she saw the ants crawling all over the butterfly during their promenade in Delaware Park, and she pushed away that macabre image as well.

"That should do it," she told her beloved patient as she finished bandaging his hand.

"My hands are getting rough. Your father would approve," he said plaintively. She nodded quietly. Did he comprehend the depth of her distress when he'd been hurt? The anxiety it would cost her from now on if he continued to work directly on his invention? He was so preoccupied that it would be difficult to steer the conversation to the topic she wished to discuss: Visions. Deaths. Ghosts.

"The machine will never work," he grumbled. "Never. Why do I keep deluding myself?"

"You shouldn't give up hope." She had to be supportive, no matter her fears for him. She believed in him, and when his own belief in himself faltered, she must sustain him.

"Hope?" He sighed. "Edith, hope is the cruelest of feelings. I normally stay away from it."

And close your eyes to things you don't wish to see, she thought.

He sat next to her. As ever, his nearness shifted her attention as it fanned a flame of its own.

"But now, something has changed in me." He gazed at her. "Why did I bring you here?" He searched her face. "Who did you marry, my darling? A failure."

"You are all that I have." Caught up in her love for him, she kissed him. She felt him stiffen, as he usually did—mindful of her mourning—and then he… *relented*. Surrendered. She was thawing his reserve.

Thomas pulled away, eager to get back to work. "The men leave at nightfall and we are racing against the snow." They both stood and started heading back, and she told herself that tonight, she would make him talk to her.

They walked out to the kitchen and reached the foyer. "Soon we won't be able to make any progress," he continued. "That's when you'll find out why they call this 'Crimson Peak.'"

She froze on the spot.

"What did you say?" she asked tightly.

"Crimson Peak," he replied. "That's what they call it. The ore and the red clay reach up from the ground and stain the snow. It turns bright red. So… 'Crimson Peak.'"

Edith stood stock-still as Thomas moved past her. Her stomach cramped again.

I was warned, she thought, stunned. *Twice.*

But I am here.

Crimson Peak.

It watched the brother leave the bride's side. Then he stopped by the foyer, hearing a noise, and turned.

Yes, there was a shadow... and a noise... but there was no one in sight. Turning away, he left.

No one that *he* could see, anyway.

CHAPTER FIFTEEN

FLOWERS ON A grave, in the snow. The Cushing belongings had been packed up, yet for Alan, there was no sense of finality.

Alan placed his bouquet at the foot of the Cushing monument, wondering if the dead rested in peace. Not even a serene death would have prevented Edith's father from watching over her and protecting her, if such a thing as ghosts existed. Alan remembered how insistent little Edith had been that her mother's ghost had haunted her shortly after her hideous death. Edith had been nearly hysterical and Alan had pretended to believe her.

But he had been the only one. Her father had soothed his fearful child by reminding her that she possessed a "fevered" imagination, which Mrs. Cushing had fed with a steady diet of fairy stories that they read together. Ghosts were not real, he had insisted, and had bought her books with more sensible themes, such as home management.

"But they are real," she had told Alan, as they stood together making pretend spyglasses with their hands in their "pirate lair" up in the apple tree in his back yard. "Mama was there. I know she was." She'd shivered, her face puckering until she nearly cried. "And she was so scary."

He had listened, and nodded, and tried to make her happy. His mother had advised him that Edith might attempt to call attention to herself with wild stories and concocted illnesses out of sheer misery. It was a fact that her family life was now "imbalanced." The loving hand of a mother was absent, and girls required a strong maternal influence in order to grow into reasonable young women.

"The damage might be too great," Mrs. McMichael had speculated and Alan, alarmed, had tried to do all he could to help his fellow pirate mend. He had even secretly played at tea with her and her dollies, much to his shame.

But his sister had laughed at Edith and told all her friends about her ghost story. Girls could be so cruel; at school and church—everywhere, now that he thought about it—Eunice and the others had lain in wait for Edith's approach, then jumped out at her shouting, "Boo!"

They tortured and bullied her; and finally, one day close to her eleventh birthday, she came to Alan and said, "On the subject of Mama, Alan, I believe I was mistaken."

For years she did not mention it, and he had almost

forgotten all about it. Then she had begun her novel, and he realized that she had only buried the memory. He had shown her those images of spectral visitation as an opening gambit to discuss it, but by then, she had become enamored of Sir Thomas Sharpe. Still, she had peered at the images with acute concentration, and he wondered what had been going through her mind.

If you could come back from the dead, he told Carter Cushing, *would you tell me how you died? How did you come to write Sharpe a check for such a vast sum on the night before you left this world?*

His musings were interrupted by the crunch of footsteps in the snow. Mr. Ferguson had arrived.

"You asked to see me?" the elderly lawyer asked, as they tipped hats to one another. Then he studied the grave. "Perhaps it all ended well enough. Edith seems to have found happiness, don't you agree?"

It was clear to Alan that Ferguson was testing the waters. "I haven't heard a word," he replied.

"I have. She asked me to transfer all her assets to England."

She is giving her fortune to Sharpe, Alan realized with a jolt. Which, as a married woman, was of course her prerogative. But he couldn't help his certainty that it was wrong. And dangerous.

"Are you really?" he asked.

"Every penny." Ferguson was trying to remain neutral, but it was clear to Alan that he was also troubled. "I've sent the papers and await only her signature. She seems to be investing all of it in those clay mines of his, and I have no recourse but to obey."

With Ferguson's frank admission, Alan decided to be more direct.

"The manner of Cushing's death—the impact on his head. He had shaving cream on his cheek. He was likely in front of the mirror. That is inconsistent with the diagonal injuries he sustained against the basin's corner." He paused, for now he was about to move into damning territory.

"And the last check was made out to Sir Thomas Sharpe, on the very night he announced his departure. You were there. The night Edith slapped him."

Something changed in Ferguson's face; he was dropping his air of impartiality and letting down his guard, as Alan had done.

"If I may confide," Ferguson began, and he leaned in close. "Before Cushing died, he hired a New York man, a Mr. Holly. Very hard to track down. He digs up unsavory facts, haunts places not suitable for a gentleman." A blush of color rose in the lawyer's cheeks. "I am afraid that even I have used him, from time to time. But the very fact that Holly got involved gives me pause."

Alan was intent. "What are you trying to say?"

"Look, Doctor, Cushing was no fool. And he liked you. Always mentioned you as someone worthy of his trust." He waited a beat, and then he added pointedly, "And, quite frankly, of his daughter."

Alan was moved, and conflicted. This mystery was

far from over. Yet was he the one who should persist in unraveling it?

"I would love to visit Edith," Ferguson ventured. "But I am old and tired. A trip like that requires a younger man than me." He looked sideways at Alan, who gave him a nod.

They were agreed, then. There and then, a pact was made.

And Alan would not fail.

CHAPTER SIXTEEN

As WINTER SET in and the days went by, a strange sense of freedom overcame me. I even started transcribing my novel again, inspired by the secrets Allerdale Hall seemed to hold.

Something had changed in Thomas, and Edith was glad. She knew he had been holding back affection because of her mourning, but a man had… needs, and this she understood. And welcomed. She wanted to be his wife in all ways. She wanted that closeness for herself. And then, perhaps, she could tell him about the terrifying things that she had seen and heard—although there had been no more of them. It was all over.

And just because I saw them doesn't mean they were actually there, or that they are still there, she thought. *Or that anything is to be done about them.* As Thomas had observed, the house was centuries old. Many people had died in this house, and some of those deaths were bound to have been violent. He and his sister had seemed quite dismissive of the shadow she saw upon her arrival at Allerdale Hall, and a part of her was still that little girl who had confided the terrifying encounter with her mother's ghost to her friend, and been laughed at.

Alan showed me those pictures. I'm not certain he put credence in them. But perhaps he thought of them only as scientific phenomena. Lingering presences, memories. He spoke of an "offering," an invitation to communicate. But was he truly speaking of that, or of a need to create a state of mind that would open one's eyes in a special state of receptivity?

Am I seeing things that are really here?

Today she had dressed in shining golden satin and styled her hair much as she had worn it the night of the ball at the McMichaels'. She took a moment before she stepped into the elevator, then climbed in and pulled down the lever. As it rose she surveyed the house. Perhaps the wounded structure was letting its ghosts out just as moths and flies seemed to be emerging from cracks in the walls. In the same way that it breathed, maybe the house was simply exhaling old, poisonous histories that had nothing to do with the modern world.

The lift jerked to a stop. As with the more horrifying trip to the mine pit, the bottom of the cab did not stop flush with the floor. She had to step down. She was almost a little dizzy; she was at the highest accessible point of the house. It seemed terribly wrong to place a nursery up here. How had Lucille phrased it? "Confined." Like prisoners.

But there was no doubt that she had arrived at the nursery. The moldy, mottled wallpaper featured a little boy who appeared to be falling—Jack and Jill? The omnipresent moths clung to painted flowers and did not scatter when she approached.

The first room she entered was incredibly dusty and neglected. A cradle and toy chest occupied a corner near a window. A blackboard and student desk reminded her of her first days learning her letters at her mother's knee, before she was old enough to join the other children at school. Many more moths trembled, glued to the walls and the ceiling, staining it a deep brown. They shifted and flew, swooping close to her head. Under a skylight stood an old wicker wheelchair. As she turned her head, dust motes seemed to collect in the chair, thickening into a shape; she looked back and the illusion dissipated.

She heard the whirring of a drill and followed the sound into a dark but wonderful room full of gears and clocks and mechanical wonders. Automata of all sorts greeted her eyes—clowns, a lady in a French gown playing a harpsichord. A wigged gentleman with a flute to his lips. A comical little duck.

And there he was with his back to her, Thomas, ever the industrious inventor, refining the prototype of his mining machine, since the snow had precluded any work on the full-scale model. Still hopeful, then. He had a woolen blanket around his shoulders, putting the lie to her suspicion that her thick-blooded English husband was impervious to the cold.

"Do you like it, Edith?" he asked her without looking at her.

"It's wonderful." She raised her brows. "But how did you know I was here?"

He turned around and smiled at her winningly. "The creak of the floorboards, a shift in the light. It's easy to sense when you are not alone in this house."

She was tempted once more to speak of the things he had not seen but that she had, but held her tongue. Instead she pointed to the array of incredible fabrications.

"You made all these?"

He inclined his head. "I used to carve toys for Lucille, make her trinkets to keep her happy."

Dear Thomas. "Were you alone?" she asked him. "Here? All the time?"

"Father was always traveling. The family fortune didn't lose itself you know, Papa really had to put his back into it."

She allowed him his bitterness, for she shared it. The house had deteriorated so rapidly; the book she had perused back in Buffalo with the engravings of the hall had not been all that old. The upkeep of a home such as this must be constant; a few years of neglect and it would show its age; a few decades and it would be as if disease had ravaged it. Allerdale Hall was truly dying, and she wondered if even her fortune could save it.

But despite everything, this room was a happy one, and its occupant seemed truly joyful to see her taking it all in. He hovered over her as she investigated the figure of a white-faced gentleman with painted black hair, a red harlequin diamond outlining his left eye and two golden cups in his hands.

"This is the magician," he announced. "It takes fifty-eight clockwork movements for it to do its trick. To look human. To charm its audience."

Then he pushed a lever and the little puppet made a show of passing the cups over a tiny golden ball. Enchanted, Edith followed the passage of the ball beneath the cups until *pop!* it appeared in his mouth and he pretended to drop it into one of the bowls. Of course there was another inside one of the cups, but Edith laughed at the clever feat of prestidigitation. Thomas grinned back at her, and then he touched her hair. A now-familiar sadness crossed his features, followed by a masculine hunger.

"You are so different," he murmured, still touching her. Studying her as if memorizing her.

"Different from whom?" she asked mildly.

He blinked, coming out of his reverie. "Everyone, I venture."

And then… at last, at last, he kissed her with real passion. Skin on skin, mouth on mouth, sliding over her cheek, her forehead, her neck.

Some held that women did not feel desire, not in the way that men did. But if Thomas felt more than she felt now, she did not understand how he could have held back all this time. For she wanted him completely, utterly. She could not breathe for wanting him. It was an ache, an insatiable need, and it had been building in this space he had held between them. She saw herself bursting free of her cocoon of innocence, ready to fly into his arms and his heart and he into her flesh, to join with her and *be* with her. To forget death and tragedy and loss. She was his wife and it was her duty and her privilege to transform him with her devotion and her love.

He put his hands on her breasts, which were pushed up by the boning at the top of her corset, and she arched her back with a gasp.

"Edith," he managed, "you're still in mourning and—"

"No. It is time. It is time," she insisted.

He shoved tools and mechanisms from off his worktable and pushed her onto it, raining kisses on her face and above the neck of her dress. She knew that he wanted her; she raised her skirt as he moved to make them one flesh and she accommodated him, oh, yes—

Then he stopped and jerked away from her. He looked almost... *frightened*.

"What's wrong?" she asked, sitting up.

"I heard a noise," he blurted, moving away from her. "I thought..."

"What?" She waited for his answer as she slipped off the table. "You thought what?"

Then Lucille swept into the room. She was carrying

a tray of tea things. The *cloisonné* pot was quite beautiful.

"I was hoping to find you here," Thomas's sister said, with as much warmth as she seemed ever to be able to muster. "I made you some fresh tea."

The English certainly loved their tea. Edith watched as Lucille put down the tray and handed her a steaming cup. There was a spoon on her saucer, though not on the others, and Edith figured it must have been intended for serving the sugar. Lucille did not comment on the mess on the floor. Too polite, Edith wondered, or disinterested?

Thomas was flustered. As he rearranged his clothes, avoiding her eyes, Edith thought he looked ashamed. Perhaps he was concerned that he had placed her in an embarrassing situation. If Lucille had come into the room any later... He was truly chivalrous.

But she wished he had taken his chances.

"You're too kind," Edith said to Lucille.

"Oh, don't mention it. I heard the elevator. I needed the company." She gestured to the bowl of sugar cubes. "One lump or two?"

Sick. So sick.

Edith awoke, her stomach roiling with nausea. She had experienced a bout of seasickness on the crossing from New York to London. This was ten times worse.

"Thomas? Thomas?" she murmured urgently.

Moonlight revealed that she was alone. Hurriedly she lit a candle in the silver candelabra, and stared in shock at a bloodstain on her pillow, next to her mouth. She touched her lips.

She heard the rustle of silk.

In the air, the scent of:

"Jasmine," she said. Not her own fragrance. She wore essence of rose.

Her dog growled.

And suddenly she knew without an ounce of doubt that there was something in the room. Something with them.

Or someone.

But she saw nothing. Their boudoir, as she warily studied it, looked the same as always. On the rumpled bed, the indentation of her body as she had slept. And beside that, evidence that Thomas had been in the bed. Her empty teacup. Beside the fireplace, a half-full glass of deep burgundy wine. Thomas's, she assumed. A book. She wanted to see what he'd been reading but quite suddenly, she was afraid to cross the room to look.

She *felt* it, sensed eyes on her, a near-caress on the nape of her neck. Nerve-deep tremors shuddered through her and knocked against her ribcage, the inside of her skull. Her cheeks and forehead prickled; her lips went numb. Was it behind her? Beside her?

Could it touch her?

She wondered if someone took a photograph right now of this room, would it reveal a stretched, blurred face staring straight at her, nose to nose? Or a crimson corpse pressed against her back, caressing her hair, showering her with ghostly rose petals, humming a lullaby? Images snapped in and out of focus like a kaleidoscope: decayed headstones neglected for centuries, the restless dead rising with the mists on the heath, and something here, right now, something that was made of hunger and longing and unrequited love. Of fury and vengeance and unsatisfied malice.

She was so sick; was she delirious?

Or was she dying, and thus able to commune with the dead of Allerdale Hall? Is that why she had been able to see her mother? A hidden sickness all her life?

Why am I bleeding? Why am I so ill?

Moon shadows stole across her curtains; did the wine in Thomas's goblet ripple against the rim?

Creeping, tiptoeing, gliding. Was there a furtive pressure on the hem of her nightgown? Did someone experimentally lift a tendril of her long, unbound hair?

The tension that gripped her was unbearable. It was making her stomach cramp and now a headache pressed hard on both sides of her head. If an invisible force was trying to contact her, she should make an effort, too. An image of her stuffed toy rabbit flashed into her mind. Rabbits and sick women could die from fright.

She swallowed hard and extended her hand. What had Alan called it? An offering, an invitation.

She would invite.

"If you are here, with me," she began. She almost stopped out of sheer fear. But she could not stop. She could not hover here forever; just as when she had been compelled to identify her poor father's ruined face, she stepped over her terror and acted.

"Give me a signal," she said clearly. "Touch my hand."

There was nothing, only the sound of her breathing and the soft whining of her pet. But the room still *held* something, and she was trapped in here with it. She swayed, even more nauseated.

And waited.

Nothing. Her shoulders drooped but she felt no relief, none at all.

Very well, then, she thought, *perhaps it is only my imagina*—

Then something grabbed her hand and half-threw her to the floor. Impossibly strong and violent. The impact jolted the breath out of her and yellow dots exploded in her vision. If she'd had time to resist it, her effort would have proved useless. Such was its power. The candle went out.

Trembling, she got to her feet and struggled to light it again. *There is something here. Oh, my God, there is no doubt*—

Screams of pain—shrill, horrible—emerged from the bathroom. Without a second's hesitation, Edith raced to the doors and flung them open. Utter blankness, blackness, nothing at all and then:

There.

In the tub.

Nightmare.

Insanity.

Submerged, partially visible above brimming crimson water.

Decayed, barely recognizable as a human corpse— an outline, blurring, transparent and then solid, in bits, and giving off wisps of red, smoke-like trails that trickled upward as the other *thing* had done, the other *corpse*; clotted blood bubbling; dead, dead, dead; dead eyes and dead mouth rotted open; hands of taut stretched leather-skin splitting over knuckles, joints, bones. Clasping the sides of the tub as it soaked, head drooped forward, and Edith was paralyzed with horror.

The skull—its head was split with the blade of a meat cleaver, firmly and deeply embedded in the bone. She could see the red brain, the bone fragments, maggots crawling in the gore.

Edith could make no sound; she could only stare, only see. *I am seeing this. I can see this.*

Then the ghastly figure twitched and moved. The scarlet water spilled over the sides of the tub as the figure rose. Its—*her*—twisted face and sagging chest were covered in blood.

And Edith knew who she was.

"Oh, my dear God, no!" she shrieked.

She ran out of the room, down the corridor. "Thomas!" she screamed. "Thomas!"

Reverberating along the passageway, an unearthly voice hissed, "You! Leave now!"

The thing she had escaped was the thing she was now running towards at full speed. It stood at the far end of the hall: a naked red hag with a cleaver in its skull. Her eyes were wild with rage and madness. She pointed a skeletal finger straight at Edith.

"Edith! Leave now!" she rasped.

Edith backed away, wheeling around as she reached

the stairs, and ran into Thomas as he was turning the corner. Her savior, protector. Safe now, safe. She threw herself into his arms, sobbing.

"Edith, Edith, what is it?" he demanded, embracing her.

She focused. Gazed around fearfully, seeing… nothing. Knowing now that it could be there, still be there, coming for them both, right this moment. Refusing to be seen. It had grabbed her.

It could kill them.

"That thing, that horrible thing!" she cried.

"Your hand's like ice." He touched her forehead. "Are you running a fever? Look at me."

And when she did, his lips parted. He must have finally seen how terrified she was.

"What, in God's name?"

"I saw a woman," she told him, and rushed on before he could contradict her. "Not a shadow, not a trick of the light. Scarlet, and full of rage. Her head was open—a horrible, gaping wound." Edith's skin was buzzing with electricity as if it were trying to crawl off her body. Her knees were rubbery and she would have fallen if he had not held her. She had to get him out of there, away.

He was stunned, but she went on.

"Her face was distorted, twisted, but I recognized her." She gazed hard at her husband, willing him to really listen to her. To see in her words what she had seen with her own two eyes. "She was the woman in the portrait. She was your mother."

He allowed her to drag him from the hall, down to the sofa before the great fireplace, where shadows could not lurk. Lucille appeared with tea; Edith was shuddering, nearly losing herself again, but needing desperately to get it all out. They could only see that she was sick and incoherent. Nothing she described made any impression on them.

"There was such hatred in her eyes. And intelligence. She knew who I was. And she wants me to leave." She ground out the words in sheer misery, in shock, desperate for their help. The cadaverous whispers still knocked against her eardrums, like a seashell whispering of doomed voyages and drowned sailors. Of horrors yet to come.

"Nonsense, my dear," Lucille soothed. "You are not going anywhere. You had a bad dream. You were sleepwalking." She poured a cup of hot amber liquid.

"But I am afraid I shall go mad if I stay." Flanked by her only two relations in all the world, Edith felt herself begin to descend into hysteria once more.

"You are imagining things," Thomas insisted. "Tomorrow we'll go out." He spoke to her as if she were a child. "To the post office. The fresh air will do you good."

To the post office? She could scarcely believe what he was saying. She had crossed an *ocean* to be here with him.

"No, I want to *go*," she demanded. And then, in case he misunderstood, she added, pleaded, "Away from here."

Her hands were shaking. Lucille helped her steady them so that she could drink her tea, forcing her to hold onto the cup. Giving her an anchor point so that she would not shatter.

"Edith, there is nowhere else to go," she said kindly, as one might speak to a lunatic. "This is your home now. You have nowhere else to go."

It watched the sister eye the brother. She was frightened. He was too.

What mischief is this? her gaze demanded.

What mischief indeed?

Of course there was something in the tea to make the bride sleep. After she passed out, the two conferred in the hallway, dark clothes shifting in the blue night gloom like two black moths.

"What is she doing?" the sister whispered fiercely. "How could she possibly know?"

"I didn't tell her a thing," the brother vowed.

That scared the sister even more. "What is she trying to do, Thomas?" As if asking the question repeatedly would yield a different answer.

"I don't know," the brother said. "She is in quite a state. Tomorrow I'll go to the depot, pick up the machine parts. I'll take her with me. Let her get some fresh air."

"Yes," the sister agreed. "Get her out of here." She glared at him. "And soon as we get the final papers signed, I want this over with."

Things moved around them, *through* them, but they did not see them. But as the bride had observed, just because they couldn't see them, didn't mean that they weren't there.

Through a glass, darkly; once upon a time...

CHAPTER SEVENTEEN

MORNING IN CUMBERLAND was so different from Buffalo. The snowy mud was rutted from wagon wheels and the residences were nothing more than hovels. Thatched roofs were not uncommon, and the air between the snowflakes was a murky brown and gray. A few brick buildings stood staunchly upright but their walls were dotted with moss and smeared with smoke. There was a pub called the Red Hand; the windows were steamed up and as their wagon bumped past the door, Edith inhaled the greasy odor of boiled meat and cabbage.

"It's much more pleasant in the spring," Thomas said; then his brow furrowed and he returned his attention to some schematic drawings in a notebook across his lap. He hadn't spoken much on the trip, and she had been unable to engage him in a serious discussion of the horror of his mother's butchered corpse ordering her to leave Allerdale Hall. Like Lucille, he had patronizingly suggested that it was nothing more than a bad dream. Then he told her some ridiculous theory held by some that spoiled rye bread could bring on hallucinations. They had been eating rye bread of late, had they not? She had used some to make his sandwiches.

"Yes, and *you* have not had any hallucinations," she'd countered.

"Well, perhaps I'm used to it," he said. Then he'd given her a look. "Have you been working on your novel?"

He knew she had. He'd read bits of it aloud mere days ago and found it quite wonderful. So now he was trotting out the "it's just your vivid imagination" rationalization, was that it? That perhaps she had *not* seen a grotesque corpse shrieking her name. Rye bread, nerves, that huge, decaying house…

That woman in the elevator. He and Lucille were so entirely unconcerned. Perhaps they've both seen things they could not explain and don't want to frighten me with the truth. But if they can see them, and know now that I can too, wouldn't it be more reasonable for them to admit as much to me?

But Thomas would discuss it no longer and she finally gave up. *None so deaf as those that will not hear; none so blind as those that will not see*, she told herself. On the subject of hauntings in their stately home, Thomas could not be persuaded to entertain any other idea than that she had frightened herself.

Then I will prove it to him, she vowed.

The snow was falling thicker and faster, and the postal depot bustled with horse-drawn farm wagons loading and unloading parcels and crates in advance of the impending storm. Finlay attended Thomas as he pointed Edith toward the back of the depot, where a small postal office stood. She had a reply to Ferguson's most recent update to send.

As she counted out some coins to pay for the stamps, the postal clerk noted her name and address.

"You're Lady Sharpe, then?" he said. "Forgive me, madam, but there's a few letters for you. One came in just this morning."

He disappeared for a moment, then returned with some envelopes. As he handed them to her, he said, "Two of them are legal—certified letters from your solicitor—and another one comes all the way from Italy."

Edith frowned quizzically, examining the postmark on the Italian letter: Milan.

"It's not mine," she informed the man.

"You are Lady Sharpe, are you not?" He pointed to the handwritten name and address on the envelope. "Lady E. Sharpe?"

She nodded. "But I don't know anyone in Italy."

"Respectfully, Your Ladyship, it's quite apparent that you do. Open it and find out."

He seemed a bit too inquisitive, and so she simply took the letters without opening them. Outside, the promised storm had arrived, and as she looked for Thomas, the prospect of returning to Allerdale Hall was even more disconcerting than before. She never wanted to set foot in that terrible place again, and to travel through this deluge to get there was more than she could stomach.

She found Thomas and Finlay at the loading dock. Thomas proudly showed Edith the contents of several wooden crates as Finlay diligently carried them and put them on their wagon.

"This is a valve controller," Thomas said, showing her a shiny part. Her father's daughter, she recognized its function. "I had it fabricated separately in Glasgow. This could make all the difference. Think lucky thoughts, Edith. The Sharpe Mines might reopen if this thing cooperates."

He laughed and embraced her, and she held her mail tight. He was so excited about his machined parts that she didn't want to change the subject by showing him the strange letter from Italy.

At least, that was what she told herself. Because he did not believe her, a rift was growing between them. She had thought he would be sympathetic, but he had gently mocked her. Marriage decreed that two halves became one whole, but she felt separated from him now. She didn't feel that she could bring her fears to him with the hope of obtaining relief. She must arm herself against them, then, in any way she could.

"Look at the storm," he said breathlessly. "Do you see? Just in time. In a few days we won't be able to leave the house."

The thought appalled her. There was nothing in this world that she wanted less.

The shipping agent overheard him and deferentially approached. "The storm is getting worse. I suggest you stay the night, Your Lordship. We have a small room downstairs, if you'd like."

Thomas looked to Edith, who happily nodded her consent. She would do anything to stay out of the storm.

And away from that house.

It *was* a small room, just as the man had warned, but warm and cozy, with a humble quilt on the bed and a fire in the grate. To Edith, it was the most wonderful room she had ever been in, never mind the elegant hotels they had stayed at in London.

Now they were propped up in bed, still in their clothes, and she felt a bit shy at the prospect of readying for sleep in a more intimate manner. They had still not been *together*.

The depot manager had brought them tea and some broth and bread, and Edith devoured it, famished. Assuming that she would have to occupy herself on the return trip home once Thomas had his new valves and gears to examine, she had brought along her manuscript. Thomas had spotted it and asked to read it, and she was both flattered and a bit abashed. The ghostly subject matter would only serve to reinforce his belief that she had imagined the horrendous visitation of his mother's ghost. But he seemed most insistent upon reading her new pages, and began to read it aloud:

"'A house as old as this one becomes, in time, a

living thing. It may have timbers for bones and windows for eyes and sitting here, all alone, it can go slowly mad. It starts holding on to things, keeping them alive when they shouldn't be, inside its walls. Things like memories, emotions, people.'"

He paused, then went on. "'Some of them good, some are bad… and some… some should never be spoken about again.'"

He kissed her on the forehead.

"This is rather good. I am so glad to see you're still at it. And this fellow 'Cavendish'—your hero—has he no fears? No doubts?"

Edith looked straight at him. "Of course he does. He's a haunted man."

"Well, I like him. There's a darkness to him. But does he make it all the way through?"

She shrugged. "It's entirely up to him."

"What do you mean?" He smiled quizzically at her.

"Characters talk to you. Transform. Make choices," she replied.

"Choices," he echoed.

"Of who they become."

He grew quiet. And then he gestured to their room. "This is quite dismal, I'm sorry to say. But at least it is warm."

She moved closer to him, hoping then, to close the rift. "I like it much better."

"Better than?" he asked.

Surely he must know what she meant. "The house."

He thought a moment, and then he laughed. He

looked almost boyish, his cares lifting from him. "It *is* much better, isn't it? I love being away too."

"Away from Allerdale Hall?" she persisted. She wanted him to say it. To realize that it was a real possibility. It would mean the world to her.

"Yes. I do." He exhaled. "I feel as if I can breathe."

They embraced and she laid her head on his chest. His heart thumped, then quickened. Perhaps her nearness was affecting him.

"You could sell the house." She mentally crossed her fingers, willing him to consider the possibility that would free them both. To emerge from that dank, terrifying place and live in the wide sunny world.

"Sell it? Impossible." Then he went silent for a moment, as if reconsidering. "As it is, it would be worthless."

Hope grew in her. He *was* actually pondering it.

"Just leave it then." Close it up and walk away. Why not? All the money that they had planned to use to restore it could be put into the mine operations. Or traveling the world. Thomas could hire managers the same as her father did for projects that were too far away for him to oversee himself.

"That, too, is impossible, I'm afraid," Thomas replied. "It is all we have: our name, our heritage, our pride."

"I left everything *I* had," she riposted, though her tone was very gentle. She wanted to bring him around to her point of view. This was a very serious discussion. "Everything I was. Behind." She let that sink in, and then she went on. "We could live elsewhere."

"Elsewhere?" He sounded genuinely puzzled, as if the thought had never dawned on him before.

"London, Paris," she tempted him.

His face softened and he took on a daydream expression, seeing their future in a different way. "Paris. Paris is delightful, yes."

"Anywhere you want." And then she thought of the letter and added leadingly, "Milan…"

He jerked. "Why would you say Milan?"

"Or Rome," she covered, but she knew then that Milan was significant. What *was* in that letter? "Have you been to Italy?"

"Yes. Once." Then his mood shifted. Darkened. As if he was burdened by Allerdale Hall again. "But I can't leave Lucille. And the house. The house is all we are. Our heritage, our name."

He was saying the same thing over and over.

"The past, Thomas. You're always looking to the past," she murmured. "You won't find me there. I'm here."

He said softly, "I'm here too."

Yes, Thomas. Yes.

Willing her love for him to make him listen, she daringly moved on top of him. Her gown clung to her body and her desire for him emboldened her as she kissed him and moved sinuously against him. True, she was chaste, but she was also this man's wife. So she kissed him passionately, and put her arms around him; and she felt his response. He wanted her as much.

No, more.

As in his workroom, their passion ignited. Seemingly oblivious to his scorched and bandaged hand, he pushed her onto her back and undid his trousers, snaking them down to avail himself of her body; she opened herself to him and then he was thrusting into her—*finally, finally*—and the pleasure was indescribable.

Oh, my Thomas, my love—

They were one. Finally making love. And as bliss lifted her up to the stars, she believed that all would be well. They would love, and they would live.

Far away from Allerdale Hall.

In the morning, the world was new. There was more kissing and lovemaking, and Chinese tea and fresh bread still warm from the oven. Sunlight gave the village a charming luster; the snow, though falling, was gentle.

Edith didn't mind the ride back so much; she and Thomas talked the entire time. They were together now, all barriers down, and things would be different. They *would* leave. They *would* travel.

He kissed her when he helped her down in front of the house, drinking in the sight of her, reluctantly parting from her to assist Finlay with the crates. Gliding into the house, she gazed up at the opening in the ceiling and watched the snowflakes sparkle as they floated down, soft as feathers. She removed her bonnet.

"Lucille!" she greeted her sister-in-law. "Lucille!"

There was no answer, but she could hear a clattering

in the kitchen. They had eaten their bread and tea hours ago, and something more substantial would be nice. And something to take the chill off the long drive through the countryside. Even that bitter tea.

Carrying a few parcels—little things she had purchased, such as warmer mittens and a muffler—she walked into the empty kitchen and set them down. A pan sat untended on the stove. The potatoes in it were burning and smoking, and she took it off the burner.

"We're back!" she called.

And then Lucille approached from the far end of the kitchen, her face drawn and pale. There were rings under her eyes.

"Where were you?" Her voice was strained. She moved like one of Thomas's automata, as if every muscle in her body had been stretched to its limit.

"We got snowed in," Edith said. "We—"

"You didn't come back last night!" Lucille shouted. She grabbed the pan and slammed it on the wooden surface of the worktable.

Edith was startled. "I… we…"

"You were supposed to come back last night," Lucille insisted.

"We spent the night at the depot," Edith explained.

Lucille blinked at her. Then she began to scrape the food, which was ruined, onto plates. "You *slept* there?"

Her distress was bewildering. She could not be surprised that Thomas had at last asserted his husbandly privilege, and yet it seemed almost as if Lucille thought she should have been consulted on the matter.

"Yes, we did. What's wrong with that, Lucille? He's my husband."

But she would not be placated. "I am serious. Is this all a joke to you? All solved with a smile? I was worried sick!"

"Worried—"

"You two out in the storm!" Lucille cried.

Of course. Like Edith herself, Lucille was no stranger to tragedy. Her parents were both dead. She knew that bad things could and did happen to people she cared about. Until one was scathed in that way, one did not understand such fear. Edith did.

"I didn't know if you'd had an accident. I was all alone. All alone. And I cannot be alone…"

The house creaked. Clay oozed from the cracks between the wall and the ceiling. And Edith thought she might know another reason Lucille was so upset— Lucille had been alone in the house after that monstrous apparition had menaced her. Perhaps she, too, had sensed something. Maybe even seen something. She was overwrought.

Edith wanted Thomas to observe the state his sister was in. *We need to leave this house. All of us.*

"The house," Lucille repeated, as if she had read Edith's thoughts. "It's sinking. It gets worse every time. We must do something to stop it."

No. We must give up on it, Edith thought. *This horrible place cannot be redeemed.*

A sudden, sharp bout of dizziness grabbed hold of

her. The kitchen tilted, stretched, and blurred... and Lucille's face along with it.

"I need to sit down," she said. "I'm not well." Her forehead beaded with perspiration and she couldn't make her eyes focus. It was as if the entire house was rippling in and out of existence, losing track of itself, forgetting to remain solid.

What am I thinking? she wondered. *I'm not making any sense.*

"I'll make you some tea. It'll be ready in no time."

Lucille sounded more composed. She bustled about while Edith's stomach churned. Her gaze fell on Lucille's ring of keys, which, of course, should have been passed on to her. Lucille had fought so jealously to keep it. Perhaps she was feeling supplanted.

She noted a name engraved upon one of the keys: ENOLA. The same as the trunk in the pit. *There* was a mystery. Had there been an Enola Sharpe, perhaps? A relative? And a letter addressed to E. Sharpe had been handed over to her, *Edith* Sharpe, at the depot. She took out her letters and shuffled them to find the one from Milan. There was no first name, only the first initial. Could there be several E. Sharpes in their family? If so, it struck her a little odd that no one had mentioned it.

While Lucille filled the teapot, Edith furtively slipped the key off the ring, then returned the set to the table. Then she passed the letter to the bottom of her stack, so that she could work on her puzzle all by herself.

Another wave of dizziness hit her, and the room spun. Edith's stomach fell. She had been so happy away in the village with Thomas that she had minimized just how awful it was here. She could feel the clay-soaked walls closing in; she couldn't imagine taking a bath in that tub, ever again.

As Lucille put the now-filled pot on the stove, she saw Edith's letters and scrutinized the topmost one. "Is that from America?"

Edith nodded weakly and Lucille boldly picked it up and read the envelope.

"From your solicitor," she said, and sounded pleased. "You should read them. Rest a bit. I'll make you some tea. It'll take care of everything."

Her smile was forced, and Edith wondered if Lucille would ever truly like her. But she could not think of that now. She was sick, so very sick, and as bitter as the firethorn tea was, the prospect of drinking something to ease her symptoms was very appealing indeed.

However, the prospect of returning to her bedroom was not. Still, what choice did she have? As Lucille had said, this was her home.

At least for now.

It watched.

In the green-tiled bathroom of Allerdale Hall, the red rubber ball rolled beneath the claw-footed tub and the little dog whined and pranced, trying to cram itself beneath the tub's curved bottom. The ball remained tantalizingly out of reach. It cocked its head, staring at it with all the longing of child gazing at a toyshop window at Christmas.

The pup sat back on its haunches and barked wildly, ecstatically.

And the ball rolled out from under the tub.

Then the ball flew through the air out of the bathroom. The animal skittered on the wood and clattered after it, barking. It followed the ball into the bedroom and was about to dash under the bed to retrieve it when it slid to a stop. It put its ears back, showed its teeth, and began to growl.

Back in the bathroom, a spider dropped down from the ceiling toward the tub. It touched down on the lip of porcelain, then bounced upward to its center. It began to weave its web like an old maid at her spinning wheel. From out of the drain, a sluggish fly emerged, buzzing haphazardly, and began to spiral toward the web. Flies were summertime pests; they were not to be found in snowy climes. The hungry spider kept weaving, one eye on the prize, working feverishly to complete its snare in time to catch the fly. In the next room, the dog whined and its sick mistress got sicker.

The fly that should be dead and the dog that should be dead in the house that should be dead, and the bride, who would be dead soon.

It watched approvingly, appreciating the complexities—and fragilities—of life.

CHAPTER EIGHTEEN

ALAN WALKED INTO the hotel lobby and felt ghosts around him. This was the hotel where Ferguson had delivered the news of her father's death to Edith, possibly with Cushing's murderer at her side. He envisioned his poor darling plummeting from the elation of love to the desolation of loss in a few short moments. He couldn't imagine how that had felt. He also wondered what she had been doing alone in a hotel with Sir Thomas. Annie, her maid, had stated that her mistress had received a large sheaf of typewritten papers at home bright and early in the morning, and soon after had left in a rush. Annie had found a letter with beautiful handwriting among the pages and had been dying to read it. The only problem was that

Annie did not know how to read.

It wasn't until Mr. Ferguson had arrived at Cushing Manor to tell Miss Edith of her father's death that Annie had known that her young lady had left to meet up with a man. Unescorted.

Everything had been so rash, so tumultuous. Alan was not exactly stolid, although he supposed Edith found him so. He would never have compromised her reputation, nor dragged her away from everything she knew three weeks after her father had been bludgeoned to death. There, he had thought it, and it was what he believed.

"Are you sure this is their forwarding address?" he asked the hotel manager, looking down at the written information.

"Sir Thomas and Lucille Sharpe. Yes. In Cumberland, sir."

He supposed that was all the address you needed when you were an aristocrat. "Thank you," he said.

He sat on a round settee and made mental calculations about how soon he could travel there. After a short interval, a man—younger than Alan had expected—approached purposefully.

"Mr. Holly?" he asked. Carter Cushing's intelligence gatherer. As Ferguson had told Alan, Holly was a hard man to locate.

"At your service, sir." Mr. Holly was deferential but not subservient.

"Do you have the copy of the information?"

"Did you bring the sum?" Holly countered.

Alan handed him a substantial packet of bills, and Holly pocketed it. The man moved closer, speaking in a conspiratorial tone.

"Mister Cushing, God rest his soul, was a loyal and honorable customer, sir." He leaned in. "I am obliged to demand a satisfactory reason for your inquiry, as I do not divulge a client's information, even after his passing."

Alan remained resolute in the face of obvious extortion. "Mr. Holly, I paid you already. That's reason number one. Reason number two is that the well-being of someone dear to me may be at stake. And finally, you have the fact that I will punch you repeatedly until you do as we agreed, sir."

Holly briefly considered his reasoning and then handed him a folder. "This is the newest information I've obtained." He also handed Alan a leather folder full of newspaper clippings, which Alan opened. Holly pointed at the front page. "August 1879. People knew Lady Beatrice Sharpe was awful harsh with her children. But no one would ever dare do anything about it. Now this. Front-page news. Quite gruesome. All that blood."

Alan jerked with great disgust at a pen-and-ink drawing of a butchered woman. She lay with her head slumped forward. An axe or perhaps some sort of sharp knife had cut her head nearly in two. The victim was Lady Beatrice Sharpe, the widow of Sir Michael Sharpe, baronet. Sir Michael had died two years before in a hunting accident.

He read the article; the murder had occurred in the

upstairs bathtub at Allerdale Hall—the family seat of the Sharpes. Edith's new home. This woman would have been Edith's mother-in-law had she lived. The only other people in the house at the time of the killing were Thomas, who was then twelve, and Lucille, fourteen. However, the paper was careful to say that there were no suspects. Were the children cleared?

Did Sir Thomas disclose this family skeleton to his fiancée before their marriage? Had this horrible scandal shaped him as Edith's loss of her mother had shaped her? Edith was fanciful, romantic, and possessed of a vast imagination. But what of a young boy who had apparently suffered at the hands of his mother, then lost her in a violent murder?

He simply could not believe that Carter Cushing would allow anyone remotely connected to such a heinous murder to be in the same city as his beloved only daughter, much less invite him to dinner under his own roof.

"Cushing saw this?" Alan queried.

"No," Holly answered. "It took some time to obtain these clippings. The only relevant piece of information I could hand Mr. Cushing was this civil document here. But it was enough to impede any further relationship between Sir Thomas and Miss Cushing." He paused to see if Alan was following him. "In other words, one that would have prevented them from marrying."

Alan was *not* following. He didn't know what the civil document signified. It was clearly an English legality, not an American one.

"Why is that?"

Holly pointed to the significant section of the paper. "Because, you see? Sir Thomas is already married."

CHAPTER NINETEEN

ALONE IN THE bedroom, Lucille's fresh tea at her elbow, Edith calmed down her dog, which seemed upset about something, then opened the first of her letters from the depot. It was from Mr. Ferguson:

> *My dear Edith:*
>
> *Please be advised that the first transfer of your father's property has been completed. The remainder will require your signature.*
>
> > *Yours very truly,*
> > *William Ferguson, Esquire*

Good, she thought, but she felt a strange fluttery sensation that could almost be labeled as panic. This was what she wanted. These were her wishes. But she had to admit that the letter bestowed a sense of finality that tugged at her; she really had left everything behind for Thomas's sake. She was homesick for Buffalo and her friends. She missed the beauty of her home, and the servants, and all her books.

I shouldn't have told Mr. Ferguson to sell my books. She frowned. *I saved so few keepsakes. I was so eager to fund Thomas's invention.*

She coughed into her monogrammed handkerchief.

A circle of blood appeared and she stared at it in horror. *Another* one. Oh, God, could it be consumption? One's lungs became clumped with infection, then one lost weight and coughed up blood… and died. The damp and the miasma of the house could have brought on an attack. It could be the reason she had been feeling so ill.

She needed Thomas to get her away from here. She needed sunshine and clean air, not rot and decay and breezes that smelled of clay.

And ghosts.

She went to the window to observe her husband as he and Finlay worked on his machinery, which jutted into the sky like a jumble of metal pyramids in an oasis of snow. He was so intent, single-minded, working feverishly, though so far with nothing to show for it. Her father had refused to give him funding and eventually the other interested businessmen had withdrawn their enthusiasm as well. If he did succeed, they wouldn't have to live here. He had to be on-site to oversee the building and refining, but oh, if it worked, they would be *free*...

It watched.

It watched the watcher.

The bride had become so engrossed in her thoughts that she no longer heeded the dog, which had moved to the center of her bed and was following, following, the sound of something underneath the mattress. Nose pressed to the blue bed sheets, eyes nearly crossed, sniffing and perplexed. It could not quite understand that it wasn't something inside the mattress.

It was something underneath the bed.

The bride kept staring out the window.

What if it finally dragged itself out from beneath the mattress, and grabbed her by the ankle?

Thomas had never been closer to his dream. He could nearly taste victory. And once it was achieved, then he would be a different sort of person. He would employ dozens of tradesmen to restore Allerdale Hall and the Sharpes would once again be known for their wealth and elegance. He knew that when he or Lucille went to the village, people whispered about them behind their hands. There were many who celebrated their fall, and would not cheer to see them rise again.

Not our fault, he reminded himself. His father had been the scourge of Northern England with his whoring and gambling. His mother, confined to the house—

His mother—

He would not think of that. Of what Edith claimed to have seen.

The snow fell gently, coating the dreary landscape in pristine white. Finlay and some laborers from the village climbed all over the harvester like ants. The first snowstorm had passed, but there would be others. Soon they would be cut off from the rest of the world, and they would have to live off Edith's money until spring with no hope of recouping their investment. "The investment" referring to the machine, of course, and not the trip to America to fetch his bride.

He had planned to court Eunice McMichael, but there were… complications. And once he had met Edith, he had been dazzled by her, as a moth is stunned and lured by candlelight. She was as golden as the sun, and he could not help but turn his face to her.

Finlay pushed on the levers in place of Thomas, who could not do so because of his injury. *Oh, let it be successful,* Thomas prayed, crossing the fingers of his unburned hand.

How many times had he uttered this prayer? How many fortunes had he spent? All worth it, if it would but work.

It kicked, sputtered. Finlay glanced over at him and Thomas gave him an encouraging nod, indicating that he should try again.

Once more the old man pulled the lever. Thomas chewed the inside of his cheek. A little fantasy flitted through his mind: the machine successful, a visit to the Crown, and letters patent on the machine itself. A knighthood, surely, and they would no longer live in mortifying squalor.

Nothing. No shrill of steam from the escape valve. No grinding clank as gears meshed. Thomas winced as his stomach twisted into a knot. He would not give up. So much depended on it. He gestured to Finlay to try again.

The gods were kind: With a shuddering lurch, the machine sputtered to life. Thomas stood stock-still for a moment, almost unable to comprehend that it was working. He was so used to defeat that he could not quite grasp success. Snow tickled the back of his neck and for a moment he thought that he might begin to cry. Triumph at last! After all these long years.

Finlay and the men broke into grins and there were congratulations all around. He had promised them a bottle of gin and a sovereign if it worked today, and he would be good for his word.

I must tell Edith.

In his elation, he did not notice that his footprints were stained with red, as the brilliant clay leached up into the snow. Red bubbled up from beneath the ground and threw red light against the harvester and the witchlike visage of Allerdale Hall itself. As if the world of Sir Thomas Sharpe were coated in blood.

As if Crimson Peak would reveal itself very, very soon.

* * *

Edith watched from the window, fears about consumption slipping away as she witnessed her husband's triumph. She heard the thrilling rhythm of the machine, saw the flywheel turning, the men cheering and patting each other on the back. He was *not* a failure; she had known it all along. All he had needed was sufficient working capital; more money—hers—would mean a chance to improve his invention, and she would sign Ferguson's document immediately.

She sat down to do so, placing the document on her blotter and preparing to write out her new signature: *Lady Edith Sharpe*. She would present it to him when he came up to the bedroom to share his good news, which she anticipated at any moment.

Ceremoniously, she picked up the beautiful pen her father had given her and uncapped it. Her hand hovered above the legal form, and then her eye caught the corner of the letter addressed to *Lady E. Sharpe*. She put down her pen and studied the envelope. The Italian return address made absolutely no sense.

Perhaps it is from Alan, on a Grand Tour, she thought, and banished the tingle of wistfulness she felt. Was it wrong to miss an old friend?

She got out her letter opener and sliced open the envelope. Then she pulled out the letter. It was not from Alan after all. It was written in Italian—and it was not addressed to her. As she had attempted to explain to the postal clerk, it had been meant for someone else.

"Enola," she read aloud, bewildered. No one had ever mentioned a relative named Enola.

She coughed again into her handkerchief and tried to translate the Italian. She had studied it a little—very little—but she certainly couldn't translate the letter on her own. Perhaps there was an Italian dictionary on the shelves in the library.

She had deliberately avoided that room since the half-dismembered corpse of Lady Beatrice had ordered her to leave this place. She was afraid if she looked at the portrait, that blazing red monster would step down from it and attack her. She remembered the power of the invisible force that had pulled her halfway across the bedroom. The venom in the rasped edict to leave Allerdale Hall.

She glanced over at her silly dog, which was burying itself in the sheets. Then she left the room and headed for the library.

Moths inspected her as she entered the vast room. Dust motes spun in the blue sunlight like tiny creatures with minds of their own.

She did not look at the portrait of Lady Beatrice.

But she had the distinct impression the portrait was looking at her. That its eyes followed her every move as she found a row of dictionaries and pulled out the Italian one. There was no scandalous picture in the fore-edge—she did check—and she returned to the bedroom, where the pup greeted her with a thumping tail. She picked it up and was about to place it on the floor when it twisted its little body in her arms and wound up on her bed again.

She got out the typewriter Thomas had given her and removed it from its case. E.S. Her initials. But Enola's, too.

She kept one ear pricked for Thomas's appearance. Surely he would come soon to announce the successful trial run. She hoped something hadn't gone wrong on a second attempt.

Doggedly, she opened the dictionary and began to hunt for the proper Italian words and their translations into English.

It watched.

The bride was so engrossed that she did not see the figure stealthily crawl from beneath the bed and drag itself arm over arm toward the half-open door. The dog hopped off the bed and climbed onto a chair like a person. The bride smiled at it and it barked excitedly. Thus she entirely missed the monstrous, distorted body as it slithered out of the room.

Utterly charmed by her little friend, she returned to her work, and did not notice when the door creaked shut.

Edith adjusted her glasses as she continued to translate the letter. She was getting a bit of a headache. The dog cocked its head as she flipped through the dictionary. Edith was so glad of its company. She was a tad disappointed that Thomas still had not sought her out to celebrate the maiden voyage of his harvester. But she remembered her father's habits: Once assured that a project was on the right track, he rarely took time out to enjoy his accomplishment. Instead, he immediately reset the bar and began to work on improvements. Perhaps that had been the secret of his success, and would serve Thomas equally well.

The dog went through a barking spell, then another, which unnerved her, and she looked over her shoulder more than once. After some time, she had managed to transcribe some troubling lines:

> *Why, dear cousin, will you not answer my letters? My little Sofia is walking and talking by now, and still no word from her favorite aunt.*
>
> *Ever since you met that man, you have grown distant and away. Your only communications are bank related and only ever so often. Please, Enola, write. You have a family that loves you and wants you to come back.*

What can this mean? Edith thought. She determined to find out. She could not deny that she was already uneasy about the duplication of her initials on the trunk down in the pit. She would wait no longer to investigate. She picked up the key marked ENOLA and left the room. Her head pounded and her palms were damp.

As she passed the bathroom, she thought she heard a *clink.* Her stomach clenched. She determinedly walked on by. She wouldn't have the key forever—even though it should be hers by rights. Lucille was possessive of everything… including her brother. Edith could not understand why

Lucille wanted to remain the mistress of Allerdale Hall. There could be no sense of accomplishment, no pride of place, in overseeing this household.

Her pulse raced as she entered the lift and descended, and a wave of vertigo compounded her uneasiness. What was wrong with her?

The lift stopped about two feet above the mine floor. Perhaps it did have a mind of its own. Warily she stepped down and cautiously studied her surroundings. Snow was falling even here. The cold and damp in a place like this would seep right into her bones. Clay was impermeable, smothering. Being inside the cavern was like being inside the body of a wounded thing, seeing its capillaries, tendons, and skinless flesh.

The sound of dripping water echoed in the blackness and she thought of the inhospitable, grim landscape outside. She examined the tunnel and rails that the miners would have used to push their cars of clay along—little children with bowed backs, their exhausted mothers and their thin-faced, pale fathers. Thomas's invention would end such human misery.

Sections of the mine pit were dark as a tomb. She thought of the statue she had seen in the room upstairs, it had looked so like a memorial. *Had* graves been disturbed because of the clay pits? Perhaps the dead roamed the halls of Allerdale Hall because, like her, there was nowhere else for them to go.

Was that their mother's headstone? Perhaps they had rescued it. Despite Lucille's apparent dislike of Lady

Beatrice, the idea that her children may have preserved her monument appealed to Edith. That would mean that their childhoods had not been too terrible. Her own had been wonderful… just too short.

From what little information she had gleaned, she didn't think that their father had been at Allerdale Hall when he had died. She wasn't certain what had happened to him, and she hadn't asked. It seemed ludicrous now that she hadn't wanted to pry. As if learning the history of the family she had married into—and the father of her future children—was invading Thomas's privacy.

Well, she was here now, and if this were invasion… so be it.

She summoned her fortitude and walked to the trunk. The shadows moved, unnerving her. Nothing was quiet in this uneasy mansion.

She inserted the key into the lock, and it gave a *click!* as it opened, the sound reverberating through the vast, frigid space.

She pulled back the lid, to discover the trunk's function as a travel desk, clean and organized, containing neatly stacked papers and folders. She selected a package and examined its contents. Inside was a letter from a bank. In Milan. Addressed to a name she recognized:

"Enola," she murmured. "Sciotti." She put it together: "Enola Sharpe. Lady Sharpe. E. Sharpe. E.S."

She looked into the drawer again. There were three envelopes, each bearing cancelled date stamps: 1887, 1893, 1896. She took them. And:

"A phonograph." She remembered the wax cylinders she had found in the otherwise empty linen cupboard on the night of the first… haunting. There. She'd uttered the word—if silently.

Haunting.

Who had wanted her to find them?

She took the phonograph out. It wasn't as heavy as she had anticipated, and she was glad of that. She set it down and began to shut the trunk when—

Tap. Tap. Tap.

It was the same sound as before, and it produced the same effect: Chills ran down her spine and she braced herself for another terrifying visitation. As with the first time, the sound was coming from the direction of the vats. She put down the phonograph and tiptoed around the puddled floor toward them, ear cocked, trying to listen over the roaring of her heartbeat in her ears. It was coming from the final vat. As with the others, the lid was padlocked shut.

As she approached, it ceased.

She looked around and found a large stone. Hefting it, she slammed it down on the padlock. Once, twice. It broke. She took it off and opened the lid.

The vat was filled with clay, fresh and malleable, thick as custard. As she leaned over it, she accidentally dropped the key into it, and it sank. Dismayed, she thought a moment, then removed her blouse and slid her arm into the liquid, which was thinner than she expected. It was cold and slick between her fingers. Frightened, she leaned in further until her arm was shoulder-deep, breathing in the earthy odor as it coated her nose and throat. The rooting was strenuous and she was getting nervous. Her entire body tingled; her face was icy yet flushed with heat. The tapping in the vat had stopped when she grew near; what if she encountered... *something*...

Her courage began to fail her. Yet she had to retrieve the key. If Lucille knew that she had taken it...

What? she thought defiantly. *I am the lady of the house. By rights all the keys belong to me.*

Still, it took all her courage to keep looking. What if something grabbed her and pulled her in? Or came up behind her and pushed—

There.

Her fingers wrapped around what had to be the key. She drew her arm out of the clay. Uncurling her hand, she gazed down at her open palm. Yes. She had it.

Following the sound of the dripping water, she discovered a broken pipe and vigorously washed herself off. The clay was difficult to prize off the teeth of the key, but she managed it. She gave herself an inspection, grabbed up the phonograph once more, and darted into the lift. The lever balked but she went up.

The bride did not see the distorted skeleton as it floated to the top of the open vat. Blood-red bones. A gaping maw contorted into a soundless shriek. Hollow eyes staring, searching. It floated on memories and horrors.

It floated through sheer will.

Tap, tap, tap.

Like typewriter keys.

Thomas had called Lucille outside to share in his joy. Now here she was, as nervous and excited as he. Their fortunes depended on the success of the harvester, and it had chugged along nicely as he made his recalibrations and coaxed it to life. But this was the acid test—seeing if it would start up and perform without the constant adjustments and fiddling.

As she looked on, he ordered Finlay to start the machine again. The coal burned; the water boiled; the pressure of the steam made it all happen. The various parts of the engine moved with the precision of an automaton, and the harvester belt carrying the buckets glided up and down in perfect working order. It was a thing of true beauty, and the mechanical parts glittered against the weak winter sun.

Thomas's elation knew no bounds. "I knew it! I knew it!" he cried. "We've done it! We can reopen the factory in the spring! We can start again. Lucille! *We can start again!*"

He could see that she was genuinely moved as she embraced him tightly. After all the struggles, the disappointments, now there was victory, vindication… he was *not* a failure.

"Oh, if only Edith could see it," he blurted. The words were out of his mouth before he realized what he was saying.

Lucille pulled away. She stared at him in disbelief.

"Edith?" Her voice shook. "*I* did this with you. For you. *I* did it!"

He put his arms around her again, trying to recapture the moment, to backtrack. Mentioning Edith at this life-changing moment was a stupid blunder. He never wanted to hurt Lucille, ever.

Nor Edith, he thought wildly, panicking. *Neither of them.*

"Of course we did," he placated her. "We did this together. No one else."

"Lady Sharpe," Finlay said. "We need more coal to test the steamer."

Edith is now Lady Sharpe, he thought, but that, too, was a thought best left unspoken.

"Would you mind?" Thomas asked his sister, who, as the mistress of Allerdale Hall all these long years, had maintained tight control on their supplies. "Sparing a bit more coal?" Thomas wondered if Edith had noticed that the only room in the house that had been heated with regularity was their bedroom.

Stiffly Lucille grabbed at her key ring, hurt and uncertainty evident in her movements. Then she looked down to select the proper one for the coal bin. Her lips parted and, without another word, she ran toward the house.

It watched the sister's eyes widen in horror. Watched her bolt away from her brother and race into the house. It knew what she knew: that a key was missing. That someone had taken it. And as the sister raced to confront the culprit—for who else could have taken it?—the innocent little thief stepped from the lift and took a few steps. Then, and only then, did she realize that her high-button boots were caked with red clay. While the sister shouted, "Edith, Edith, Edith!" from somewhere distant in the house, she unfastened them with trembling hands and carried them and E.S.'s phonograph down the hall toward her bedroom.

The sister was charging up the stairs. She was crazed, wild, panicked.

The bride sailed into the bridal chamber, stashed her dirty boots and the player under her settee, then draped herself across it with a throw drawn over her clothes. She shut her eyes, feigning sleep, but it could see her chest heaving, her arms trembling.

Then she said groggily, "I'm here."

The sister swept into the room, fighting to catch her breath without giving away that she had been running. An earnestness born of cunning supplanted the violence of her expression.

"I want to apologize for my behavior this morning," the sister said, as if all her care and thought were for peace between the two of them. Then, "Child, are you feeling all right?"

Equally adept at performance, the bride groaned and turned weakly. The sister put down her key ring and laid a hand over her forehead, taking her temperature. Glanced at the document that the bride's solicitor had told her to sign.

She had not done it.

"I felt a little sick," the bride murmured. "That's all. Do you mind getting me some cold water?"

"Of course, of course," the sister replied. A consummate actress.

Deliberately leaving her keys in the bedroom, she went into the kitchen to pump some water. Her face was grim, set.

While she was there, the bride slipped the key back onto the key ring, then settled back down on the settee.

The sister returned with the water. Handing it to her brother's new wife, she said kindly, "I should let you rest. You'll feel better soon."

Then she grabbed up the keys. A quick examination revealed that the key labeled ENOLA was no longer missing.

That the bride had furtively returned it.

That there were small clumps of red clay on the floor of the elevator.

And that the sister *knew*.

Night had fallen on the day of Thomas's greatest triumph, and he had come to Lucille's room to discuss everything that had happened on this momentous occasion. Lucille's room was a vivarium for her living insect colonies and a crypt for the unfortunate many she had chosen to kill and display instead. Vast arrays of mounting tools, pins, and knives cluttered nearly all the flat surfaces, and curio cabinets contained bizarre trinkets such as a shrunken head from Borneo, a voodoo doll from the American city of New

Orleans, and misshapen animal fetuses suspended in for-maldehyde. Her bed, however, remained free of her bizarre proclivities and was always clean and sweet-smelling. She had kept the finest linens that ever Allerdale Hall contained and sprinkled them with herbs to keep them fragrant.

His sister fed all her idiosyncratic passions.

Now she faced Thomas as they conferred. She seemed unusually animated tonight, frantic in the old way, the bad way, but when he asked her what was wrong, she would not say. Her eyes glistened with need and fear, and he remembered all that she had done for him. What she had endured for him. He had to be here for her. It was their pact.

"Just for me, Thomas," she said. "Say that you love me."

He regarded her. "Ding, dong, bell," he began, and she sat back, delighted.

> "Ding, dong, bell,
> Pussy's in the well.
> Who put her in?
> Little Johnny Thin.
> Who pulled her out?
> Little Tommy Stout.
> What a naughty boy was that,
> To try to drown poor pussy cat,
> Who ne'er did him any harm,
> But killed all the mice in the farmer's barn."

They seemed *odd* now, these rituals of theirs. Over time, spending nearly all their waking hours together until…

well, until they hadn't, they had created their own rites and ceremonies, dreamed of other lives: of parties, and friends, and Christmas. During the troubled times, they had done anything to comfort one another, keep each other sane.

He was no longer certain that it had worked.

He held out his arms and she slipped into his embrace as he led her in a waltz. Chopin soared in his memory and he found himself thinking of Buffalo. So very different from here. Not as cold, not as dark, not as dead.

Why did I take Edith away from all that? Why did I go through with it?

He whirled his beautiful, dark-haired sister around the attic, swirling in a circle as moths revolved around them. Her black fairy attendants, she used to call them. She had cultivated generations of moths to make them as sooty-hued as ravens.

Lucille was gazing into his eyes and he could feel her weaving her spell around him. How old had he been when he had first surrendered? She was incredibly strong-willed, far more so than he. That was both a blessing and a curse. Lucille had kept them alive. Now they would begin to thrive. She had worked out the plan and except for a few unexpected hiccups—bumps in the night, literally—it was going well.

They danced. She was his most perfect partner. When they waltzed, a candle contained in their shared clasp never, ever went out.

One-two-three, one-two-three…

In the darkness, a *danse macabre.*

CHAPTER TWENTY

THE ATLANTIC OCEAN

ALAN WORE A heavy beaver coat over his evening clothes and stood at the railing of the transatlantic steamer in his top hat. The magnificent dinner was concluded, but in truth, he had not eaten very much. He was proving to be a disappointing table companion, of that he was certain: circumspect, brooding, taciturn. A young lady and her mother were on the hunt for a suitable husband, and he was certain he had been struck off the list the previous night. Even if he had been able to be charming, their obvious disappointment at his profession had been almost comedic.

Some of the male first-class passengers were gathering

for port and cigars in the smoking room, but he had no stomach for conversation and he was very tired. Since boarding the night before, time had taken on a new urgency: Having determined that all might not be well with Edith, he could not wait to be at her side.

He stared down into the rushing dark water so far below, recalling his first voyage to England to go to medical school. On the way home he had pondered the nature of visions and studied some of the hair-raising photographs he had purchased from a classmate. Mediums were conducting séances all over Britain—and many of them were being exposed as frauds. People wanted so badly to believe in an afterlife where their loved ones continued to exist.

But what he had spoken about with Edith was something different. It was not so much continued existence as continued *expression*. An emotion, a presence, continually repeated but unnoticed by most until someone with the mechanical or organic means became aware. Glowing emanations of ectoplasm also signified such manifestations. He had seen pictures of such phenomena as well. But a spirit with volition and purpose was a different entity altogether, was it not?

The arctic air prickled his face. As he absently toyed with the backs of his gloves, he caught the scent of cigar smoke on the frigid breeze.

"There is so much more below the surface," said a gravelly voice close to his elbow. The British accent belonged to a distinguished gentleman perhaps ten years older than he, also dressed in fur, with a large Cossack-style hat that nearly covered the entirety of his head. He was barrel-chested under the greatcoat, with ruddy cheeks and a pointed beard flecked with gray. The man gestured toward a huge mountain of ice floating on the water. It seemed dangerously close, but they had passed several that evening at roughly the same distance.

Alan tipped his hat but said nothing. The man positively reeked of brandy.

"…of the iceberg," his fellow passenger continued. "What we see above the surface is estimated to be one-tenth of the mass of the thing. There's ninety percent more below the water line, stretching out in all directions."

When the man took a puff on his thick cigar, tears welled in his eyes—from the cold air or the smoke? Or was he maudlin from drink?

"I am sure that we're sailing too close," he confided nervously. If we scraped against it, it would gouge a hole in our hull." Steadying himself on the rail, he looked down at the oily black sea and shuddered. "What a terrible place to die."

"But surely the captain knows his business," Alan countered, wishing to calm the poor man.

The man grunted. "I only hope that God does." He reached inside his fur coat and pulled out a silver flask. Unscrewing the top, he offered it to Alan. "Napoleon brandy," he said. "The finest."

"Thank you, sir, but no," Alan demurred. "This is a unique experience and I do not wish my senses to be dulled."

"That's the only way I can endure it." The man took a swallow and kept the open flask in hand. "Dear Lord, there are more of the bloody things ahead."

Indeed, an entire family of them, large and small, glittered in the moonlight. Safely guiding the ship through them would be a singular challenge. It was clear from the expression on the gentleman's face that he was beginning to panic. Alan determined to distract him as best he could.

He extended his hand. "I am Alan McMichael," he said. "At the risk of sounding patronizing, I've crossed before this time of year, and all ended well, sir."

"I see." The man managed a weak smile and inclined his head as if acknowledging Alan's kindness. "I am Reginald Desange." His expression did not change as he stared at the icebergs.

"Is your final destination Southampton?" Alan inquired, attempting once more to engage him.

"I have business in London," Desange replied, prying his gaze from the horizon and looking directly at Alan for the first time. "And you?"

"I'm off to Cumberland," Alan replied, and the man made a face.

"The weather in the north of England is beastly this time of year. Well, actually, it's beastly any time of year. The proper word is 'brutal.'"

Alan smiled resignedly. "And yet I must go."

"May I be so rude as to inquire as to your business there?"

It was a bit forward to ask, but Alan could see that

the distraction was helping the man calm down, and truth be told, Alan could do with distracting, too. He permitted himself to think for a moment of Edith and all her lovely books and dreams. "Well, I am Sir Galahad, sworn to rescue a dear lady in distress." He shrugged, abashed at his attempt at poesy. He was a man of science, not a fanciful writer like Edith.

"In Cumberland?" The man seemed incredulous.

"Yes."

"You'll find no castles there. But I believe I read about some Roman ruins. Mining or some such. There is an ancient pit in that region…"

Alan nodded. "As a matter of fact, my destination concerns mining of clay."

The man raised a brow. "Now I remember. Some wine vessels in the British Museum, quite red, were donated by the family who own a modern-day adjoining mine." He slid a glance at Alan, who realized he shouldn't speak further for fear of revealing too much about the identity of the lady in question. He did not want to cause a scandal.

"How interesting," he said blandly.

The Englishman must have sensed that Alan was done speaking on the subject. He put his flask back in his pocket and lightly tapped the rail with his gloved hand.

"Well, Sir Galahad, I wish you luck on your quest. And I exhort you to dress warmly for your journey to the north."

"Thank you for the advice," Alan replied. "I'll be sure to take it."

The man cocked his head. "You're an amenable chap. I say, won't you join me for a proper drink in the Grand Saloon?"

The night air was bitter, and Alan felt that he had achieved a victory by easing this man's great anxiety. Though he wasn't certain that more brandy would serve his new companion well, Alan said, "I'd be honored, Mr. Desange."

CHAPTER TWENTY-ONE

EDITH WAITED, HEART racing, for Thomas to come to bed and then to fall asleep. Her dog was restless, and kept shifting, unknowingly waking her up a couple of times when she began to drift off. Her stomach was cramping and her headache had gotten worse. Her eyes itched and her mouth was as dry as cotton wool.

Her best guess was that he was in his attic workroom, tinkering with his mining models. It was difficult for her to judge when he might walk into the room, but what of that? She wasn't a prisoner. She could come and go as she pleased.

So she stole out of bed, picked up the phonograph case and stepped into the hall. Rubbing her arms to ward off the chill, she looked fearfully up and down the long, elaborate hallway with its mullioned arches. Light from the moon tinted the air a dreary blue. Moths that perched on the walls turned out to be shadows in the wallpaper. She could almost see human faces, even letters forming words that she couldn't quite make out.

Was that the elevator? She had better get to work or she would miss her chance. Gingerly, she crept to the linen closet and faced the closed door for a good minute before she gathered the courage to open it. The box of wax cylinders was still inside. She accepted now the possibility that she had experienced supernatural guidance in finding them. To what end, she was not yet clear. She had also come to believe that neither Thomas nor Lucille could see these ghosts or phantoms or whatever they were. They had no idea that they were there.

Unless Lucille is a better actress than I give her credit for. She certainly can't hide the fact that she sees me as an interloper.

She grabbed the cylinders and tiptoed down into the kitchen. With each noise, each shift and creak of the house, her sore stomach spasmed. There could be something in the room with her. It could be standing behind her, or crouching under the table.

By the moonlight, she arranged the cylinders for playing on the phonograph, and examined her clutch of envelopes from the trunk with their faded lettering:

Pamela Upton, London, 1887. Margaret McDermott, Edinburgh, 1893. Enola Sciotti, Milan, 1896.

Her memory cast back to her father's first fateful

meeting with Thomas. Carter Cushing had stared straight at him and said, "You have already tried—and failed—to raise capital in London, Edinburgh, Milan…"

Her throat tightened and she almost faltered, but she put down the needle on the cylinder and listened:

"*I cannot take it anymore.*" The speaker was a woman with an Italian accent. "*I'm a prisoner. If I could leave him, I would. If I could stop loving him. He'll be the end of me. Hush, hush now…*"

And then, as the scratchy recording ended, the cooing and wailing of a baby. She blinked, stunned.

I have seen no baby here. Those things in the attic… I assumed they were Thomas and Lucille's. But did another child live here? She looked back at the date. *It would be four years old now.*

She thought of the red rubber ball. It could have belonged to a child, not a dog. That would make more sense, since the Sharpes had not owned a dog.

That day in the tub when she and the dog had played fetch, and the ball had rolled back on its own… and she had heard something in her bedroom… *Could it have been a little child?*

Perhaps there was something wrong with it. With *him*. Maybe the speaker was his mother, and the child was so sick or malformed that his mother had stayed by his side rather than leave him. Maybe she had died and left him on his own here, and Lucille had concealed that fact from Thomas.

Or maybe Thomas knows. What if all those automata he has made are for that child, and not Lucille when she was a little girl?

Shakily, Edith pulled the cylinder off the spindle and put on another. Then the next, and then a third. And when she was done…

No.

…everything in her heart and soul stopped working for at least a full minute. She simply could not believe what she had heard. It wasn't that she didn't want to. It was that she couldn't.

Once upon a time…

It was like a wicked fairy tale. Like Bluebeard, with his haunted castle and the one room his new wife was forbidden to enter.

The room with the forbidden key. Thomas had told her never to enter the clay pit.

Enola Sciotti's trunk was in that pit.

Once upon a time:

There lived three young women. One was named Pamela, one was Margaret, and one was Enola. They did not know each other. Each of them had fallen in love with Sir Thomas Sharpe and left everything to move to Allerdale Hall to be his wife.

Like me, Edith thought.

And each had been so happy at first, so loved. Then they had gotten sick. They had grown steadily weaker, unable to leave Allerdale Hall. They had suffered terribly. Wept. Cursed Thomas's name. Tried to warn others with these recordings… or at least leave a mark upon the world: *I was here. I was murdered.*

Oh, God, Edith thought. She began shaking from head

to toe. Her heart thudded thickly; her head pounded. A sensation like sharp pins moving through her veins traveled throughout her body. Icy fear and the deepest dread she had ever known clasped her in invisible arms and drew her inside that dark, evil room she was not meant to enter. This couldn't be right. This could not possibly be the secret of Allerdale Hall those red-boned wraiths wanted her to see.

It could not be, because it was too horrible.

Not Thomas.

Quaking, she shuffled through the stacks of photos she had found in the envelopes and matched them to the voices on the cylinders. All featured Thomas and one of a trio of women, proudly smiling.

Pamela Upton, from 1887, was thin, and seated in a wheelchair with a cup of tea on the arm. Edith jerked as she studied the conveyance. Was it the one she had seen in the attic nursery?

Margaret McDermott's photo was dated 1893. She was a little older than Pamela, and older than Thomas, who stood beside her. Margaret was already graying, but what one might call "handsome," in a straw hat. She was holding a cup of tea.

Wait, Edith thought. She went back to the picture of Pamela Upton. She was also drinking tea. Were the cups the same?

They were.

And it was the same cup Lucille had used to make tea for her.

Her throat constricted so tightly she couldn't swallow.

She teetered on the brink of bursting into screams; through sheer force of will, she sat in the chair and saw her sister-in-law in this very kitchen putting on the kettle. Saw the tea leaves steaming in the pot. Saw the cup on a tray brought up for her.

All on that very day, that first day, when Thomas had told her about firethorn berries. And urged her to drink her tea. And had stayed away from her, claiming to respect her mourning, when in reality he had not wanted to make love to a dead woman.

No, I have to be wrong. I'm tired and scared.

"They put poison in the tea," she whispered very distinctly, forcing herself to face it, believe it. In *her* tea. Her stomach clenched hard and she tasted the bitterness in the back of her mouth and the odor of it singed her nose as she absorbed the shrinking horror of it; she had been murdered. She couldn't even count the many cups she had consumed since arriving at Allerdale Hall. She recalled with crushing clarity how, when she had made sandwiches and tea for Thomas, he had asked her which tin of leaves she had used—the blue or the red? She remembered his guarded expression, which had obviously masked real fear at the prospect of drinking only one cup. Had he ever poured her a cup himself? Had she drunk down her death deliberately prepared by him?

She forced herself to move to the next picture. By the date she knew that this was Enola Sciotti. Also with tea… and by her side sat the cute little dog that now belonged to her, Edith.

Edith remembered what Lucille had said just after she had come in from the post office: *What is that thing doing here?* They had pretended not to recognize it. But they had thought it was dead. That all evidence of the Italian woman... the Italian *wife*... had been erased.

He had released it onto the moors, anticipating that nature would run its course. He hadn't cared a jot that it might starve, or fall into a ravine, or drown in an icy stream. That sweet little pup had come to her emaciated and half-frozen. *And Thomas had let it happen.*

More frantic, she made herself look at the next picture: Enola.

Holding a newborn baby.

It had to be the baby in her recording, the one Enola had soothed as it cried. But surely there was no four-year-old hidden away in this enormous mansion?

There are parts of the house that are unsafe. So Lucille had claimed. Unsafe for whom?

No, dear God, Edith thought, as the room began to spin. *All evidence erased... they would not do such a thing.*

But they would.

And they had.

They *had.*

The very last picture was of the baby, alone.

And clearly dead.

Its little eyes closed, mouth slack, cheeks pale.

Edith choked, coughed. A drop of blood escaped her lips and a stain bloomed on the image of the baby. For a moment her terror was too great to do anything.

She couldn't think, move. Her mind simply refused to put together what her soul knew. What they had *done*…

She tried to feel some hope; reminded herself they had failed to kill a little dog, but—

These were, in their way, spirit recordings, spirit pictures. Images from beyond the grave telling her their stories.

Warning her to beware of Crimson Peak.

"I cannot stay here any longer," she said aloud, to force herself back into the world of thoughts. "I can't."

Galvanized, she stashed the envelopes in the phonograph case and hid everything in a cupboard. Then she grabbed her coat from the rack and threw it over her nightgown. Sobbing back hysteria, fighting through an overwhelming panic, she lurched for the front door and threw it open.

Snowdrifts were piled up high in front of the door, two feet tall at least. She staggered outside, choking back fear, so numb she did not feel the cold. But as she ventured out, the moonlight shone on the snow and she stumbled in shock.

The snow was bright red, extending out to the gate; the madhouse was surrounded by a scarlet ring like a moat of fresh blood.

There was too much of it, and she was too sick—too *poisoned*—to venture out into it. She was trapped. It was as Lucille had said: She had nowhere else to go. Nowhere, and they were going to kill her just like the others.

Thomas, she thought, *help me.* Her field of vision filled with his deep blue eyes, so often sad, haunted. Had he never loved her?

I don't believe that. I don't, she thought. That night at the depot, when they had talked of a new life…

When we made love. It was love. It was. It was. He loved me. He still loves me.

But what did it matter? He was a killer. And he was going to kill her.

She remembered the night they had danced. He had come to America for Eunice, not her. Why had he changed his mind?

Alan, she thought. *Alan, help me.* He had told her to proceed with caution. He would have had stronger words for a sister, and the possibility of his interference had no doubt spared Eunice from this hellish fate.

Beware of Crimson Peak. Her mother had come back from the grave to warn her. She knew it now. And she had not listened.

Because she had not *known.*

Edith backed away from the doorway, doubling over in a fit of coughing. Blood gushed from her mouth, as red as the snow. As if Allerdale Hall itself had been poisoned and was hemorrhaging its lifeblood beneath a cold, uncaring moon.

"Oh, no, no…" she begged. She had to get out. She had to escape. She had to leave.

But instead, she fainted dead away.

BOOK THREE

CRIMSON PEAK

"All that we see or seem, is but a dream within a dream."

— EDGAR ALLAN POE

CHAPTER TWENTY-TWO

YELLOW LIGHT SPILLED across her face, and Edith opened her eyes to defeat. She was back in the bedroom she shared with Thomas, tucked in beneath blankets that were wrapped tight around her legs. Lucille was there, waiting, holding a breakfast tray. When she saw that Edith was awake, she smiled, all sweet concern.

"Edith?" she said cheerily. "Edith? Darling! We found you next to the door. Do you feel better?"

Sick, so much sicker. And in mortal danger. Edith tried to get up. The room tilted crazily. Even in her semi-delirium, she knew she must reveal nothing. Her life depended on their ignorance. She had not signed away her fortune yet, and she must make them believe that she fully intended to. They would need to keep her well enough to hold a pen and scrawl her signature. To write Ferguson and tell him to give Thomas every penny she had to her name.

And *then* they would kill her.

Still, the extreme nausea and cramping were beyond her capacity to endure in silence.

"I need to go to town… see a doctor," she slurred.

"Of course, of course," Lucille soothed. "But I'm afraid we're snowed in. Perhaps in a day or two."

Lucille sat down and held up a spoonful of porridge, tempting Edith in the way one would an infant.

That baby, that poor baby, Edith thought, and gave her head a shake. There had been pictures of a baby last night, yes? She was muzzy-headed. Confused. So exhausted. She had to get out of here.

Away from Crimson Peak.

I have to pull myself together. I need to think clearly. Her heart stuttered, skipping beats, and she feared she would have a heart attack.

"Now you must eat, my dear. You must get stronger." Lucille tried again to feed Edith some porridge. "I tended Mother in this bed. I can care for you too, my pet."

Edith listened but made no move to eat. Undeterred, Lucille set down the bowl and poured Edith a cup of tea. "You see? Father hated Mother. He was a brute. Broke her leg. Snapped it in two under the heel of his boot."

Edith's lips parted in shock. She had never heard anything about this. Was Lucille making it up? To what end?

"She never quite healed. She was bedridden for a long time. I cared for her. Fed her. Bathed her. Combed her hair. I made her better. I'll do the same with you. I'll make you better."

Remain calm, Edith reminded herself. But she was even more afraid. The Sharpe legacy contained depths of violence and madness she had not dreamed of. If what Lucille had just told her was true, it was no wonder that the dead prowled the halls and the ground bled.

Lucille was about to say something more when Thomas entered the room pushing a wicker wheelchair. Edith's hair stood on end. That *was* the wheelchair Pamela Upton had sat upon in her picture. With Thomas. Holding the very teacup that Lucille had used to make her numerous cups of firethorn tea. Too numerous to count. Burning away her insides, torturing her, killing her.

"What is that?" Edith asked, her voice shrill.

"Just to help you get around," he replied, falsely cheerful. But he couldn't pull it off. His smile didn't reach his eyes, and he faltered. He turned to his sister. "I'll take care of Edith," he said. "Leave it."

Lucille threw him a defiant look, but he held his ground. Lucille backed down, rising and planting a loving kiss on Edith's forehead as she placed the deadly teacup between Edith's hands.

"You'll be out of this bed soon," Lucille cooed. "I promise."

She swept out of the room. As Thomas sat down, he took the tea away from Edith.

CRIMSON PEAK

"Do not drink that," he said.

Hope billowed through her like the frosted winds that pushed air through the chimneys and gave breath to Allerdale Hall. He didn't want to harm her. So he would spare her. He would. But she was so *sick*…

And perhaps that was why he took the tea away from her. Not because he had had second thoughts, but to keep her from dying until she gave him her money.

Nevertheless, he fed her the porridge very gently. Kindly. The way a loving husband would minister to his sick young wife. It was very sweet, laced with honey and butter.

"Just eat," he urged. "You need to get stronger."

"I need to see a doctor," she pleaded.

A shadow crossed his face, and then light came into his eyes. He seemed… transformed. As if a terrible weight had just lifted from his shoulders. Everything in her waited. Everything prayed, even her fingernails and eyelashes.

"Finlay is gone for the winter but I'll clear a path to the main road. Take you to town."

Oh, thank God, thank you, God, she thought in a rush. *Thomas, love me still. Keep loving me. Save me.*

"Yes, yes," she said eagerly, almost crazily in her desperation. "I would very much like to go. Just us. Alone."

He gave her another spoonful of porridge. And then his face altered again, and she was terribly afraid that she had misunderstood him… or that he had changed his mind.

"Thomas?" She fought to keep the terror out of her voice. "What is it?"

"Those apparitions you spoke of," he began. He paused. "I have felt their presence for some time."

She stared at him in astonishment. "You have?"

He inclined his head. "Out of the corner of my eye at first. Furtive, almost timid. Then I felt them. Figures, standing still in a dark corner. And now I can sense them, moving and creeping about, watching me. Ready to show themselves."

"It's time. They want you to see them," she declared. "But why? Who are they, Thomas?"

He seemed to look somewhere that she could not. Was he reviewing his life with each of the women he had failed to save? Whom he had murdered? Were those the apparitions? But what of the ghost of his mother? So evil, raging at Edith to leave?

"They are tied to this land. To this house. Just like I am," he said. "I will tell you everything, in time. Now eat. Get well. You must leave this godforsaken place as soon as you can."

She did not know why he had decided to save her. She didn't know what it meant, or how they would manage it. But she would do exactly as he bade her: She would eat, she would get well, and she would leave. Though it cost her dearly, because she was so ill, she made herself eat the sickly sweet porridge.

And she forced herself not to break down in tears as her stomach clenched and her abdomen burned.

* * *

Thomas's hand shook as he fed Edith, but she didn't seem to notice. She was in terrible shape. She had nearly frozen to death outside in the snow, and her mouth had been smeared with blood. The poison was taking its course. He prayed it was not too late to reverse the effects. The end was always agonizing. After Pamela, he had made it a practice never to be home when it was happening. He'd gone riding during Margaret, and into town for Enola. Lucille had stayed with them. Lucille had made sure.

After Edith had eaten all her porridge, Thomas carried the tray into the kitchen. Lucille was there, pacing, and he wondered how on earth he would spirit Edith out of here without her knowledge. She would stop him if she could. They would have to plot and plan.

How can I do that to Lucille? he thought. *Edith will tell the world.*

"She knows everything." Lucille's dark eyes flashed as she violently washed out the teacup. She was in turmoil. Thomas knew the signs very well.

"She's sick," Thomas said urgently. "She may be dying."

Lucille stared at him as if he had completely lost his mind. She was so stunned that for a moment her lips moved, but no words came out.

"Absolutely, she is dying. I've made sure of that," she announced, peering at him as if she was making sure he could hear her. Then she moved on quickly. "She stole the trunk key." She showed her ring of keys. "You see? She returned it, but it's facing the wrong way. She went down into the clay mines, too. And I believe she might have stopped drinking the tea."

Lucille enumerated the sins she was laying at Edith's feet, although Thomas had been the one to stop Edith from drinking the tea. He had seen Lucille do all this before, under different circumstances. Back when they had still had servants, Lucille had dismissed her maid for chipping a teacup that she herself had dropped. The girl had defended herself, insisting that the mistress *knew* she had done it herself, and Lucille had taken the cost of the cup *and* a few pennies to cover the wasted tea out of the girl's wages as punishment for her insolence. She had even accused Finlay of failing to repair the hinges on her bedroom door, claiming that it opened during all hours of the night. She had "fined" him for this breach and warned that if it happened again, Thomas would dismiss him.

But Thomas had observed Finlay working on the door while the two had talked about the harvester. He had returned Finlay's wages to him with his apologies.

Thomas didn't ever directly defy Lucille. He just went around her. That was what he was doing now, with Edith. But he had never taken his duplicity to such extremes.

Lucille paced again, faster, balling her fists. "It doesn't matter at all. I put the poison in the porridge." Then she began washing the tea things.

His heart dropped to the floor. Why had he not even considered that? The time had come, then. He must speak up. He must defy her.

"Lucille... stop," he said. His nerve almost failed, but he pressed on. For years she had been his defender, his champion. She had borne the brunt of their father's fury, the abuse and debasement from their mother, in order to spare him. She had kept them from starving. It was she who encouraged him to modernize the mining process, and had also come up with the scheme to marry the heiresses. Why not? It was what their father had done. And they had paid him back for that.

They had struck a bargain, vowing never to be separated. And in so many words, to kill anyone who tried to force them apart. Though he had been but eight years old when that pledge had been made, the memory of that day had never left him. It had haunted him all his life.

CHAPTER TWENTY-THREE

ALLERDALE HALL, TWENTY-FIVE YEARS AGO

"Raving lunatics!" Sir Michael Sharpe bellowed at the three bleeding men who cowered before him. Thomas and Lucille were hiding behind the draperies in the library and Thomas peered between the gaps at his huge, strapping father, who was as terrifying as an ogre. Sir Michael had a wild mane of thick black hair and eyebrows to match, and he was dressed in his hunting attire—red coat, trousers, and thick black boots. The men were not bleeding. They were covered in red clay.

Lucille had been showing Thomas that when you bent the pages of various books in the library like a fan, you could see the most indecent pictures imaginable. Thomas had been agog. Then their father had stomped in, and the miners with him, and Lucille had dragged Thomas out of sight.

"Try heating your stoves with clay!" their father went on. He was tapping his riding crop against his boot. *Tap, tap, tap.* "Firedamp is a gas that occurs in coal mines. And there are no coal mines on my land."

"But, sir, summat 'appened," the oldest of the three men said. He was stooped and bowed. "Summat blowed up. There's children burned."

"For the love of God, man, speak like a human being." The *taps* became *thwaps* as he snapped the crop harder against the leather boot top.

"With respect, Your Lordship," the man said. "It's our children wot's been burned and we was 'oping Lady Sharpe, she'd come, or if we could 'ave a doctor."

"Like a human being!" the great man thundered. His eyes blazed. "And Lady Sharpe will not be coming to salve up your brats! Lady Sharpe is a cretin, and she's upstairs loaded to the gills with laudanum, and is of no use to anyone, most especially not to me."

"Then the doctor, sir," the old man wheedled. "Them's 'urt summat awful."

"Dear Lord!" Sir Michael shouted. "Get out of my house! You have damaged your brats through your own ignorance and now seek to steal my money to right your wrongs. Get out before I put *you* in need of a physician!"

Then he began to whip the old man, who put up his

arms to protect his head as the other two hurried him out of the room. Thomas was both horrified and excited; in his exhilaration he yanked on the curtain—and the entire thing came crashing down.

"What the devil?" their father shouted.

"Under there," Lucille whispered to Thomas beneath the drapery, pushing him toward an overstuffed love seat that sat on very long legs. "Now!"

Thomas darted away just as the heavy pounding of their father's boots stomped close. He slid beneath the love seat and peered out. Sir Michael had been gathering up the damask fabric and threw it back down when he found Lucille beneath it. She gazed up at him in terror; he grabbed her wrist and yanked her to her feet. Her eyes were enormous. Her face was dead white.

"What are you doing? By the devil, what did you…"

And then he trailed off. He was bending over, staring. The books. He saw them. He picked one up and held it for a moment. Then he turned to stare at Lucille as if he had never seen her before in his life.

"You little *bitch*," he said in a tight, furious voice. "Whatever possessed you?"

Her breathing was shallow. "I'm sorry, Papa," she said. "I—I…" She began to cry. "Please don't hurt me. I'm so very sorry."

"Where is your brother?"

"In the nursery," she said quickly, not looking over at Thomas.

"Did he see these?"

"No, no," she said. "He's a good boy."

"And you are wicked beyond the telling." He raised his crop over his head. "Say it."

She cringed. "I am wicked," she whimpered. "Please, Papa."

"Again."

"I am wicked." Tears streamed down her face.

The crop came down hard on her shoulder, and she buckled. Thomas caught his breath.

Down again, and she fell to one knee. He began to scrabble back out and she flashed a warning look at him and said, "No!"

"'*No*?' You dare say that to your father?"

"No, Papa, I mean, I do not dare!" He brought the crop down on her hands as she put them on her head. She screamed. "Please, Papa!"

"You're as bad as your mother. She is a wanton slut. Say it!"

"She is a wanton slut!" Lucille cried.

"Come with me then and say it to her face!"

He reached down, grabbed up a book, and gripped her by the forearm. Lucille glanced in Thomas's direction and gave her head a firm shake, ordering him to stay hidden.

She was sobbing as they left the library. As soon as he thought it was safe, Thomas scooted from beneath the sofa and tiptoed out. Panting with fear, he crept up the stairs and snuck into the attic, where he sat unmoving until the shadows came out and the moths emerged from their hidey holes.

He kept waiting for Lucille, and he was so very sorry

she had been punished for something they had both done. But the fact was that he was also so very glad that he had not been caught. His shame warred with his relief.

He decided to make her a present. He looked at the moths as they swirled around, and then he cut out two pieces of black paper from his collection of art supplies. He made her a moth with wings that opened and closed when you pulled on a string that connected the wings to a thread down the moth's back.

He had just finished it when Lucille staggered in. She looked awful; her black hair was sticking out every which way and her eyes and nose were swollen from weeping.

"Oh, Lucille!" he cried, throwing his arms around her. She winced.

"Thomas, you must never confess that you were in the library," she said, "or it will go doubly hard for me. Papa thinks you are the good one, and if he discovers that you are not, then I shall be punished for it."

His lower lip quivered. "Am I not the good one?"

"No," she said sadly. "I wouldn't have got in trouble if you hadn't asked to see the books."

"See…?" He frowned. "But I did *not* ask to see the books."

"Yes, you did," she replied firmly. "Don't you remember? You said that Polly told you about them. And so we got them out and I showed you how to look."

"I did?" He was baffled. Polly was one of the maids, and she was very pretty, but he couldn't recall anything of the sort.

"And Papa likes Polly better than you. Or me," she added bitterly. "He will blame you instead of her for being so bad."

"But I didn't…" he began, but then he wasn't sure. He was confused. His cheeks were hot and his palms were wet.

"This moth is wonderful," Lucille murmured, picking up the toy he had made for her. "How did you manage it?"

"See, I attached the string this way, and so when you pull down, the wings flap open." He smiled hopefully. "I made it for you. I did it because I was so sorry that you were hurt. So that must mean that I'm good. Is that right, Lucille? That I'm good because I'm sorry?"

Lucille shook her head. She made the moth flap. "Papa told Mama that he wants to send us away. You will go to boarding school and I will go to an academy for young ladies in Switzerland."

"No!" He was aghast.

"We can never let that happen," she told him. "We must make a promise that we will not let them separate us, ever."

"I promise!" Thomas cried. He held up his hand. "I promise with all my heart."

Silver tears ran down Lucille's cheeks. "It's just… your heart is very little. You are my sweet boy, but what can you do to stop him?"

"Cut him to bits!" he cried. "Push him into the mine and make it blow up!"

"Oh, Thomas." She smiled wanly through her tears. "If only you could."

* * *

Two years later, while Thomas had stood watch, in the small hours before the dawn of a great fox hunt, Lucille had cut the girthstrap of their father's hunting saddle nearly in two; she had pulled two nails out of his horse's shoe. He had been thrown, and his neck broken. It had dawned on Thomas that Lucille had also drugged the man so that his fall would be all but assured.

"Mama showed me how," she had told Thomas sweetly.

And two years after that, Mama was dead.

Thomas roused himself from his reverie. She had wound him up so many times and he had done as she had directed, always, like one of his automata. And it had worked well for them. For him.

But now… cracks were appearing in their foundation. He was not of one mind with her. Gazing at his sister, sensing her energy radiating like the steam that propelled his machine, he felt strangely dizzy, and very frightened.

"Must this be? Edith? Must we…?"

She turned to face him, incredulous, as she dried her hands. He saw in her brown eyes the supreme will he had assured Carter Cushing that he himself possessed. But Lucille had always been the puppeteer behind their elaborate performance.

"Yes, Thomas. We must. And I will."

But he couldn't bear it. Edith was not like the others.

Those doting women had been like Eunice McMichael—charmed by his social graces, in love with his title. When they gazed starry-eyed at him, they saw Prince Charming—as they were meant to. Eunice had been the most mesmerized of all, asking him the most naïve questions, such as what he wore when he called upon the royal family, none of whom he had ever met, and if he owned a crown.

But Edith had seen a man, and a clever one at that. He *was* intelligent. He *was* inventive. Like her father, whom Thomas had admired deeply. Like an American, that nation of builders, where a person was defined by their achievements rather than their surname. Edith had her own dreams. And she had wished to help him achieve his. He was the one who had become hypnotized. He had fallen in love with her, and that love was changing him. But could he *be* different? Push a button, and he performed—could that magician upstairs perform any new tricks?

No.

But I can. I have free will.

It was a terrifying notion.

Lucille read his refusal on his face, and *he* saw *her* terror.

"You have no idea what they would do," Lucille said shrilly. "We would be taken away from here. Locked away. We would lose our home… each other. They would hang you."

She was right. They would not hang her. They rarely executed women, and anyway, he would accept full blame.

But only if they were discovered. Only if their story was told. And where would Lucille be then?

She had always been right. She did know what was best for them. And he owed her everything.

But could he give her Edith's life?

He blazed inside, ice and fire, pure temptations, polluted intentions. He envisioned the brilliant scarlet of his lineage rushing through his veins; the aristocracy put such store in their blood but his was brimming with rot. It was all he knew; all he was.

His eyes welled; he was utterly perplexed. Rudderless. Oh, Edith! If only she knew what they had been through. She would understand, would she not?

"We stay together, never apart," Lucille intoned. It had been their vow through the long nights of torment; helped them weather the insanity of both their parents. No one in their lives had ever tried to help them. School mistresses and masters, churchmen and physicians had seen the misery on their faces, the hollowness in their eyes, but no one dared to speak up. Their father was too powerful, their mother too terrifying.

No one but Thomas had seen the whip marks and bruises on poor Lucille's body. Their mother had reveled in punishing her, not even bothering to determine whose fault it really was before she attacked Lucille. Once his sister confessed to whatever infraction had occurred, it was like opening the floodgates of their mother's wrath.

Lucille always taking the blame: *It was I.*

And little Thomas, too afraid to speak up.

Now, in the kitchen, he was crying, too. "I know. I know."

Lucille looked as small and frightened as he had been back then, when he had let her take his punishments. When he had not spoken up. When he had not been a man.

He had to be, for Edith. She had finally brought light into this house, his world. His *soul*. He could save her, when he had not saved Lucille.

But he loved his sister, he did; she had been his world for his entire life.

"You couldn't leave me, could you?" she asked.

"I couldn't, I couldn't," he sobbed.

She kissed his tears away. They clung to each other, orphans who could have been freed by the deaths of their nearly demonic parents, but were too haunted instead. Stripped of everything but darkness. Too late, too late for light?

It watched, it exulted. It had them where it wanted them.

And the sad little specters that cried out for justice?

Inconsequential.

And delicious.

Outside, the scarlet ring of snow grew, a sucking bog of bloody clay, the sins of the Sharpes made visible for all to see.

Behold, I show you a miracle.

I show you the seventh circle of hell.

CHAPTER TWENTY-FOUR

IT HAD BEEN snowing back in Buffalo when Alan began his crossing nearly two weeks before.

In London, he had been told that the snowfall was at record levels. But here in Cumberland, it was the worst—another in a series of violent snowstorms that had shut down most of the roads. He had not seen another soul in days.

By the time he reached the village's postal depot and climbed down from his covered carriage, he was more than half-frozen. Despite growing up in Buffalo, he had never been so cold. He wished he could linger for a hot meal and a hotter bath, but nothing could stop him from getting to Edith now that he was so close. Ever since

Holly's revelation that Sir Thomas Sharpe already had a wife, Alan had existed in a perpetual state of fear for her. Cushing had known that Sharpe was a fortune hunter, but had he realized the Englishman was a bigamist? His supposed sister, Lady Sharpe... was she his real wife?

Leaving his luggage for the moment, he walked stiffly over to an official-looking man and said, "I need directions for Allerdale Hall."

The man shook his head. "Can't get there on that horse. And there's none to be had. We're closed for the winter."

Alan groaned inwardly.

"Can I get there by foot?" he asked.

The man grimaced and looked meaningfully at the snowstorm. "It's well over two hours following the road."

Alan set his jaw. "Then I better get going."

He made provision for the storage of his trunk but decided to take his medical bag. Heads turned his way as the postal clerk wrote him a receipt and villagers frowned at the young man's stubborn ignorance. A few muttered under their breath, and he heard what they were saying. An American, then, with no idea what could happen if the weather got *really* foul. A man in a bright yellow muffler argued that someone should go with him, but did not directly offer to do so.

Irritated and more than a little worried about the likelihood of his survival, Alan wrapped his muffler around his face, pulled his hat on firmly, and headed back out into the weather. The snow was falling harder, and to make matters worse, it had begun to sleet.

An older man shuffled after him, hand raised, but seemed to think the better of it. Behind Alan, the depot gate shut, and he was all alone in a world of ice and snow.

Hours later, gusts of sleet buffeted Alan as he staggered down the road.

> *"Then move the trees, the copses nod,*
> *Wings flutter, voices hover clear:*
> *'O just and faithful knight of God!*
> *Ride on! The prize is near.'"*

He set his face in a tight, grim line. If only he *could* ride.

He had been reciting Tennyson's poem about Sir Galahad over and over to keep himself going. He was caked in frozen sweat and thirstier than he had ever been. And tired. So very, very tired. To walk he had to lift the weight of the heavy snow with the tops of his boots, every step a strain, and the snow kept falling, filling, masking the footsteps he left behind.

There was nothing for it but to press on, despite the temptation to collapse in the slush. He should have listened to the man at the depot, rested, and eaten. If Edith was in trouble, what possible aid could he offer her? She would bear the burden of his hubris. No knight in shining armor, he.

His right foot broke through the powdery crust and he slid into ice crystals. He began to pitch forward, arms windmilling, dropping his doctor's bag. He brushed a spindly tree trunk with his right hand and grabbed hard. He gripped it with his left and steadied himself.

His thigh muscles seized up and he grimaced, drawing in shaky breaths. Then he realized that his means of support was not a tree trunk but a pitted and weathered signpost, crusted with snow.

The top had broken off, and so, there was no indication of its intended purpose, except that it was planted in front of a fork in the road. He frowned. His directions to Allerdale Hall had not included any intersections such as this. A freshet of anxiety trickled down the back of his neck; he hoisted each foot out of the piled-up, bluish chunks of snow and studied the jagged end of the post. Then he scanned the area for the top of the marker, but a visual sweep revealed nothing but a few thin sticks and a couple of large rocks. The howl of the wind created a counterpoint to the crunch of the snow under his boots; reluctantly he walked a circle around the post and experimentally kicked at a few chunks of snow. The first three collapsed but the fourth held. He knelt and picked it up.

With anxious fingertips he gradually unearthed the remnant of the wooden sign. It had lain beneath the snow for so long that it had begun to decompose. He read — DALE —— 3 MI—. So did this mean that Allerdale Hall was perhaps only three miles away? An hour, maybe two, then, if he maintained an average pace.

And if he went the correct way. Should he go right or left at the fork? He could not tell from the sign. His attempt to hold it resulted in the wet, fibrous fragment shredding in his grasp.

Alan swore and dropped the pieces, which were carried into the snow by a heavy, mean wind. Layers of snow and gusts sharp as razors; he couldn't imagine himself fighting his way through it for half a mile, let alone three. Or six, if he discovered that he had chosen the wrong road.

Was that a human shape standing in front of him? He squinted at a thickened blur hovering in bold relief against the white, and every sleepless night on the steamer crashed down on him. He waited, every molecule of his body quivering with anxiety. He needed help; if the dead ever intervened in the affairs of the living, he prayed that they would do so now. Panting from cold and fatigue, he was poised for revelation.

But it was only the signpost. He set his jaw, feeling foolish and desperate. There was so much snow he was afraid he might drown in it. It had buried his ankles and was piling up around his shins. Dear *God*, he was so exhausted. If only he could lie down and restore his strength.

If you lie down, you will never get up again, he told himself sternly. *Make a move, man. Otherwise you'll die here.*

He looked left, scanning a treeless horizon… and then it occurred to him that the view on the right was forested. Though it was cloaked in heavy snowfall, he could see that the barren land to the left dipped into a bowl shape. It was unnatural; the rest of the area consisted of low, rolling hills. He thought a moment. What had Mr. Desange told him? That there had been another mine carved into the landscape by the Romans. And that that mine had been located adjacent to that of a present-day mining family— very likely the Sharpe property.

Then he blinked. Was he seeing properly? He staggered forward. Puddles of blood dotted the snow. He rushed closer.

No, it was clay. Of course it was clay. The brilliant scarlet treasure that had driven Sir Thomas Sharpe to deceit and perhaps even to murder.

To the left, then.

> *"Then move the trees, the copses nod,*
> *Wings flutter…"*

Alan resumed his trek.

Edith woke up, weak and wobbly, but grateful that she was still alive. Then her stomach clenched into a thousand knots of burning pain. With a grunt, she staggered into the bathroom and fell down on her knees before the toilet. She vomited gouts of blood, her stomach cramping in merciless spasms until she feared she had no blood left.

I thought he had saved me, she thought. *He took away the tea.* He had sworn. He had promised…

But she was sicker than ever. The pain was more than she could stand, and it shook her to her core that he could ever have considered doing this to her.

That he *had* done it to other women. Or, rather, allowed Lucille to do it.

She staggered back into the bedroom, wondering if he had actually slept through all the noise that she'd been making. He could not possibly have lain there and ignored her. No human being could be so cruel.

"Thomas," she rasped. "Thomas, I feel very sick. I need help."

She pulled back the bed sheets. There was no one there.

The wheelchair, then; she fell into it and began to push the wheels with all the remaining strength she possessed. She couldn't think past her immediate need for aid. Killing her was one thing, but to make her suffer like this?

The wheels squeaked. She had to stop and start many times. She had barely made it into the hall, but her body was bathed in sweat and her trembling arms seized up from the exertion.

As she inched along, a threatening net of menace dangled above her: If anyone came after her, she would not be able to outpace them. She was a hapless target. But she had been all along.

She pushed the wheels, dismayed by her increasing weakness. She wouldn't be able to fit the chair into the elevator and she would never be able to make it to the bottom of the stairs unless she fell down them. And what difference would that make? She couldn't leave.

But she could get to the kitchen and put something in her stomach to soak up the poison. Bread. There was cream for tea. She needed something to shore up her strength.

She needed, she needed.

Where was Thomas? Had he abandoned her? She had dared to believe that she would live. But now, as the horrible poison cloyed her organs, she almost wished to die. But she would not give him the satisfaction, nor give herself permission to give up. Were he and Lucille even still in the house? Is this how they killed their victims— glutted them with poison, then left them to die alone? It would be the coward's way.

Thomas's way.

Why promise to take her side, then do nothing? Did he find pleasure in raising false hopes? Perhaps he had lost his nerve.

Or perhaps he was outside right now, clearing the road. Harnessing the wagon.

He must do it faster, she thought. *I am running out of time.*

She could not die here. She could not become trapped, tapping out warnings for the next unsuspecting bride.

Unless I am the last. With my money, he will have the funding for his machine. Black anger washed over her as in her mind's eye, his jubilant face projected over her father's ruined body. Thomas had so rarely smiled around her. He had not masked his wickedness with the same ease as Lucille. He had not enjoyed hurting her.

But Lucille had.

I will not give her the satisfaction of my demise. And if Thomas killed my father, I will show him no mercy.

She pushed on the wheels with aching wrists. Maybe he would come soon to check on her. Or maybe Lucille would. That thought urged Edith to move faster, and she winced as the effort tore at her stomach muscles.

The corridor stretched out before her like an endless blue-gray mine shaft. What catastrophes skulked behind those doors tonight? She prepared herself to roll past them, toiling with her sickened body, struggling not to unnerve herself with harrowing fancies. It would have proved impossible for Edith to be more frightened than she was.

Then a whisper wafted down the corridor. Breathy, unnatural. Echoing from everywhere and nowhere.

Edith jerked as cool air crested over her head like a giant sigh. Smoky syllables twined around the curtains and scattered the black leaves littering the floor. Cobwebs quivered like dead hair.

No one came forward. No one appeared.

This, then, was a speaker for the dead.

Edith pushed the wheelchair forward, and then into an icy chill that slid fingers into her rib cage and squeezed her heart. The syllables became words:

"*Lasciare ora. È necessario lasciare ora.*"

She stopped wheeling and listened hard. It was Italian. "*Ora*" meant "now."

There was something on the stairs. Shudders ran up and down her spine like a hand trilling the keys of a piano. The thing shifted. Edith couldn't quite see it; she thought of Alan's spirit photographs and concentrated.

Believing is seeing, she told herself. *And I believe.*

Then there it was, hovering in the air: a crimson ghost. It was a woman covered in blood, holding a child,

and her long hair wafted as if she were underwater. It had
to be Enola Sciotti. The baby was tangled in her hair, and
the expression on her face was one of extreme trepidation,
as if she were more afraid of Edith than Edith was of her.

Perhaps that was true.

Summoning all her strength, Edith pushed herself
out of the chair and walked toward the ghost. The pain
that clawed at her was physical, but by the expression on
her scarlet features, the phantom's agony was soul-deep.
There was such profound grief and anger on Enola's face
that Edith almost looked away. She felt as if she were
seeing far more than she was meant to, invading the dead
woman's privacy.

Enola Sciotti, who had loved Thomas Sharpe so much
she had left her home and family and allowed herself to be
imprisoned here.

Just as Edith had done.

They had killed this woman and her child. They
had taken her life, cup by poisonous cup, and she died
vomiting blood. Had she held her poor tiny baby in her
arms as it had died? Was that unimaginable heartache the
reason she had lingered all these years?

How could they do it? How on earth?

She locked gazes with Enola. They were sisters in this
foul madness. Their fates were entwined, and Edith would
do all she could to ease this dead woman's suffering.

"I am not afraid anymore," Edith told her. "You are
Enola Sciotti. Tell me what you want from me. Tell me
what you need." *Trust me. Believe in me.*

Still floating, Enola stared back at her. Then Enola raised her hand and pointed down the passage where Beatrice Sharpe's ghost had once appeared and ordered Edith to leave Allerdale Hall. Edith understood that she wanted her to go there. Despite her weakened state, Edith began to walk, and as she did the ghost faded.

Edith was alone again.

She heard someone humming and recognized the tune Lucille had played on the piano in the library. Haunting, sad, and yet tender. A lullaby. For the dead baby?

The melody wound through the gallery, with its blue tracings and fluttering moths. It seemed to go on forever, and she had the strange thought that the objects behind all those doors had been rearranged since she had taken the cylinders. That all the objects, when seen as a whole, could tell her a story.

What did Enola so desperately want her to see?

She followed the sound up the stairs to the attic. Taking a deep breath, she pushed open the door and stepped into the room.

Thomas was there, standing with his arms around a woman, his face in profile against her long dark hair. Her bare shoulder was there for his lips, his touch, and his face was passionately buried in the soft hollow between her breast and shoulder. She was clinging to him.

Who was this? A mistress?

The woman in the elevator. His secret. At last I meet her.

He jerked, turned, and in so doing, the woman turned too.

Edith gasped. It was Lucille.

And this was her room, spilling with moths and dead things, a shelter for Thomas's horrible secret: Lucille was his lover.

CHAPTER TWENTY-FIVE

THOMAS AND LUCILLE heard Edith's sharp intake of breath and turned as one to look at her. She could not believe it; Thomas's face was a study in panic and guilt.

But did he speak?

Not one word.

Lucille flew at her; Edith backed away, then turned on her heel and stumbled into a worktable. A mounting kit upturned, clattering; jars rolled and broke, releasing moths and butterflies that harried Edith as she picked up speed and broke into a run.

This cannot be. I did not see that.

Lucille was closing in.

The elevator. It was Edith's best hope for escape. She

pressed the button and begged it to come. To no avail: Lucille caught up to her and grabbed her brutally by the collar of her nightdress and her hair. Edith felt the mad frenzy of her grip as she struggled to free herself. But Lucille was stronger. Her face was contorted in hatred and fury.

"It's all out in the open now," Lucille said triumphantly, turning her around to face her. Edith's back slammed against the gallery railing. "No need to pretend. This is who I am. This is who he is!"

Then she grabbed Edith's hand and tried to rip the garnet ring off her finger. The Sharpe family heirloom, treasured by the dead. The metal scraped along Edith's flesh and burned as if it were molten.

Lucille tugged again, and again. She pushed Edith to the edge of the balcony; Edith's heels brushed the decaying wood and she teetered, close to a fall. She looked down at the parquet floor and held on for dear life. This could not be her end. Enola Sciotti had not sent her to her death.

The front doorbell rang.

At the same instant, Thomas appeared in the hallway, hand outstretched toward Lucille and Edith. His face was pale and blank, his eyes swollen. His features were contorted in fear—was he afraid for Edith, or for himself?

"Someone's at the door!" he shouted. "Don't do it!"

Lucille was uncommonly strong. Her face spoke of implacable determination. Edith fought back as best she could, holding onto her, but she was outmatched and her grip began to fail. Sick, off-balance, struggling for her life as the red stone caught the light, she understood finally that the ring was important to Lucille not because it was a family treasure, but because of what it signified—marriage to Thomas.

"I knew it!" Edith cried. "I felt it all along! You're not his sister!"

Then Lucille finally slid the ring onto her own finger and slapped Edith with tremendous force across her face.

"That's delightful," she sneered. "I *am*."

Then she pushed Edith backwards off the balcony. Edith fell headfirst, her nightgown streaming behind her like wings. Moths skittered out of her way and pelted as she plummeted. This would be a better death, a cleaner death, than what they had planned for her. At least she had saved herself from that.

As if in slow motion, she saw a railing, but couldn't avoid it and smacked hard against it. The breath was knocked from her lungs. The parquet floor rushed up to meet her and she slammed against the rotted floorboards. A brilliant flash of light exploded in her vision on impact. Clay oozed out from beneath her body, or was it her own blood and brains?

A doorbell rang again and again. The irritating sound roused her. Or maybe the ringing was inside her own head?

She struggled for breath, but she had none. She was completely empty and when she tried to draw air, nothing happened. Her chest did not move, and suffocation squeezed down on her like a hand over her mouth.

The doorbell, again. It was real, not imagined, outside not inside.

Find me, save me, she begged whoever had arrived. *Come now. Please.*

But Lucille's face appeared in her field of vision, eyes spinning with madness and victory, and then all went dark.

In Edith's dream, the sun was shining on a field of green grass, and she was holding hands with her parents. Her mother on one side and her father on the other. And Mama gazed down at her and said, *"Thomas and Lucille don't even have this. They have no happy memories to draw from."*

When she opened her eyes again, she knew that she was still dreaming. Peering at her intently was Alan McMichael, and he could not be real. He was back in Buffalo… or had he gone to Italy? Why was she thinking that?

Enola Sciotti's letter, she remembered, and it all came rushing back.

"Hello, Edith," he said warmly, but in a subdued, professional tone. "Don't try to talk or move just yet. You are heavily sedated."

Alan, listen to me, oh, dear God, she thought. But she looked around and realized she was still at Allerdale Hall. Thomas and Lucille stood close together, observing. Two vultures circling carrion. Dear God, what would they do to Alan?

She tried to warn him, but it was just too much to manage. His face blurred in and out of focus; was he a ghost already?

"It's a shock seeing me, I warrant," he said to her.

Then he turned to Lucille and Thomas. "Forgive me for dropping in unannounced."

Lucille simpered, the very picture of a worried sister-in-law. "Heaven-sent, as it turns out."

"I arrived in Southampton yesterday. I should have sent a wire." His smile took in all three of them. "But I thought you'd enjoy the surprise."

Tell him, tell him, she ordered herself, flailing at him. But she was drifting in and out of awareness. Part of her was back with him in their pirate lair in his back yard, and she was trying to tell him about Enola Sciotti. And Eunice was there, laughing at her.

No, not Eunice.

Lucille.

"We'd have been at a loss. It's a miracle," Lucille told Alan. "She's been sick. Delirious."

Edith looked down. Her left leg was bandaged and braced. Alan must have done it.

"She spoke to me—" she began.

"Who spoke to you?" Alan asked gently.

"My mother was delivering a warning." She *had* to make him understand. "Crimson Peak—"

As she reached toward him, he dropped his gaze toward her hand. She followed his line of vision: It was her ring finger, red and swollen, from where Lucille had torn off the ring.

"Delirious, you see?" Lucille murmured. "Poor thing."

Alan looked at Lucille.

She is wearing the ring. See the ring, Edith begged him. But even if he did, it wouldn't mean anything to him. He had probably never noticed it on her hand, although she had begun wearing it the second that Thomas proposed. Men didn't see things like that.

Tears of fear and frustration rolled down her cheeks, but deep gratitude rushed through her as well. Alan had relinquished his work, crossed the sea, and searched her out in the stormy moors of England to save her life, at grave risk of his own. She had not understood his true mettle or the depth of his feeling until now, and she felt deep remorse for not allowing herself to see it before. It had been there all along, like the air around her and the ground underfoot. Because of her blindness, Alan was like her, a butterfly for these two dark moths to devour. If he discovered what was going on, they would kill him. If they convinced him to leave her with them, they would kill her.

"Here, drink." He held a cup of tea to her lips. *The* cup.

"No, no, no, please, no!" she cried, batting at it. She felt herself fainting. She was going to die. And he, too.

Alan...

Edith's "sister-in-law" put on every air of the utmost concern as Edith slipped back into unconsciousness. Alan made a show of putting away his equipment as he pondered his next move.

"I'm only sorry that you have to see her like this," Lucille said. "Really, for all her city upbringing, she's taken to life here in the hills." She paused and then she said,

"You will stay here, with us? Wait for the storm to pass."

"If you insist," Alan said, although etiquette demanded that he make at least a token refusal. This was certainly no time to stand on ceremony. "But then…" When she raised her brows, he knew he must not reveal that he had a terrible suspicion that Edith's fall had been engineered. Did they actually mean that she had plummeted from the topmost floor? It was a miracle that she was still alive. He, too, for that matter, if his suspicions were correct. "…I'll need a moment alone with my patient," he finished.

Lucille paled and Sir Thomas nervously came forward. His apprehension and culpability were written all over his face. It took everything in Alan not to strike him.

"I beg your pardon?" Sharpe said.

"Would you mind?" Alan asked in a friendly, innocent tone. "Just a moment more. We must all do our best to see her through this."

Lucille pulled Sharpe by the sleeve. "We'll leave you then, Dr. McMichael," she said. "With your patient."

Once out of sight of Dr. McMichael, Lucille was relentless, taking the stairs so quickly she skipped half of them. Thomas followed, near-paralyzed with apprehension. Everything was spiraling out of control. When he had seen Edith fall…

He thanked Providence that the floorboards were rotten, and the viscous, bright clay had softened her landing.

"Where are you going?" he asked her. But he knew where: to the attic. He followed after her, as he always did.

She whirled on him. "Somebody has to stop him. I just want to know, brother. Is it going to be you this time? Or me, as usual?"

His face fell. He couldn't even name all the emotions that were swirling through him—shame, horror, bewilderment. Reaching her room, she rummaged in a drawer and pulled out a familiar-looking knife. He recoiled, and she huffed.

"Thought so," she snapped.

Alan knew that Edith was almost out of time. He touched her cheek, concerned by how clammy it was. His mind raced, working out various scenarios to get her out of here as fast as possible. These people must own horses. Could he get her to the stables? Would he have time to hitch a horse to a carriage or a wagon? How far would they go to stop him?

They will do whatever it takes, he thought.

Edith roused slightly. That was good. If she could help him make their escape, so much the better.

"Edith, listen to me. I am here to take you away. You hear me? I am going to take you with me now."

She gazed into his eyes, but he wasn't certain she was able to understand him. He checked her pupils and then her pulse, and saw her fighting to regain mastery of herself.

"Help. Help me," she said, gasping. She grew frantic. "They are monsters. Both of them. *Alan.* Somebody has to stop them."

He tried to keep her calm. "Shh, shh, I know. I *know.*

I will not let them harm you any further, you hear? We are leaving."

He took her by the arm. "You have signs of poisoning. You're weakened. So you have to show me you can stand up."

Suddenly a little dog at her feet barked, startling him out of his wits. He shushed it, realizing that the Sharpes must have heard it. Time was up.

They began to walk, but she was swaying, stumbling.

"Keep quiet," he cautioned her. "We'll be out in no time."

She lurched forward; it was no good, so he lifted her into his arms and carried her down to the foyer. She cried on his shoulder, clinging to him. Dear God, he had gotten here just in time. If he had been too late... He looked down at her, their faces inches apart, the kiss he had dreamed of his entire life within his reach.

"Things are getting a bit emotional, I see, Doctor," Lucille Sharpe said from her vantage point on the staircase. Her brother was with her, but Alan saw at once that it was the sister he had to fear.

He raised his guard and assumed a more authoritative demeanor—a doctor and friend concerned for his patient. "She's exhausted, showing signs of anemia. I'm going to take her to a hospital immediately."

She advanced like a wild animal stalking prey. He reminded himself that she was very dangerous.

"That won't be necessary," she said coolly. Thomas Sharpe followed her, his gaze on Edith.

Alan stared at her for a moment, weighing his options. This woman was not interested in playing cat and mouse. Very well, then.

"It is. You've been poisoning her. I know everything."

He set Edith down and pulled out his folder of newspaper clippings. He showed the brother and sister the gruesome drawing that Holly had shown him: a butchered woman lying in a tub, her head hacked open. "I'm sure you remember this. Front page, the *Cumberland Ledger*. Lady Beatrice Sharpe was murdered in the bathtub. One brutal blow, almost split her head in two."

He gestured to the caption: *Shocking Savage Murder at Allerdale Hall.*

Edith gaped open-mouthed. Though he was sorry to upset her, perhaps the shock might stir her into action.

"No suspect was ever arrested," Alan said. "There was no one else in the house, only the children. The truth was too horrible to consider."

Edith stared at Sir Thomas as if she had never seen him before in her life. And Alan suspected that she never *had* seen him. Not the real him.

"You?" she said to the man. The monster. "You did this?"

The man stood awash in self-disgust and desolation. "Stop it, please!"

"You, Sir Thomas, were only twelve at the time. After questioning by the police, you were sent to boarding school." Alan looked at his sister. "As for Lucille, at fourteen, her story is less clear. A convent education in Switzerland, the news account says. But I suspect a *different* sort of institution."

Lucille glared at her brother, who was in a paroxysm of despair. She narrowed her eyes. "What are you waiting for?"

"Sir Thomas is married, Edith. Your father obtained a copy of the certificate. But he couldn't bear to show it to you. He married Pamela Upton—"

"And Enola Sciotti—*E.S.*," Edith cut in, ice-cold, her chest heaving. "And Margaret McDermott. He married all three, and got their money."

"Edith—" Sir Thomas begged. But for what? Alan wondered. Forgiveness as she left him? Or absolution because he would never let her go?

Boldly, Alan took Edith's hand and walked away from the Sharpes. He was resolute, although finely trembling, aware of the intense peril they were both in.

"Edith and I are leaving," he announced, and he threw open the door.

The snowdrifts were mountainous, and Edith wore only her nightgown. But better to face the elements out there than sure death in here. He took one step—

—and Lucille darted forward, stabbing him in the armpit. The pain blazed like a branding iron. Edith screamed, falling away from him, and he arched backwards, the knife jutting out. He flailed at it, staggering forward, realizing too late that Edith was not beside him.

Then he saw a flash of white as Edith attempted to catch up. He heard a crash and half-turned; Lucille had thrown the groggy Edith against the wall.

No! he protested, but he was unable to speak. He could only gasp. The knife point, he feared, had nicked the upper lobe of his lung.

He could not leave Edith at their mercy. They would set upon her like rabid dogs and rip her apart. He struggled against his failing body. He was bleeding profusely and knew he was going into shock. His pulse was rapid, his breathing shallow, and he was getting light-headed. Edith was crying, shouting his name but she sounded as if she were very far away, or speaking to him from underwater.

He had to do something to save her. But the pain was excruciating, and he could barely think. As he lurched onto the ice-coated doorstep, he ordered himself not to pull the knife out. If an artery had been cut, the pressure of the metal might be tamping the blood flow. If removed, he might bleed to death.

Don't do it, don't, he thought, but he couldn't stop himself. He drew out the knife. As he had feared it would, blood gushed from the wound onto the stairs. So much, so much; he lost his balance and fell, hard. The knife bounced off the stone. He didn't hear it clatter.

All he could hear was Edith screaming his name.

And all he could see was the murderess bearing down on him in the center of an inferno of crimson snow.

CHAPTER TWENTY-SIX

It watched as the sister rushed the hero. It breathed in the hatred, the fear and madness; her soul was as poisoned as the bride's body.

Perhaps Allerdale Hall had been a happy house, filled with fat children and prosperous parents. It did not remember such times, and its madness doubled, tripled at the thought that such joys had once filled these walls, to be replaced by torment.

It breathed out the clay, the crimson clay, and the ring expanded out into the snow. Let them all drown in it, and walk the floors forever with the murdered wives and the mother and the child, with the sins of the Sharpes sucking the life out of the land, out of each other, *parasites*.

Black moths feeding on carrion and butterflies.

The death's-head carnivore was stalking the hero, each step a toll of his funeral bell.

As Alan rolled over, Lucille calmly picked up the knife. Thomas trailed behind her, and so did Edith's little dog, yipping with excitement. Alan scrambled backwards, understanding at some level that he was probably dying, that he would surely die if he did not flee, but that nothing in the world could compel him to abandon Edith.

But instead of finishing him off, Lucille held Edith down and handed the knife to Thomas.

"You can do this!" she shouted at him. "Get your hands dirty!"

Alan yelled, "No, Edith can't die here!" He had seen Sharpe's tortured look, understood that the madman did love Edith. That was the only weapon Alan wielded at the moment—an appeal to whatever shard of a soul Sharpe still possessed to spare the woman he loved.

Numb, Sharpe stared at the knife in his hand, and Alan dared to hope that he had gotten through to him.

"You've never done anything for us," his sister spat at him in disgust. "Look at you!"

"Edith's stronger than both of you," Alan said. "She can't die here."

In a rage, Lucille pushed Sharpe forward, toward Alan. Changing targets, then, from Edith to him. Good. So be it.

"Do it!" Lucille shrieked.

Alan readied himself, regretting with all his heart that he could not do more for Edith. Wondering if, because he loved her, by some miracle he would be able to save her from beyond the grave.

Sharpe was grim-faced, dirty, and bloody as he approached Alan. Gone was the dapper fortune-hunter, perhaps as much a victim in all of this as the mother his sister had slaughtered. He stank of fear.

"She will not stop," Sharpe whispered to Alan. "Her will is so much stronger than my own. I am so sorry. I will have to do this."

Shielding his actions from his sister, who stood at some distance behind him, Sharpe closed in on Alan, and to Alan's astonishment, discreetly encouraged Alan to guide the knife.

"But you are a doctor," Sharpe added. He took a breath. "Show me where."

Where to stab me so that it is not fatal, Alan translated. *Sparing me. He will spare Edith too, if he can.*

So he, Alan, *must* live. But he couldn't think straight. He was one giant sinking throb of agony, withering inside.

Sharpe was wrapping Alan's hand around the hilt. This was the apotheosis of their duel at Cushing's funeral: on the black day, he and Sharpe staring down one another, Alan quitting the field with a tip of his hat. Today their positions were reversed. Sharpe had surrendered everything. If only he would dare to turn that knife on his sister... but he wasn't man enough for that. This was the best Sir Thomas could do.

As he swayed, Alan pictured the inside of his abdominal cavity. The bowel, the intestines, the appendix…

There. Right there. That will inflict the least amount of damage.

He eased Sir Thomas's willing hand a few inches to the right, locked eyes with Sharpe, and nodded once, nearly imperceptibly.

The regret in Sharpe's eyes was palpable.

And then Sharpe sank the knife in.

The dog yipped frantically as the hero doubled over and collapsed. The bride fell, sobbing, as the brother turned away from his bloody deed, averting his gaze.

"You are monsters! You both are!" the bride cried.

The sister almost chuckled. "Funny. That's the last thing Mother said, too."

The last.

The last of the Sharpes.

It was coming to an end.

The house bled a river of blood, a filling gulley to drown the hapless creatures as they flailed out their last moments in the snow. It had no foundation; it was sinking, yes, down into the pit, gleeful and furious and busy. And as mad as the Sharpes themselves.

CHAPTER TWENTY-SEVEN

FINALLY.

Pride, relief, joy. Her brother, her beloved, her soul mate had torn his way out of his cocoon. Through the cut he had sliced in McMichael's body, he had emerged a beautiful, black-winged moth. Her heart was soaring as the interfering American collapsed to the ground, blood gushing everywhere. Thomas had come into his own—at last, at last.

For years and years, she had borne the burden, performing every necessary task to safeguard them. She had to accept the blame for spoiling and shielding him, which made this moment all the sweeter for her. McMichael had come here to save Edith, and Lucille had goaded Thomas into killing him in front of her, an act that was guaranteed to destroy any affection that Edith had left for Thomas. The stupid little bitch was a witness to the murder and she was now utterly alone. Lucille had no doubt that Edith Cushing would never leave Allerdale Hall alive.

Edith knew it, too. Dazed as she was, it had been easy for Lucille to restrain her and drag her into her room. She was in there now, wringing her hands like some princess in a fairy tale.

Lucille would never have let such a thing happen to *her*.

Barely able to restrain her high spirits, she watched Thomas drag the dead doctor into the elevator. Look how sure he was of himself! Gone was her "doubting Thomas;" in his place was a *man*. It was all ending so perfectly. There would be no need for other women once Edith had signed the papers that transferred her entire fortune to Thomas. And she *would* sign.

Thomas pressed the lever and the elevator hiccupped, then began its descent toward the mine pit, and the vats, where they had submerged other inconvenient… persons. No matter if Alan had told the entire village of his plans to come here. Lucille had searched for a horse and carriage and deduced that the fool had *walked* here. Through a *snowstorm*. He had deserved to die.

And speaking of dying…

She still had the boning knife, and that ridiculous, yipping dog was still alive.

"Come here, doggie," she said sweetly. "Come see what I have."

* * *

Blood is only crimson while it's fresh, Thomas thought, as he tried to make Dr. McMichael as comfortable as possible within the confines of the pit. *Brown blood means that it is no longer flowing.* There was a very little bit of brown mixed in with the red, and Thomas hoped that meant it was no longer pumping because it was thickening… not because McMichael was dying.

Lucille did not, could not know that the man was still alive. She would realize that Thomas had betrayed her… and then she would kill McMichael herself. Could she not see that the last act of their terrible Grand Guignol had concluded?

Thomas looked the man straight in the eye. "Can you hold on?"

McMichael nodded weakly, and Thomas handed him his handkerchief. As if that could possibly staunch the flow of blood. So much of it. Thomas prayed the doctor had guided his aim true, and that his wounds, while gruesome, were not fatal.

"I have to go," Thomas told him. "Lucille has taken Edith to her room. She has the papers. The minute she signs them, she's dead." He felt so different, as if he had finally become a man. The key in his back was gone, and he was moving under his own volition for the first time in memory.

He added, "I am getting you both out."

* * *

Things in the clay vats bobbed and tapped. Things under the stones shifted.

One very sharp thing gleamed.

And waited to be used.

CHAPTER TWENTY-EIGHT

THE KILLING ROOM.

Edith was dazed. Lucille had hit her over and over and dragged her into her workroom, then forced her to sit in an overstuffed chair while she left to fetch something. Edith had almost summoned enough strength to bolt when Lucille had sailed back in and dropped some papers in her lap.

"No need to read them, just sign."

Edith didn't move. She knew she was in shock. Thomas had stabbed Alan to death right in front of her.

I am so, so sorry, Alan. Please forgive me. She wanted to cry but she couldn't yet. She must stay alive.

She must stop Thomas and Lucille Sharpe by any means necessary. Alan would not have died in vain; these monsters must never be allowed to hurt anyone ever again.

Frigid and dank, Lucille's room was like a crypt, brimming with the corpses of hapless insects and dozens of bat-like black moths. Living moths fluttered through the dust motes and hovered around Edith's head like a crown of powdery black thorns.

Edith stared down at the death warrant placed before her: the legal papers from William Ferguson that would transfer all her assets to Thomas. Next Lucille handed Edith a different sort of weapon: the golden fountain pen her father had given her. Whoever it was that had said that the pen was mightier than the sword had not faced a madwoman with a sharp, bloody blade.

Edith held the pen. In her mind, she was little Edith again, and the blackened figure of her mother was materializing in front of the grandfather clock. She trembled, more terrified now than she had been then.

"What are you waiting for?" Lucille demanded angrily. "You have nothing to live for now. He never loved you. Any of you. He loves only me."

"That's not true," Edith replied, dizzy and soul-sick. Thomas *had* tried to save her. He had wanted to change. But he was trapped in a mad waltz with this house, and this woman, and he couldn't stop dancing until the music stopped. He was cursed, and the curse had not yet been broken.

And she was struck with the terrible realization that the only way that the curse would be lifted was through his death.

Could I do it if it came to that?

The question was moot; first she had to live through these moments with Lucille. Edith saw the madness in her eyes and wondered how she had missed it before, how they had all missed it. Lucille hadn't been in Buffalo long, just a sufficient amount of time to set the trap for Edith.

Glaring at her, Lucille picked up the pages of Edith's novel. With a flick of her wrist, she began to feed the manuscript page by page into the fire. It was a move calculated to hurt her and nothing more.

"It's indisputably true," Lucille countered. "All the women we found—in London, Edinburgh, Milan—"

"America," Edith reminded her.

"America," Lucille concurred, as if she were humoring Edith—and she didn't really count.

She kept tossing the sheets into the fire. As the flames rose to destroy Edith's story, Lucille's mood brightened considerably. She was a sadist; she was enjoying this. No doubt she had celebrated each heiress's agonizing death with glee.

"Yes, America. They all had what was necessary: money, broken dreams, and no living relatives. Mercy killings, all of them."

Not "all of *you*," Edith noted. She was not yet included among their victims. Thomas had said she was different. She had thought it a compliment born of true love—that she was unique because she was his soul mate. But the hideous truth was that she simply violated their pattern of chosen prey: she had had a father. They had killed him so that she would have no protection, only a lawyer who would do her bidding.

They had not counted on a friend like Alan. A man who had loved her all her life, whom she had overlooked, taken for granted simply because he had always been there. Her eyes welled but still she did not cry. There was so much to cry over, so many deaths.

Alan had doubted her father's cause of death. She had observed his unease and dismissed it. He had urged caution; she had ignored even that. And her father had paid. Who had done it, Lucille or Thomas? Could the man who had kissed her so passionately have destroyed her father with such savagery?

"Is that what I am going to be? Is that how you explain it to yourself?" Edith asked defiantly. She flared with anger. How she hated this woman.

"I did what I had to do." Lucille was thoroughly unrepentant. Another page, and another. The sheer number of pages attested to the fact that Edith's dreams had not been broken when they had picked her out. She had been pursuing her dream of becoming a novelist with a full heart.

And with Thomas's encouragement. That had been genuine; he had loved reading her ghost story. He had seen himself in Cavendish and followed his path to redemption with interest.

For Thomas, there would be no redemption.

"And the Italian woman?" Edith asked. "You killed her baby."

Lucille froze, her hand halfway to the fire. She did not

look at Edith as she said, "*Her* baby?" But Edith saw the somber expression on her face, her eyes stained with tears. So somewhere in Lucille's body there *was* a heart.

"Didn't you kill her baby?" Edith pressed, hoping to probe that heart, soften it.

"I did not. None of them ever fucked Thomas. Don't you understand?"

Edith did not. None of them... except her. And if he was not the father...?

"Then?" she asked.

Lucille's gaze went distant and her shoulders slumped. She stared downward as she said, "It was mine."

Edith was speechless. Was she implying, was she actually saying...

"It was born wrong. We should have let it die at birth. But I—I wanted it. She told me she could save it." Her voice went hard. "She lied."

"No," Edith whispered. Lucille had given birth to her brother's child? She had not thought she could be more sickened. But this secret... all their secrets together... while he had been with *her*...

"All this *horror*... for what? For money? To keep the mansion? The Sharpe name? The mines?"

Lucille whirled on her. "What vulgarians you Americans are. The marriages were for money, of course—quite acceptable for people like us, expected, even, for generations. But the *horror*?"

And now the madness overtook her again. "The *horror* was for love."

She went to a narrow set of drawers and opened one to reveal a gleaming set of dissection tools and a row of scissors arranged in perfect order. She took out a narrow scalpel.

"The things we do for a love like this are ugly, mad, full of sweat and regret." She advanced on Edith, who tried very hard not to scream.

"This love burns you and maims you and twists you inside out. It is a monstrous love and it makes monsters of us all."

She darted forward and grabbed Edith by the hair. Then she sliced off a lock with the scalpel and moved away, braiding it with great care. Edith was gasping.

"But you should have seen him as a child." She sighed. "Thomas. He was so… so *fragile*, like a porcelain doll. And I had nothing to give him. Nothing. Just myself."

She opened another drawer and placed the braided ring of hair next to another four. One of them was gray and covered in blood. Beatrice Sharpe's, Edith guessed. Was she the first person Lucille and Thomas had murdered? Or the first they had been caught killing?

"You know how many times I was punished instead of him? I couldn't bear his beautiful, pale skin being marred by scars. He was immaculate. Perfect." She smiled at the memory.

"So from all his small infractions—from my father's riding crop and my mother's cane—I protected him."

She took out a pair of shiny bone scissors. So many sharp, cutting things.

"And when she found out about us… well, I protected him too."

She killed her mother. It was Lucille. And now she's here with me.

"All the love Thomas and I ever knew was from one another. And the only world that kind of love can live in is this one. These rotting walls. In the dark. Hiding."

Edith barely listened. She was looking at the fountain pen, the only weapon that she had.

"Sign your name! Sign your bloody name!" Lucille shrieked at her.

Edith wanted to burst into tears but she clamped down hard on her emotions. She would not let them win. She would not.

"While I still have a chance… *you* killed your mother? What about my father?"

Don't let it be Thomas. Please. At least grant me that.

And Lucille's tight smile of triumph gave her that. Edith tightened her grip on the pen.

"Such a coarse, condescending man. But he loved you. You should have seen his sad face when I smashed it on the sink—"

No! Edith silently screamed. She would deny Lucille that smile. Deny her victory, her life.

She signed her name with a flourish, and Lucille grabbed the papers from her, scrutinizing them, exulting. Edith took her chance: She plunged the golden pen into Lucille's chest. She jerked it out, hammered it back in with all her strength, the arc of her swing finding the same hole.

She felt the point drive in deeper. And again, a third time. Deeper still.

Lucille staggered backwards. She grabbed at her wounds, gaped at the blood on her hand.

"No one hurts me! No one!" The words tore out of her throat. She was bleeding badly and her face was draining of color. Could she be dying? Could it be that simple?

It watched.

Wind her up, wind her up…

Edith lurched to her feet and staggered toward the door, falling against glass cases, the tombs of insects; desiccated butterfly wings fluttered and rained down.

Behind her, Lucille tore open her dress, undamming a waterfall of blood. She stumbled to the washbasin and poured water over her injury, a visible, bleeding gap.

She almost fainted.

Put her down and make her spin…

The house's favorite toy still had tricks to perform. And miles to go before she slept.

Edith did not so much walk as collapse in a forward motion as she aimed herself toward the staircase, aware that Lucille still lived. The stairs canted crazily and she knew she would not survive a second fall. She had to live. She had to stop them. If she could have set the house ablaze she would have, and died inside if it meant that Thomas and Lucille would be destroyed.

And then she saw him coming at her, and she tried to scream. Thomas held out his hands in a gesture of innocence, surrender.

"Edith, wait!" he cried.

She only hesitated because she was too wobbly to move.

"You cannot take the steps," he said. "You have to use the elevator. Come with me."

Mutely she raised her pen, her weapon. His face blurred.

"You lied to me!" she flung at him.

"I did," he confessed, holding open his arms.

"You poisoned me!"

"I did."

"You said you loved me!"

"I do." His face snapped into sharp focus and she saw the truth: He did love her. He had, and he loved her still.

She staggered, and he sustained her, holding her in an embrace very like a waltz… a dance of death. Night's candles were all burned out. He had drawn not a moth but a butterfly to his flame, and she hovered on the brink of annihilation.

"I will take you to McMichael," he told her quickly, seriously, honestly. "He is still alive." He nodded as if to make sure his words were registering, and Edith was overwhelmed. Alan! So Thomas had found a way to spare him?

"You can leave through the throw shaft. I will deal with Lucille," he promised.

At the eleventh hour, a hero. Not a knight in shining armor, but someone who had finally seen the light. Who had ever said that love was blind?

They got in the elevator, she leaning against him. It was almost over. They had to get Alan to a doctor as fast as possible, and the village was far away. But with Thomas on their side, his chances were ever so much better.

He looked at the pen in her shaking fist and his face changed suddenly. "Wait. You signed the papers?"

"I don't care about that," she said. "Come with us."

"No. It's your entire fortune," he insisted. And she understood that he believed his sister would outlive him, and plunder her wealth, and then kill her. His fear frightened Edith; in this haunted house, was Lucille somehow indestructible? Immortal?

"I will get them back," he said. "I'm going to finish this. Stay here."

She could do little to disobey; she was too tired, and she needed to rest. She leaned against the back of the elevator and watched him dash off. At the last, a reformed man, a redeemed soul. And Alan alive—these were mercies, blessings. Hope was real. She would cling to hope.

CHAPTER TWENTY-NINE

MY LOVE, THOMAS thought, as he walked into Lucille's room. He saw the destruction of her entomological specimens, the mayhem. In that decaying house, Lucille had catalogued species like a delicate god; he had built toys. She had laid traps and snares; he had retrieved their wounded doves.

How did I ever think this was right? he asked. *How did I not see that we are monsters? How could I justify my love for my own sister?*

Pain.

Terror.

Torment and cruelty, and never knowing when they would be visited upon him. Such abuse as no child should ever have endured, and no one to stop it. No one but Lucille, who suffered for the both of them. It was the least he could do; she had told him that over and over again. Whatever she wanted, the least. What she wanted was for the mine to reopen and the house to be made whole again. To triumph over the squandering of their fortune, the sullying of their name.

She had loved him beyond all reason; she had assumed that other women would, too. They had. And they had died for it.

Lucille wasn't in the room, but the bank papers were. They had spilled all over the floor. He spotted Edith's signature page, transferring every penny she owned to Sir Thomas Sharpe, his heirs and assigns. With a shaky hand, he set his knife down on a small table and began to gather them up. He knelt down, head bowed, as if begging the universe to accept his atonement. Then he threw the papers into the fire, an offering to the fates.

There was a heap of accumulated ash in the grate. A large amount of paper had already been burned, and he wondered what it was.

Then he saw, and his jaw clenched. It was Edith's novel, and he could only assume that Lucille had burned it out of sheer spite. The first three of his wives—Pamela, Margaret, Enola—brother and sister had been kind to them, had doted on them as they sipped their poisoned cups of tea and slipped away, slipped away. Lucille had monitored their mail and, of course, the only letters that had been allowed to reach the post were requests for money. No one inquired after them, at least that Thomas knew of.

Thank God Alan McMichael came, he thought. He prayed that the doctor would survive. A man like that would be good for Edith. Of course he, Thomas, would let her go. Their marriage was legal in the sense that he was not a bigamist, as Carter Cushing had assumed—for the simple reason that Lucille had murdered Pamela Upton. As divorce was so uncommon in England, and they hadn't reported Pamela's death, he and Lucille had forgotten to account for the Civil Registry. He had married Enola in Italy and Margaret in Scotland. Incestuous adultery could easily be laid at his door, but it was far more likely that Edith would be freed through widowhood, for he *would* swing. If he could spare her that scandal by other means, he surely would.

A shadow stepped from the corner and for one moment he thought it was one of the ghosts Edith had seen. But it was Lucille, his own black phantom, and blood coated her bodice. His eyes widened in shock.

"What the devil are you doing?" she demanded in a shaking voice.

More blood soaked into the fabric. He reached for her.

"Lucille, you're injured."

She brandished the knife at him. At *him*. Her eyes jittered but her jaw was set. He knew that look. What it meant. It was a look that meant she could kill, and would. But kill *him*?

"Stay where you are. You burned them?"

"She will live. You're not to touch her."

Her lips parted as she held out the knife. Her look cut him as sharply as if the blade had found its mark. "You're *ordering* me now?"

"We can leave, Lucille. Leave Allerdale Hall." They could free themselves of this horrible curse—

"Leave?" she echoed, as if she couldn't understand the word. He wouldn't have been able to either, before Edith had spoken to his heart. Given him hope. He felt as if he were looking at their world through different eyes. He stared at his sister and partner in mortal sin, and he swayed, dizzy and thrilled and terrified. There could be redemption for them. They were standing at the edge of a precipice and for the first time in his life, he grasped that they could soar high above Crimson Peak. Wings weren't just for butterflies and moths. Gargoyles could have them, too.

"Yes," he insisted. "Think about it. We have enough money left. We can start a new life."

She gaped. "Where? Where would we go?" She was listening to him. Perhaps believing him. Considering the possibility that he was right. That they could make it happen.

"Anywhere. We can leave it behind."

"Anywhere," she said, testing out the word, groping toward the prospect like a blind woman. Standing beside him on that cliff, defying death.

He was elated. They were saved. There *was* hope.

"Let the Sharpe name die with the mines. Let this edifice sink in the ground. All these years holding these rotting walls together. We would be free, Lucille. Free of all this. We can all be together—"

"*All?*"

He realized only then what he had said. And that he had said exactly the wrong thing, at exactly the wrong moment.

"Do you love her?" The agony on her face stabbed him through the heart. He remembered all the times she had taken the cane, a slap, staring at him as tears rolled down her face, bearing the brunt, loving him. There was more pain on her face now than in all those times combined. He didn't want to hurt her. But to free her, to give her a life, a real chance, he had to be cruel to be kind. It was the same thing that Carter Cushing had demanded of him, and he knew, unfortunately, that he was good at it.

Beyond that, he must quell her rage, for Edith's sake, and Alan McMichael's survival. Lucille had withstood torture at the hands of their parents. The blood on her dress was no guarantee that she could be stopped from doing anything she set her mind to. And that included seeing their plan through to the end.

By killing Edith.

They spoke at the same time:

He began, "This day had to come."

And she, speaking over him like someone drowning out horrible news that, once uttered, could never be retracted: "Do you love her? Tell me, do you?"

"We've been dead for years, Lucille. You and I in this rotting place… with an accursed name. We are ghosts."

Lucille's face drained of color. Blood loss, shock, disbelief. "Do you love her more than me?"

"But she is life. *Life*, Lucille. And you won't stop her."

Her breath was hitching. He felt as though he had just pushed her off the cliff, and she was falling.

"You promised—*we* promised we would not—that you would not fall in love with anyone else—"

Falling to her death.

He delivered the death knell:

"Yes, but it happened."

Yes, but it happened.

The watcher moaned, exhaling its poison into the heart and mind of the last of the Sharpes. For the brother was a Sharpe no longer; he had renounced his name, his legacy… and his curse.

So the house reserved its love for the sister, the murderess, the one who would serve and love evil for the rest of her days. Who would not waver from filling the halls and walls with ghosts. And it whispered at her to *do it, do it*—

And with a shriek, she stabbed her brother in the chest. He tried to grab the knife but she slashed at his arms and hands, wildly. Clay oozed through the floorboards and the ghosts wept crimson tears in all their prisons of Sharpe misdeeds and malefactions as the prison bars shut again. No more free than the puppets and dolls in the attic, to be wound up again and again and again.

"Is this how it ends?" the sister screamed in the throes of anguish. "You love her? *You love her?*"

Hate him, it cackled.

* * *

Thomas looked down at his belly as blood poured from it; out of his mouth came the faintest sound—a discreet surprise, a quiet, nearly casual sigh:

"Oh, Lucille…"

She stabbed him again, almost as if she had to prove to him that she had meant to, weeping half in rage and half in pain.

The pain was so great that he went numb, which was more than he deserved. He had done this… to her, to them. To all of them. Still, he tried to save her from ripping him apart, because he must save her, and Edith, and the doctor.

"No, no, stop, please. I can't…" He trailed off. *I can't*, the litany of his life. *I can't*, and so she had been forced to. He had turned her into this.

The look on her face. Would it be the last thing he ever saw? He knew that all she wanted now was for him to be silent, to stop looking at her. He hurt everywhere; the numbness was gone, and every blow, slap, and kick that she had endured for his sake hit him full force. Engulfed him. He was bobbing in a boiling vat of crimson clay, and torment sucked him down toward a scarlet hell.

With a shriek she drove the knife in one final time; it lodged itself firmly into his cheek, almost to the hilt. *That* he felt, and he staggered as he moved away from her. He shuffled a few steps forward. He dislodged the knife, though the effort cost him, and he sank wearily down into a chair. Everything was growing dark.

In the distant recesses of his mind, he heard the lullaby she had played for him through the years. He remembered their child, a poor, sick little thing, born of a very sick love. Enola, how she had rocked that baby. Lucille's bitter tears.

She could not lose her other child: him.

We can't live in the mountains,
we can't live out at sea.
Where oh, where oh, my lover,
shall I come to thee?

Then he heard the melody transformed into the Chopin waltz he had danced with Edith. Holding the candle; the light had flickered but was not extinguished.

Oh, Lucille, Lucille.

"I will… it will be fine," he promised her. "Or… I… the things we do…" He gazed at her and for a moment he thought he saw the sun. But it was an illusion; dark moths circled Lucille's head, and his vision began to fade as he gazed into her eyes. What could he do for Edith now? How could he save her? For he must. That was the only way he could go on.

"Oh, sister, you killed me," he murmured.

Then he saw a white light, and in it…

CHAPTER THIRTY

LUCILLE HELD HIM and in her mind he was so little and scared, she but two years older, and she sang to him as she played the piano:

> *We can't live in the mountains,*
> *We can't live out at sea.*

But he wasn't listening. He wasn't singing with her.

Because he was… because she had…

Edith Cushing has murdered him, she thought. Everything inside her exploded. Her face changed. Her eyes filled with hollow rage. She grabbed the knife and dragged it across the floor, opening the veins of the house, making it bleed.

* * *

Something *rippled* through the house as Edith opened her eyes in the elevator. With a start she came to full consciousness. Apparently she had passed out pressed against the bars while waiting for Thomas to return; she had no idea how long she'd been there, but she knew she couldn't delay. Alan needed help and so did she, if they were to survive this day.

Beyond the elevator's gaping skeletal gate, beyond the filigreed-iron, protective fence, she saw someone moving towards her. Her tired heart leapt in hope. Unable to stop herself, she called out, "Thomas?"

But it was not he.

Lucille marched out of the half-light like an avenging spirit, her bloody knife raised high overhead. When their eyes met Edith shrank away from what she saw: the promise of brutal death, and shameless, diabolical pride.

No, she has killed him! She's lost her mind.

Oh, dear God, Thomas…

Desperately, Edith slammed the insubstantial cage door shut and jerked the elevator's control lever to the down position.

Nothing happened.

Nothing at all.

She looked fearfully back at Lucille, who was picking up speed, charging to reach her before the car could move. Beneath its dripping sheath of blood, the knife gleamed and flashed in the gloom. Catching her breath, Edith raised the handle to STOP, then lowered it again, throwing her full weight upon the lever. Nothing happened.

Fear shot up from the soles of her bare feet and crackled through her body like an electric wave, threatening to take off the top of her head. She was trapped in a cage that offered absolutely no protection from attack; the bars of the gate were too far apart to block a knife thrust, the back of the tiny car too close to the front, offering nowhere to retreat. No matter whether Edith stood or cowered, she would be cut to pieces. If she couldn't get the lift to move, then she had to get out of it *now*. She would have to outrun Lucille. And though wounded, her adversary was clearly in better shape than she—poisoned and sedated, her damaged leg bound in a brace. How could she hope to escape a raging madwoman?

As Edith gripped the bars, determined to wrench back the gate anyway, pounding footfalls made her look up. It was already too late. Lucille was closing on her fast and the cloying, coppery scent of blood—Thomas's?—rode the frigid air before her. There was no way Edith could exit the car and survive.

Moaning, she pounded on the lever once more. And she was finally rewarded with a jolt of motion. There was a clank, and then a sickening lurch, and the little elevator began to creep away from the landing.

As Thomas's sister rushed forward, lunging over the low fence, straining outstretched to drive the point of her knife into warm flesh, both the car and Edith dropped out of her reach. Lucille stabbed at empty air.

But that did not stop the harpy's pursuit; if anything, frustration maddened her even further. As the elevator bearing Edith descended at an agonizing crawl, she saw Lucille flying down the wide, mahogany staircase, her gown billowing out behind as she rounded a landing's newel post, one hand grazing the polished rail, the other holding aloft the bloody knife, racing to catch up to her before she could reach the ground floor—and freedom.

Over the erratic whir of the contraption's gears and pulleys, floating across the vast emptiness of Allerdale's entrance hall, a string of curses made guttural counterpoint to the trample of feet rushing down the staircase. Though Edith willed the elevator to speed up, the lethargic pace continued—perhaps Thomas was right, the machine born a slave had acquired a mind of its own, and it had decided to let his sister take her life.

Maybe Thomas isn't dead. The realization sent a sudden pang of tender feeling deep in her chest. *He has risked everything to save me. His honor. His future. His very life.* She wanted desperately to believe in his remorse, in a transformation that she had wrought, in his need to find redemption. One thought led to another. *But if it isn't his blood, then whose gleams upon that blade? Maybe Lucille only wounded him. If he does not appear, I will go back for him if I can.*

As the ground floor rose up to meet her she decided her next move had to be finding a weapon. Lucille was falling behind now, clearly badly hurt, but she had a knife. Edith knew she had to seize her best chance to arm herself. She looked across the great hall to the main fireplace, where a long iron poker leaned against the mantel. To reach it on her bad leg would take an eternity, and leave her open to attack from all sides. The kitchen seemed a better choice. It was also on the ground floor; if she could beat Lucille to the entrance hallway, attack could only come from one direction. And, safely there, she would have quick access to a variety of cutlery, frying pans, kitchen shears, and roasting skewers with which she could hope to defend herself. Her plan was to quickly grab up something she could use and hurry back to the elevator by the same route. She realized that if Lucille saw where she had gone and came after her, she would have to fight her way back to the lift.

Edith stopped the elevator on the ground floor and without hesitation pulled aside the cage door. She stepped out and hurriedly padded down the hallway, limping barefoot, heart hammering, constantly looking back over her shoulder and fearing the worst. Once in the kitchen, she scanned the counters and seized the first weapon she found. A butcher's knife, well used but the stained blade was massive. She gingerly felt the edge with her thumb. It was razor sharp from tip to heel. Gripping the handle, she tested it with a downward stab into the cutting block. It pierced the wood easily and so deeply she had to wrench the handle back and forth to free it. It would do. Yes, it would do nicely.

In the next breath Edith whirled away from the counter. *No time to waste, I have to get to Alan.* And Lucille was coming. If she hadn't found her yet she soon would, that was guaranteed.

She hurriedly retraced her steps down the hallway,

hobbling on her bad leg, her whole body tensed, knife point raised to ward off frontal assault—but there was none. A wave of relief flooded over her as she finally lurched into the elevator. Their escape suddenly seemed at least possible, if not likely.

As Edith pulled the cage door shut she jolted at the sight of Lucille's face on the other side, not two feet away. Eyes slitted, corners of her mouth upturned, teeth bared. There was no misreading the expression of triumph— her intended prey could not escape. No mistaking the blood-smeared fingers and steady hand that held the weapon—murder was more than a livelihood to this creature; it was her ruling passion. No matter how many people Lucille Sharpe slaughtered, that ravening thirst would never be slaked.

A scream leapt from Edith's throat as the woman threw herself at the flimsy barrier that separated them. The red hand thrust the blade between a gap in the bars. Backing hard against the rear of the car, Edith attempted to use her own weapon to fend off the attack, but that proved useless. Stretching over the protective barrier Lucille could almost reach the car's back wall with her knife's point, and twisting her wrist, she turned the long edge to sweep at an angle. The flurry of frenzied slashes backed Edith into a corner, folding, shrinking down into the smallest possible space. But it was not near small enough.

Once, twice, thrice, as the knife thrust and then drew back Edith simultaneously felt the tug at the sleeve of her gown, the drag of sharp steel across her bare skin, and shrill pain. Three deft, shallow cuts, and blood began to freely flow along the curve of her arm. Lucille was toying with her, like a cat with a caged canary. A one-sided game that could go on and on. The prospect of being slowly hacked to pieces sent her into a panic. As the knife came at her, Edith grabbed the blade with her free hand. She only managed to grip it for a second before Lucille wrenched it from her, making the edge slice deep into her palm. But the violent backward effort sent Lucille reeling onto her heels.

Desperate to gain advantage, Edith cracked open the cage gate. As the other woman leaned forward, overcompensating to recover her balance, Edith made her move, seizing the outstretched wrist, using Lucille's momentum to pull her arm into the car and pin it to the edge of the iron bars.

For a second the tables were turned: Lucille was the helpless one. Edith used the heel of the hand still holding the butcher knife to pound down the elevator control lever. With a familiar lurch, the car began to descend. In seconds Lucille's arm would be broken or perhaps torn off at the shoulder as the roof dropped past the level of the parquet floor. Edith leaned into the trapped arm to hold it fast. The gory fingers clutched wildly at her gown. Though they touched her, they could not reach her. She was beyond that. Had Lucille had empathy for her as she had smiled and fed her poison day after day? And what of the other murdered women? The ones whose anguished spirits lurked behind rotting walls and floors. What of Alan and Thomas?

As the car fell, the arm rose closer to the ceiling. When it climbed above her shoulder, Edith could no longer use her body weight to pin it. She dug her nails into the wrist and pulled down as hard as she could.

At the very last second, frantic to avoid having her limb shattered or amputated, Lucille managed to twist free and draw her arm back. As the elevator continued down, Edith heard howls of frustration from above her. She wished she could have hung on just a little longer. Though the idea of cradling a dismembered arm horrified her, Lucille deserved no less. And it would have certainly ended the matter.

The cries of anguish grew fainter and fainter as she descended. By the time the car reached the clay-mine level they had gone silent. Struck by a wave of penetrating damp and cold, Edith began to shiver uncontrollably. As she took in the surroundings, once more she felt like she had been swallowed by a dying animal, immense, red-fleshed. With an effort Edith shook off the disorienting vision.

When she opened the gate she saw that the elevator had once again stopped two feet above the floor. An easy jump before, but now she had an injured leg. She sucked in a quick breath and stepped out. Though she tried to land on her good leg, her bad one took some of the impact.

Screaming in pain, she lost her grip on the knife. Her only defense skittered across the floor and she watched helplessly as it clattered down a recessed grate. Unable to fish it out, she tried to pry up the drain cover with her fingers but it was slick from the red clay and meltwater oozing from the walls and so heavy she couldn't budge it in her weakened state.

Straightening up, she could barely make out Alan crumpled in a corner. He wasn't moving. She hurried over to him and knelt by his side, a terrible pain welling up in her throat. His face looked drained of all color and he had been grievously wounded. There was an obvious puncture wound on the right side of his chest, and the fabric around it had turned purplish-black from congealed blood. More blood had puddled on the floor at his elbow. It was difficult to be certain, but it appeared that the bleeding had stopped. His eyes were closed, his jaw slack. She couldn't tell if he was breathing. When she touched his cheek the skin felt as cold as her father's dead hand in that wretched excuse for a morgue. She lowered her own cheek next to his nose and mouth and felt a faint but unmistakable rush of warm air. He was still alive!

Carefully she helped him up into a sitting position, caressing his hair, trying to gently but firmly rouse him. After a second or two his eyes opened, and, seeing her, he instantly brightened. Just as quickly his smile turned to a grimace, eyelids squeezing shut, and his face lost its color again.

"We will get out of here," she told him as she helped him to his feet. "We *will*. Now you have to trust me."

The sound of her voice echoed off the walls of the mine. As they began to move back to the elevator, she heard rapid footfalls coming their way. They, too, echoed.

It had to be Lucille.

Edith stopped, propping Alan upright against the rough, dank wall.

The footfalls slowed, then stopped.

Though Lucille could not see her, and vice versa, that didn't stop the madwoman from shouting an accusation.

"Thomas is dead because of you. You killed him!" she shrieked.

As the insane proclamation echoed and faded, Edith's blood turned to ice. Was she telling the truth? If Thomas had indeed been killed, it was by his sister's own hand. She eased Alan more deeply into the shadows. She would have to leave him there. Abandoning him there was one of the hardest things she would ever do, but if Lucille found her while she was holding him up, there would be no fight, no hope. It would be a slaughter and they would both surely die.

Crouching low, she watched Lucille gliding like a ghost over to the pile of objects beside Enola Sciotti's trunk. In the silence Edith was again aware of the sounds of dripping water, *plip-plop, plip-plop*, like the ticking of a hundred unsynchronized clocks. Bending down, Lucille grunted and struggled with something at her feet. At first Edith couldn't tell what she was doing; then she saw the woman lift aside one of the stones set in the floor.

"Before they put me away, I kept a little souvenir from Mother," Lucille announced over her shoulder to her unseen audience. Then she took from the hole a meat cleaver—it appeared to be the same one in the illustration on the front page of the *Cumberland Ledger*, which had been driven into Beatrice Sharpe's skull. The same nightmarish cockscomb worn by the dead woman's spirit.

Lucille rose, turned, and started coming in Edith's direction; in seconds, she would be on top of her—

Edith drew back further out of sight. She needed to lead the murderess away from the defenseless Alan and then find something to fight her with. Panting for air, she looked wildly around…

At the perimeter of the dimly lit cavern, the entrance to the mine tunnel opened onto blackness. She caught the faint gleam of metal in the floor, and remembered what it signified. Embedded rails that were designed to carry crude, wheeled carts that the mine workers loaded with clay, then pushed and dragged to the surface. The light glinting off the rails was coming from above.

Steeling herself for the ordeal, she lunged from cover. It didn't matter that Lucille would see her; there was no way to avoid that now. She had to cross in front of her; she had to beat her to the entrance. Hurling herself forward despite the pain, she reached the tracks and ran into the tunnel, turned her face toward the soft flow of light. The source of the illumination became clear: a tiny, bright rectangle in the distance. How far up the steep incline, she could not tell. It looked like a postage stamp.

A howl of anger close on her heels spurred her to flight. As she ran up the tunnel's slope she stumbled, lurching awkwardly on her bad leg and waving her arms for balance. On either side of her, the narrow, rusted rails were held together and cleated to the soft substrate by perpendicular wooden ties. Though muck-covered and slick, the ties' rough front edges gave Edith's numbed feet purchase. Supported by ancient, rotting timbers and braces, the shadowy ceiling hung low and dripped red tears on her head and shoulders; the walls were shored with sodden planks to keep the sides from collapsing inward and burying hapless workers alive.

Fighting to stay ahead of Lucille, Edith pushed her legs, the good one and the bad, to their absolute limit. And when both began to tremble and fail, she used her hands and arms to scrabble forward, digging her fingers in the muck. For an instant she thought she could feel Alan gazing down upon her, urging her on. She prayed that no matter what happened he would remain silent; if Lucille discovered he was still alive, he wouldn't be for long.

If he is still alive. Oh, dear God, what if he's already dead?

Then what is there to live for?

Don't think of that now. Keep moving!

Her guttural gasps for air and whimpers of pain roared in her ears; savage, animalistic, inhuman, they were all she could hear. The atmosphere below ground was as poisonous to her as the tea, a wretched miasma of pungent clay and snowmelt that coated the inside of her mouth and her throat. She could feel the cold, wet weight of it filling her lungs as she inhaled, making it more and more difficult for her to breathe. Without turning her head to look over her shoulder, she couldn't tell if Lucille was suffering from the same difficulty. But she knew the other woman was gaining on her: Out of the corner of her eye, she glimpsed the dark scrambling shape behind.

Keep going. The command was almost a whisper in her ear, uttered by someone else. *Mama? Pamela? Enola? Margaret?* Or was she hearing the voice of her own spirit fighting to survive?

Sweat streamed down her face and stung her eyes; her arms were slippery with putrid clay. The rectangle of light at the end of the tunnel had grown larger and brighter, she could just make out the timbers framing the exit, but the slope at this end was steeper—every yard upward was agony. The hem of her voluminous nightgown wound around her legs—dragged through the muck, caught on rail spikes and splinters of wood, it seemed to grow heavier and heavier. Her long, plaited hair kept falling into her eyes but she didn't dare pause to brush it away.

I do not want to die here. I do not want to die here.

Lucille was gaining; she could feel it. Then came a sudden pull from behind—hard, determined—and she knew Lucille had grabbed hold of her gown.

Edith looked up and saw that she was mere feet from the surface. She lowered her head and with a backwards kick and desperate burst of effort, fought free of the restraint. Crawling frantically on all fours she tumbled out of the tunnel's red mouth.

But she had not escaped hell.

CHAPTER THIRTY-ONE

THE HEAT OF the fading afternoon sun had melted the snow that lay thinnest upon the ground, and the condensation mixed with freezing air had caused a dense, choking mist to rise and cling to the grounds. Visibility had shrunk to a ring of no more than a half dozen yards across. At the edges of the haze, crimson-tinged fingers of fog caressed the boiler of Thomas's harvester, filtered between the skeletal legs of the poppet, hid and then revealed a long-dead conveyor and an oven where bricks had once been baked.

A gust of bitter wind ripped the air from Edith's lungs and slapped her full in the face; the impact made her groan. She tried to move forward and found all her joints had gone rigid from the flash of intense cold—suddenly she was wearing the iron boots of Cinderella's stepsisters. The icy air had penetrated the marrow of her bad leg as well. It felt like it was being slowly sawed off at the point of the injury, the imagined saw moving in time with the beating of her heart. Back and forth. Back and forth, the pain sharp, deep, and excruciating.

Then Lucille burst out of the mine a few feet behind her. Hair matted with red clay, face and arms likewise smeared with a gouache of crimson. In the center of her chest bright blood oozed forth in a steady trickle from the wound Edith had given her. She still clutched the obscene cleaver firmly.

When Lucille started scrambling to reach her feet a fresh rush of fear coursed through Edith's body. Adrenaline animated her like a puppet or a wind-up doll. She jumped up and ran as fast as she could for the cover of the fog bank. The air inside it was thick as soup; it burned the inside of her nose to breathe it in.

I need a weapon.

She scanned the scaffolding of the poppet, the snow-filled buckets of the conveyor belt, and climbed up on the harvester. The machine burst into life, and the chugging of its heart matched her own.

Her hiding place revealed, she clambered back down. Lucille would know where she was now.

Dear God, let there be a mislaid hammer, a wrench—no, something to give leverage, something to overcome Lucille's advantage in strength and speed.

The face of the man who had taught her about

mechanics swam before her eyes, crushed and broken. Then she stumbled over it, the thing that she sought.

A shovel!

She grabbed the tool and hefted it in both hands. The connection between blade and handle felt solid and the blade's edge looked thinned and sharpened by use. She turned back toward the tunnel mouth, the one place she would be able to see Lucille coming at her. She used the shovel as a crutch, hopping on her good leg, conserving her strength, easing her pain, groping her way through layer upon layer of swirling fog, which thinned to a haze when she reached the cluster of machinery.

"What do you want, Lucille?" Edith called out.

"I want to smash your face in with a stone—and then to count your teeth as I break them off…" shouted a voice almost lost in the mist.

Edith had already reasoned the answer to her question; it was the sound and direction of the voice that she was after.

Wielding her shovel in both hands like a lance, Edith moved through the roiling murk. As daylight from above faded in and out, shadows and shapes half-seen and blurred seemed to shift of their own accord in the haze. She mock-parried with the weapon, defining the boundary she could easily defend. The edge of steel was far too wide, the point too dull to stab with—but it could chop and hack bone-deep. She could not let Lucille get hold of the blade, though. That would reverse her only advantage.

"…cut you into pieces and make you disappear. That's

what I want. Can you give me that? Or must I take it?"

Lucille's voice seemed to emerge from everywhere and nowhere. As Edith neared the harvesting machine, whose base was still banked with drifts of clean snow, Lucille darted out of the red mist and slashed at her with the cleaver. She was too slow bringing up the shovel to block it. Searing pain shot through her cheek just below her eye, and before she could strike back, her adversary had vanished into the fog.

Lucille's speed and accuracy on the run made her heart sink. Perhaps she wasn't badly injured at all? A hot trickle of blood rolled down her cheek. She swiped it away with the back of her hand. A sound behind her made her turn. She seized the end of the handle and swung it with both hands like a medieval broadsword.

Getting it moving was easier than stopping it once it was in motion. Before she could recover from the wasted blow, a dark form burst from the mist to her left. Lucille brushed against her hip as she used the cleaver's edge to make another cut. The shovel clanged against the side of the boiler as Edith tried and failed to hit her assailant in the back. With her bad leg she could not give chase; she had to watch as her tormentor disappeared into the swirling mist.

Silence descended on the hazy clearing, searing, malevolent silence. Edith strained to hear, to see as she turned and turned again, making the landscape of dead machines and bleeding earth revolve around her. She had no idea where Lucille was, where she would come from next. She had no idea if Alan was still alive.

As seconds became minutes, the tension of remaining on her guard began to drain away her last ounces of strength. The weight of the shovel blade made her back bow and her arms from shoulder to wrist spasm and quake. When she could no longer carry it, she let it drag behind her as she searched. It was not a ploy to draw out Lucille, but it functioned to that end.

A dark human form moved between a jumble of machines, then back into the mist, but no longer in haste, as if testing, observing her vulnerabilities. Edith stopped turning and listened, drawing the shovel's handle into both hands, poised for the attack that was sure to come.

Out of the fog, with cleaver slashing wildly, Lucille sprang at her weak side—the bad leg side. Edith managed to evade her this time by backing away as she kept the shovel blade between herself and the cleaver's edge. Steel rang on steel, the sharp clatter instantly swallowed, muffled by the surrounding fog. The shovel was long and slow to swing, even with two hands; Edith persisted because she had no choice now, parrying with answering force every time Lucille attacked. As she drew back, the cleaver flashed down with blinding speed, chipping the wooden handle above her hands, knocking the blade aside. Before Edith could recover, she was cut again. Desperate now, she brought the shovel around, jabbing it at Lucille's face and eyes. Again, too slow, even slower than before because her arms were growing weaker, and then the cleaver slashed inside her guard. It bit into her flesh more deeply this time and hot blood jetted down the inside of her nightgown's sleeve.

Edith knew she could not withstand the frantic onslaught much longer. She retreated with shovel raised, and kept on retreating, back into the fog where she hid, trembling and shaking bright red drops into the drifts of clean snow. It was no comfort to her that Lucille did not follow. Lucille was that sure of the kill, and more than content to draw out the filthy business as long as possible.

Edith was grateful that her nightgown concealed the full extent of her injuries; she was afraid that if she knew how bad they were, she would lose heart and fall to her knees to await the inevitable. More than ever she needed to believe in herself. She needed to weave a story so powerful that it would allow her to survive. *Once upon a time, there were:*

Love.

Death.

And ghosts.

And a world drenched in blood.

A scarlet fog veiled the killing ground, then dripped down through the greedy, starved mineshafts and into the tortured vats of claret clay that bubbled and gasped on the filthy, bone-white tile. Crimson earth seeped back up through the walls of mud. Allerdale Hall was ringed with brilliant red—a stain that clawed toward Edith's bare and battered feet.

But that was the very least of her troubles.

Because hell's own child, Lucille Sharpe, was coming for her. Implacable, unstoppable, a creature fueled by madness and rage, that had maimed and murdered and would kill again, unless Edith struck first. But she was weak, coughing blood and stumbling, and this monster had already claimed other lives—other *souls*—stronger and heartier than hers.

Snowflakes blinded Edith's swollen cornflower-blue eyes; red droplets specked her golden hair. Her right cheek had been sliced open; the hem of her gauzy nightgown had soaked up blood, rot, and gore.

And crimson clay.

She braced herself for the last battle, the duel to the death. Everywhere shadows and shades loomed, red on red, on red. If she didn't survive, would she join them? Would she haunt this cursed place forever?

Ghosts are real. That much I know.

She knew much more than that, of course. She knew all of it, the whole brutal story. If only she had pieced it together sooner—the warnings, the clues. But had she learned it too late to save herself *and* Alan, who had risked so much for her sake?

Behind the snow and scarlet gloaming, she caught a flash of running feet. Lucille was coming for her.

Beside the monolith of Thomas's excavating machine, near a brick oven, Edith waited, tears streaming down her face. Her leg throbbed and she was freezing, yet her insides burned so hot she expected black smoke to plume from her mouth. She backed up a few steps, whirled around, eyes searching, her breath a rasping sound in the back of her throat. Then time stopped, and her mind cast back to how it was that she, Edith Cushing, had come here to fight for her life.

It seemed too much to wish that she could live happily ever after.

Lucille stepped out of the fog and walked towards her; there was no longer need for guile. The dark eyes boiled with hatred and madness, and lust for revenge. Lucille had killed Thomas but, in her deranged mind, Edith had delivered the fatal stab because he had chosen her over his own flesh and blood.

"I will not stop," Lucille said, panting heavily, "until you kill me or I kill you."

"I know that…" Edith's voice quavered, but from exhaustion, not fear. What did it matter? At this point she was half-dead already.

I am no match for her by myself.

And then… she had the strong sense that she was not alone. *Someone* or *something* was with her, though she could see nothing in the swirling haze. Insane Allerdale Hall towered above them, but it was not the source of this… presence.

A presence she knew meant her no harm.

Was it Enola? Pamela Upton, perhaps? All three of the murdered brides?

Edith slid her glance from Lucille's contorted face to the churning ether. She dared to believe what she could not see.

"If you are here with me—" she extended her hand "—show yourselves. Give me a sign."

There. Edith was flooded with joy as she gazed at

the one who had come to help her, out of love. She was ready now.

As she closed distance with Lucille she dragged the shovel like an exhausted berserker trailing his battle axe, building momentum for a final, desperate blow.

Apparently blind to the specter, Lucille's face radiated triumph. "There's no one to help you," she flung at Edith. Her smile was cruel and vindictive; it was unforgiving. "I don't see anyone, do you?"

"You don't?" Edith smiled. "Because I do. You see them only when they want you to. Only when it's time." She raised her chin. "And one of them—" she faltered, so tired "—one of them wants you to see him now. It's time."

She watched Lucille as a luminous specter emerged from the fog.

Thomas.

His ghost was pale. From his cheek a plume of blood rose, swirling into the air like smoke. His eyes and lips were golden; he was shimmering with sunlight from within. He was no longer a creature of the dark, a denizen of Allerdale Hall and all the madness and barbarity of his tragic, passionate family.

Lucille stared, amazed.

"Thomas? No…"

The sight of him brought her weapon down. Tears streamed down her cheeks. The sight of Thomas's ghost was the only thing that could vanquish her—that could suffocate her rage.

Edith called softly, "Lucille?"

At the sound of her name, Lucille turned. And as she did Edith crashed the shovel blade against the side of her skull. The jarring impact staggered Lucille backwards, and she fought gravity with knees that would no longer support her weight. Seeing her falter infused Edith with a sudden burst of strength. It was now or never. Press the advantage. End this or die trying.

She swung the shovel, smashing the back of the blade into the woman's head. Only when Lucille fell to the ground did she pause to gasp for breath.

Though down, Lucille was not done. She blurted out, "I will not stop, I will not." She groped for the cleaver she'd dropped, blindly clawing at the crimson muck. "Until I kill you or—"

Edith already had the shovel in motion again, a blow that started in the soles of her bare feet, and corkscrewed up through thighs and hips. Before Lucille could finish her words, the shovel came down on her head with a crack that echoed off the walls of the manor, driving her face into the blood-colored snow. There was no need for another blow. Well short of the cleaver, Lucille's outstretched fingers quivered in frantic palsy, then went forever still.

"I heard you the first time," Edith said, heaving for breath.

Leaning on the shovel for support, she looked down upon the corpse of Lucille Sharpe, who had once been a tiny, innocent baby in her mother's arms. A toddler who had wanted nothing but love, and warmth, and to be safe and cherished.

Or could it have been that Lucille had "come out wrong," just as her own poor baby had? Thomas's child?

Edith's face was suddenly lit by shimmering, warm light. Thomas's ghost moved closer, suffused with gold, in contrast to the dark, mad creature lying dead in the mud.

He smiled at her, really smiled; she remembered the glow of flame in his eyes when they had danced the Chopin waltz; the radiance of the firelight on his face in their humble honeymoon sanctuary at the depot. Need had driven him into the darkness, but love had brought him into the light. It had redeemed him.

Letting the shovel fall, she opened her arms to embrace him one last time, but the diaphanous figure dissolved away into the mist... into white light.

CHAPTER THIRTY-TWO

I KILLED HER.

Edith gazed down at the ruined body of Lucille Sharpe, the deeper red of her head wound darkening the crimson snow. She tried to summon pity or remorse, but she could be nothing but fiercely glad. Lucille would have killed her, and would have gone on to kill others, if Edith hadn't stopped her.

Snow fell on the back of Lucille's head flake upon flake, each crystalline shape soaking up the blood and sparkling like rubies. The sight was beautiful in a horrible way.

Trembling as the adrenaline in her body burned off, Edith hobbled to the narrow tunnel of the mine and called, "Alan?"

The word echoed but there was no answer.

She went cold. *He must be alive. He must.* After all this, his incredible bravery, his sacrifice… after loving her for his entire life, he must not die.

"Alan?"

Still nothing.

And then she heard him call her name, deep beneath the earth in the clay pit and Edith choked out a sound that was halfway between a sob and a laugh.

"Alan!"

She started to climb back down the rail track but her whole body rebelled. Her muscles would not obey, her joints would not bend.

"Alan, hang on!"

Allerdale Hall glared at her as she staggered through the front door. Her injured leg had stiffened further, from ankle to hip. The memory of Thomas's arms around her as he carried her over the threshold brought tears, which she held back as she summoned the elevator. She could not break down now, not when Alan needed her. She had been right that first day; it *was* colder inside the house than out in the snow. *Colder than the grave,* she thought. A grave's contents rotted into earth, to someday return to the sunlight and warmth. There was no hope of renewal in Allerdale Hall; what died there stayed there, frozen in place by a cold beyond imagining.

The elevator did not seem to want to come. Eventually it rattled up to her. Blood had pooled on the floor and smeared handprints ringed the cage bars like the stripes on a barber pole. The coppery smell was overwhelming. For the briefest of instants she couldn't make herself go inside, and then she knew she had no choice. She had to get to Alan.

"I am not your enemy," she told the house. There was no answer, no scattering of leaves in the hallways or huge, moaning breath. There were dozens of black moths circling the snow that filtered through the hole in the ceiling, as if they did not dare test themselves against the light.

Edith entered the elevator and closed the grate, holding her breath all the way down. As usual, it did not stop flush with the floor; she lowered herself to a seated position and gingerly put down one foot and then the other.

She heard a moan.

"Alan, Alan!" she shouted.

Water dripped. Vats bubbled. The foundation groaned.

There was no tapping.

She limped and half-fell and staggered and lurched, and somehow miraculously made it to Alan's side before she collapsed. His eyes were closed and his mouth slack. He looked dead. His forehead and face were icy to her touch. She felt no breath. There was so much blood. Was she too late? Had the house claimed another?

Wrapping her arms around the still form, Edith burst into sobs.

Not this. Not Alan.

"You loved me," she wept. But more importantly, "I love you."

Alan grunted.

And opened his eyes. He tried to raise a hand and moved only his fingers instead.

"Edith." He smiled weakly. "You found me."

Edith did all she could to help Alan into the elevator and then out the front door of Allerdale Hall. He couldn't bear to stay inside the house while Edith went to the stable to harness the horse to the carriage.

She came back with bad news: The horse must have smelled the fresh blood on her, for as soon as she had pulled back the gate of its stall, it had bolted and run out of the building, and from there, Alan assumed, out onto the moor. Given their physical condition, there would be no recapturing it. He was bleeding still, and it was a long walk, but it seemed the only chance either of them had for survival. He had already beaten the odds, as he figured it.

Edith Cushing had declared her love for him.

And so they began the trek.

With Alan's heavy arm and most of his weight across her shoulders, Edith limped upward in the mist. She and Alan left tracks in the blood-red snow. The black hulk of Allerdale Hall was perched half a mile away ringed with a moat of scarlet.

"Will we make it?" Alan asked in a tired, faint voice.

She decided to be honest. "I don't know, Alan. Nothing seems sure."

"No," he agreed. "To think… to think that *I* came to rescue *you*."

Edith smiled as she held him. "We have a long way to go. We have each other's shoulders. We should be grateful for that."

No sooner had the words left her mouth, she caught sight of torches bobbing a distance ahead of them, growing larger as they approached. They were men from the village. She could hear their voices, suddenly excited and shouting, but couldn't make out what they were saying. One wore a bright yellow muffler as brilliant as a sunbeam. Upon spotting Alan, he raised his hand in greeting.

Rescued, she thought. *Both of us.*

She looked back at the house and the opening lines of the novel she would begin again popped full-blown into her head:

Ghosts are real. That much I know.

They fade away, along with the past, like mist in the daylight…
Leaving only small lessons behind. Small certainties.

EPILOGUE

I<small>NSIDE THE HOUSE</small>:

The blood of Alan McMichael on the floor.

The broken banister where Edith had fallen.

The chimney in the library, raising as the house took a deep breath of poisoned air.

There are things that tie ghosts to a place, very much like they do us. Some remain tethered to a patch of land or a time and date. But there are others that hold to an emotion, a drive: loss, revenge, or love…

…a terrible crime…

And the ghost of Lucille Sharpe, alone, all alone forever, seated at the piano in the unforgiving cold. Playing the first note of the lullaby.

Those, they never leave.

Let the wind blow kindly
in the sail of your dreams
and the moon light your journey
and bring you to me.

We can't live in the mountains,
we can't live out at sea.
Where oh, where oh, my lover,
shall I come to thee?

THE END

"To learn what we fear is to learn who we are."

—GUILLERMO DEL TORO

ACKNOWLEDGMENTS

MY THANKS TO my agent, Howard Morhaim and his team; to my editor, Natalie Laverick, and to Alice Nightingale, Julia Lloyd and everyone at my Titan Books home. I'd also like to acknowledge the University of California at San Diego for an education in film and TV production that has served me well all these years. My friends Beth Hogan, Pam Escobedo, Julia Escobedo, and Amy Schricker so often went above and beyond while I was on deadline; and Mark Mandell shared my joy, hope, and anxiety about this project as only another freelancer could. Thank you to Anna Nettle and everyone at Legendary, who proved so helpful. My appreciation to the cast and crew of *Crimson Peak*, whose artistry continues to astonish, delight, and terrify me. But most of all, I would like to extend my deepest gratitude to Guillermo del Toro, whose brilliance blazes bright in every frame of *Crimson Peak*. *Muchas gracias por invitarme a su casa.*

ABOUT THE AUTHOR

NANCY HOLDER IS a multiple award-winning, *New York Times* bestselling author (the Wicked Series). She has won five Bram Stoker Awards from the Horror Writers Association, as well as a Scribe Award for Best Novel and a Pioneer Award from RT Book Reviews. Nancy has sold over eighty novels and one hundred short stories, many of them based on such shows as *Highlander*, *Buffy the Vampire Slayer*, *Angel*, and others. She is the vice-president of the Horror Writers Association and teaches in the Stonecoast MFA in Creative Writing Program, offered through the University of Southern Maine. She lives in San Diego with the writer Mark Mandell, Tater the corgi, and McGee the cat.

You can visit Nancy online at www.nancyholder.com